He Only Died Twice

He Only Died Twice

Chris Elgood

First published in 2008 by Hallmark Press as More Deaths than One
Re-published by Chris Elgood 2011

32 West Street, Tadley, Hampshire, RG26 3SX. United Kingdom

www.chris@chris-elgood.co.uk

ISBN 978-0-9568948-1-6

Printed by CPI Antony Rowe, Eastbourne

Chapter One
Cautious Approaches

Mike Fanshawe stood up to shake hands with the clients. He thought about leaving with them but changed his mind. Had he done so, Jeffrey Hicks would not have met him at The Hog in the Pound and would not have seized a chance opportunity. After all, there were many ways for Jeffrey to fulfil his brief. Had he chosen another one, his employers would never have made contact with Nshila Ileloka. She would have continued with the conventional and respectable life that had occupied recent years. It was not as if that life lacked interest and reward. She had her own successful business in an unusual and challenging field. If her witchdoctor skills were never required again, it would hardly be the end of her world

Mike went for a small brandy instead - to be consumed peacefully without pressure. Negotiations such as these were demanding. You not only had to get the facts right, but you had to convey the right impression. You couldn't allow personal quirks to emerge – like the over-developed sense of humour that often compelled him to make jokes when others were deadly serious. You had to be regular and professional.

The corner table to which he returned with his brandy, offered a good view of what used to be the saloon bar of The Hog in the Pound. The whole room was horseshoe-shaped with the bar partially separating a bigger half from a smaller half. In the old days there had been a partition extending from the bar to the outside wall so that the Saloon Bar and the Public Bar were quite separate. One had been 'respectable'. It had featured triangular Victorian love seats upholstered in red velvet, mahogany tables, flock wallpaper and paintings in heavy, dull frames. In the other had been stools, darts, shove-halfpenny and glass-topped tables. Today there was no difference between the areas. Both had light

1

yellow walls hung with two sorts of picture frames. Old world maps – Essex, Middlesex, Surrey and Kent – alternated with modern counterparts that showed the principal wine-growing areas of the world with the local grape varieties shown in bright colours. Multi-paned windows had been replaced with large single panes that let in far more light and frequent visions of red London buses. Simple but sturdy tables had bench seats on the wall sides and pine chairs opposite, both upholstered in green leather. The Hog in the Pound had become family-friendly. Discreetly stored in one corner, folded up, were high chairs for children. Three relics only survived from earlier days; the 'Yard of Ale' suspended from the ceiling above the bar, a wine glass about three foot high which adorned one corner of the bar, and a reproduction of Landseer's Stag at Bay. Successive landlords claimed that it had been signed on the back by the Prince of Wales, when he visited the pub in 1936. A less welcome trace of the past was unevenness in some parts of the floor. In three places the tables had slivers of wood under one leg to keep them steady. In one more place it was just a folded-over envelope.

Most lunch-time customers had gone, and the barmaid leaned over the bar to talk briefly with Mike – a favourite customer. Mike's reply must have been heard in the other section of the horseshoe, because a man came round the corner.

'That voice has got to be Mike Fanshawe.'

Mike and Jeffrey Hicks were contrasting types, drawn to each other in university days by a common dedication to rugby football, racing and beer. Mike came from an old county family - one that had somehow managed to preserve its wealth and had showered him with advantages. His toys – from rocking horse through to cabin cruiser – had always been the best and most expensive. Yet Mike was also gifted in other ways. He was intelligent and socially skilled. Those qualities had brought him an excellent degree and acceptance by a firm of stockbrokers in the City. He had progressed thence to a merchant bank and regularly handled multi-million deals. In bad years his bonus was significant, in good years it was obscene. Outwardly, Mike was a perfect hate-figure for social reformers, keen on a more egalitarian society.

Yet he had friends of all types and backgrounds, and seldom aroused envy or enmity. While other silver-spoon children lied to themselves and everybody else about their personal merits and deserts, Mike's attitude was relaxed. 'I am dead lucky to have all these goodies. If I don't share them around I expect the gods will take them away from me.' His appearance helped, of course. Mike was just less than six feet tall, broad rather than fat and had an ugly, slightly squashed face enlivened by a startling smile. He had short fair hair that stood out all round like a bottle-brush and made women want to re-order it. He had been described in a university magazine as 'The Friendly Thug from Trinity'. Mike was inclined to think the best of everybody and had often been conned out of money. That, perhaps, was why he had no immediate suspicions of Jeffrey.

There is nothing Scottish about the name Hicks. Jeffrey's family were descended from a soldier in Butcher Cumberland's army who had deserted in 1746 to marry a highland girl. Several generations later, Jeffrey's father had become a Presbyterian minister in the lowlands near Jedburgh. He was a man of strict and narrow principles with little intelligence and no imagination. Jeffrey was the reverse. He was academically brilliant and acquired a mastery of deceit and subterfuge in evading the prohibitions imposed by his father. When his success at school made it obvious that he was university material, he used all his skills to enter one that was a long, long way from Jedburgh. Cambridge, he decided, would do. Jeffrey was small, agile, wiry, tough and unreliable. He was tolerated, and even liked, because the results he achieved from any endeavour seriously undertaken were quite excellent. The feeling was, 'Don't rely on Jeffrey to do what he has promised, but if he does do it, you can be sure he will do it well.' His friendship with Mike worked. It worked because he was reliable in just one respect - consistency behind the scrum. When Mike or one of his fellows got the ball backwards, Jeffrey directed it well.

Mike welcomed him, of course, but minor doubts affected his mind when Jeffrey responded to, 'What have you been doing these five years?' He was vague, and full of generalisations. He had worked in Financial Services, it seemed, and Market Research and Investigative Methodology, whatever that was. His present employers were, 'A small firm of Research Consultants. You wouldn't have heard of them.' Mike wondered why he was not more open, and remembered times when Jeffrey had been numbered with the bad guys rather than the angels. Conventional morality was not his strong suit.

And then he asked, just ten minutes later, 'Do you know a woman named Nshila Ileloka?' There was no reason for him to expect that Mike knew her, any more than he should know a particular film star or footballer. The question showed awareness that Mike was acquainted with her – as indeed he was. Jeffrey wanted an introduction.

'I know her, yes. Why are you interested?'

And why am I being cautious? Mike was surprised by his own behaviour. What was it that gave him bad vibes about a meeting between these two?

Nshila was unusual, certainly, but hardly unique in modern, cosmopolitan Britain. Born in a remote African village, chosen to receive a good secondary education, winner of a scholarship to the London School of Economics, owner of her own business and holder of an MBA from the Open University. The facts spoke of a successful, impressive immigrant, well able to take care of herself and give Jeffrey the brush-off if she wanted to. Why did Mike suddenly feel protective?

Perhaps the feeling came from the facts he didn't know – the facts that might underlie the sharp, clever, competent almost powerful image that she projected. It's common, Mike reflected, for people to disguise their own inadequacies behind convincing outward behaviour. His friendship with her was a simple thing based on convenience and superficial compatibility – not on any in-depth knowledge. She seemed to need the security offered by his stable, rooted background and unthinking loyalty to an

4

inherited culture – the Englishness that almost reached cartoon proportions. She sometimes seemed torn between the tribal culture in which she had grown up and that in which she now lived. And what about that witchdoctor? Old Kwaname, who she sometimes spoke of with love and sometimes with fear. What of the rituals in the hut under the baobab tree at which she sometimes hinted. What had she learnt through the accident that made her his pupil? Was she still influenced by dark beliefs and practices? Did part of her still live in an environment in which human life was expendable and the checks and balances of civilised society unknown? There was plenty of scope, surely, for psychological conflict.

Why do I value her friendship? What do I get out of it? Mikes rhetorical questions provoked guilty feelings. He valued the image and the skills so highly that he had thought little about the true personality. Her upright carriage, her ebony colouring and her perfect dress sense made her an immediate success at the many parties Mike went to. Those were packed with city types, conceited and apt to boast about money. Nshila was a total contrast, and gifted with an ability to produce one-line put-downs that were hilarious to everybody except the target.

What had she ever really told him about her past? Had he simply heard the words and not seen their significance? He did recall asking her once about the witchdoctor business and teasing her about supernatural skills she might possess. Her reply had been guarded.

'Mike, if an impressionable young girl is friendly for two or three years with an established guru, in whatever society, she is bound to learn things. You can describe the contact as friendship or schooling or apprenticeship. It doesn't matter. Knowledge rubs off on the less experienced one. There are things I can do that you might describe as witchcraft or magic. There are doubts in my mind about the values of your modern European society, and moments when I feel the rough, pragmatic rules of tribal life were actually better. But let's not get into those areas – you and I. It's better if we just enjoy what we have got and put philosophy on the back burner.'

'Calling Mike Fanshawe! Calling Mike Fanshawe! Come in, Mike!' A finger was dug forcefully into Mike's ribs.

'Stop dreaming for a moment and I'll tell you why I am interested! I've seen her once or twice at parties and I've heard rumours that she has peculiar psychological talents. A part of my work is what we call "perceiving and connecting". My bosses argue that human knowledge is too compartmentalised today – each area placed in a neat little box and assumed to have no likeness to what goes on in other boxes. What they want is cross-fertilisation. Whenever I come across some talent that is weird and unusual I'm asked to tell them about it. Nshila sounds odd enough to qualify.'

Mike saw the answer. He would tell Jeffrey about Nshila, but refuse an introduction till he had got her OK.

He told Jeffrey about her brother winning the lottery, and how the money had opened the door to secondary education. He told of her purchase of The Rain Consultancy and the occasional rows with the Meteorological Office. He told of the rather flamboyant life-style that suggested resources greater than any small business could afford. And then he dried up. 'Let Nshila tell you more if she wants to. How about rugby? Are you still playing?'

Chapter Two
Conflicting Opinions

Judgements about Nshila varied wildly. The most sympathetic one would have come from the landlady of the digs in Golders Green where she arrived one autumn evening – her first day in England – worn out by the London underground, carrying a battered suitcase and shivering with cold. Mrs Mayhew had taken her straight into the kitchen to get warm and consume first hot tea and then gin. She remembered their hysterical laughter as Mrs Mayhew tried to get her name right.

'The 'N' sound, Mrs Mayhew. You make it by putting your tongue just behind your upper front teeth. Then it's Sheila, just like the English girls name.'

Mrs Mayhew's first attempts were poorly formed grunts with no 'N' in them at all. Finally she got it, and came out with N-Sheila. The surname was easier, for Nshila wrote it down for her as 'Ee – lay – lo –ka and Mrs Mayhew got it straight away. She liked Nshila from the start.

'A sweet girl. Nothing wrong with her except that she had never been loved and never learned how to respond to it.' It took Mrs Mayhew three months to forge an open relationship with Nshila, but gradually she heard of a mother who was worried only about her own status as a third wife and her failure to produce a male child. She did not hear of real neglect, but rather of maternal behaviour rooted in convention and carried out with little warmth. She learnt of an environment in which Nshila came to feel that she was somehow personally to blame for not being a boy. She learnt of two older half-brothers and their hateful behaviour. She heard of relief found at school as the teacher saw her as talented. She heard how any tiny victory over the brothers won no respect and no change of attitude. From time to time she scored a point or two, but it was done by cleverness, so it served only to make them hate her more. 'She never expected love', Mrs Mayhew would say, 'One freezing winter day I found that she had been saving old newspapers to put between the blankets on her bed for extra warmth. She was afraid to ask me for extra blankets because she thought I might be offended.'

'Was she clever?' Mrs Mayhew would have had no doubts. 'Clever? My goodness, yes! I get some really silly overseas students who must have got here through powerful friends. Nshila was in a different league. I'm not bright – shrewd enough they all tell me – but not educated. Yet I hear them talking about their college work and Nshila never showed any concern at all. She was always looking forward to the next step, anticipating it and eager to learn.' If a questioner persisted, Mrs Mayhew might have elaborated. 'She had great self-reliance. It was as if relying on other people had always been a disappointment and she believed she had no security other than through her own capabilities. She would do almost anything to acquire new skill, or new knowledge. Experimental – that's what she was. A bit like those crazy doctors I've read about who think they have discovered a new remedy and try it out on themselves. Catch me doing that!

'She was really smart about people, too. Summed them up quickly and got it right. That crooked plumber had been just two hours in the house when she said, "Get rid of him, Mrs Mayhew. He's not honest and he's a lousy workman". Two weeks later I found that he had conned Jean Darby out of £150 for replacing a tap that just needed a new washer.'

'She cried when she left me. I was sorry, too, but I understood. We are a long way out, and the travel is tiring and expensive. Girls want a place of their own, too, and she was going to share a flat with friends from her college. I'll always remember what she said to me. "You've given me something I never had before in my whole life".'

Walter Vokes - the South African failed assassin - would not have recognised that picture. He was an adventurer who had completed just two assassinations before accepting that he was

8

psychologically unsuited for the work. 'Nshila Ileloka? A very clever, competent, ruthless woman. I first heard of her when I was hired to dispose of a bent politician. The man was also being targeted by a witchdoctor. The witchdoctor got to him first, and I wondered how he had done it. During my enquiries I learnt about this young girl who had served her tribe by destroying a cattle thief – using a mixture of witchcraft and physical violence. It was an extraordinary story: Women don't have much status in remote African tribes, yet this one had acquired astonishing skills and qualities.

'I had an assignment in England later on that proved beyond me. I knew she was studying there, and I sought her help on a sub-contract basis. It was wildly successful. I'll never know how she did it, but the target apparently blew himself up like a suicide bomber – only out of range of any other human or animal! I have heard some people talk of her as if she was a different creature altogether. They use words like "gentle" and "considerate" and "insecure" and "confused". That's got to be rubbish. How can you be those things if you kill people – even really bad people who are otherwise untouchable? I've also heard talk that she's gone legitimate and given up witchcraft. I don't believe it. She may want to, she may try to, but she's quite incapable of turning down the big one when it comes. You'll hear of her again!'

At St Alban's, the school on the outskirts of the capital city, they kept some school reports for fifteen years. Not all the reports – just those on pupils sponsored by an organisation. That included the National Lottery, and meant that the headmaster's final comments on Nshila Ileloka existed.

'Intellectually, Nshila is outstanding. However, I am concerned that she has difficulty integrating the pragmatic values of her tribal background with the values of modern Western society. She finds our high regard for the individual hard to accept: where she comes from, the good of the community matters more than the well-being of one member. She also has a psychological compulsion to press relentlessly against all restrictive boundaries and conventions. She's got no evil intent, but her self-belief is high: she feels confident enough to take big risks. She will never miss a chance to experiment. She's sure to achieve distinction, but it won't be in any normal way.'

Different again would be the image offered by Gillian Harker, who worked for Nshila in The Rain Consultancy. 'Don't you say a word against her! She's given me a job that exactly suits my talents and a splendid environment to work in. She bought this company without having any special meteorological knowledge and it's great to feel that I'm the expert who keeps it going. She values me and relies on me. It's fun, too, helping her learn about the technical side – almost like having a pupil. And the things that I hate doing – she likes them and does them marvellously. You should hear her talking to clients!

'She's great on woman things, too. She's a bit older than me and helps me with dress, make-up, social behaviour and so on. I get on better with men than I used to before I knew her.

'And I like a touch of mystery. There are things she knows and does which are a bit scary. I can remember three events for which we were asked to give a forecast and all the science said "Fine. Warm. Sunny". Nshila had me forecast a thunderstorm instead, and three times it happened. As a child, she was befriended by a witchdoctor. They can make rain, can't they? Can she do it, too? Sometimes I really believe she can.'

Nshila's half-brother was a science teacher at a school in Margate. 'My little sister, Nshila? She's great if you keep the relationship superficial. She's smart and educated and fun to go around with. But don't get too close to her, and if you sense that she is mixed up in some dodgy activity, then run away fast. When we were children she got involved with our local witchdoctor. I don't know how it happened. I came home for the holidays and found that she was getting far too close to him. I doubt if he intended to teach her so much, but she's intelligent and imaginative and intuitive. She worked out a great deal for herself by listening and watching and experimenting. She's inquisitive beyond belief and takes extraordinary risks just to find out what will happen. One day she will call up some spirit and handle it the wrong way and get carried off into darkness.

In fact, many of her experiments pay off and give her ego a boost. Personal growth seems to be a psychological compulsion. She has considerable power in the paranormal field. You can call it witchcraft or magic or voodoo or whatever you like, but she has it and can use it. When I am with her I act the strong, dictatorial elder brother. It works, because of the tribal respect for older males, and because she owes me. It was my lottery win that paid for her education and got her away from tribal life. Without me she would never have a BA from LSE and an MBA from the Open University. Recently she's been almost normal. But it won't last. Just watch her eyes light up when somebody offers her a challenge. She's one of those people who are compelled to live life on the edge.'

Zach Kawero would have similar views. Dr Zach Kawero, as he has recently become after acceptance of his thesis on 'The myth of electronic privacy'. Zach revels in the change of status. No longer is he just 'A tall scruffy black nerd with glasses'. He is a respected academic, and tries to show it by horn-rimmed glasses and an unkempt haircut. Of course, those things don't stop him being a hacker.

'Nshila? Wow! Keep well away from her if you want a quiet life. I'm devoted to her on account of my MBA degree. I'd never have passed the exam if she hadn't seen all the questions in that greasy cauldron of hers. There are times when she scares me stiff, but I go on accepting work from her. Why? She pays well, and the assignments are exciting and challenging. And perhaps I do things for her because we are alike in seeking to break new ground. I'm good at manipulating the electronic world, and it delights me whenever I increase my skill. I think it's the same with her in spiritual things.'

If Kwaname could communicate across the void, he would have two comments. 'She's good. I still have things to teach her, but she's good. Her weakness is that she likes people and gets too friendly. Liking people is bad for a witchdoctor – it can weaken his will to act. The best relationship is mutual dislike and, towards the witchdoctor, fear. She's not feared the way I was. But maybe that's an advantage if targets don't take care the way they should.'

Chapter Three

In The Carpenters Joint

When Mike Fanshawe spoke to Nshila about Jeffrey some hint of protective intention must have come through. It riled her.

'What's wrong, Mike? Why shouldn't Jeff want to meet me? It could be a business proposition, or cultural research, or an offer of millions for my pent-house flat. He might even fancy me. I'm not married. Perhaps I want to be.'

'Nshila, I'm aware there are chunks of your life I know nothing about. You never talk about them, but tales are told. There's a mystery about you; I've thought you might have a double life – like Jekyll and Hyde. You might be vulnerable in ways I can't guess. You certainly don't tell me everything, and sometimes you have asked me to get the weirdest things for you – things that go with my passion for big boys toys but are way outside your areas of interest. Why did you want me to get a steam whistle from one of those old road rollers? Things that make a noise like Dracula screaming. What did you do with it?'

'So you think there is a secret part of me that might be vulnerable?'

'Well, Jeffrey wants something, and we don't know what it is. He might be looking for something in your past - something that he or his masters could use against you.'

'Fantasise a little, Mike. What's your worst scenario?'

'His vagueness tells me he's into some dodgy activity. And he might be in it on either side. He might be tied in with some sort of clandestine agency.'

'Like what?'

'Well, before we got round to talking about you, he was very interested in the amount of foreign travel I do. I wondered if he might not be an undercover operative: maybe a customs officer - hoping to nail me for importing drugs or illegal immigrants.

Perhaps he imagines a secret compartment underneath my old Lagonda.'

'How do you think he rates in terms of being powerful and dangerous?'

"I never thought of him like that in the old days. Why do you ask?'

'Because of this hypothetical double life. I'll tell you that it exists right enough, and that "powerful" and "dangerous" are words sometimes used about myself. I don't think your friend is going to damage me. It might be the other way round. You can fix up a meeting, Mike, but I don't want you present.'

Nshila agreed to the meeting – and was attacked straight away by doubt. Was it wise? Ought she not to slam the door on any borderline activity and stick with her emerging taste for respectability? It was a repeat of old arguments between different halves of her mind. Almost, it seemed to her, there were two little men inside her skull, fighting to decide who she would be. Her risk-taking self reminded her now that it had never been her style to back away from a challenge. And what was wrong, this self asked, with her semi-legal practice? She was no evil-doer, was she? The practice had grown over the years, starting with minor things – things that were perhaps questionable but not seriously wrong. The love potion business with Patrick Quinn had harmed nobody. The cattle thief episode back in the village had been justifiable action against a tribal enemy. He had died, yes. But people do die in tribal conflict and nobody agonises about it. Both events had left her with the euphoric feeling of a challenge surmounted – a good job done. The death of Frikkie Verloppen was more questionable, but bringing that one to it's dramatic, explosive conclusion had been a technical – and spiritual – triumph. The evil nature of the victim made it easy to live with. If Jeffrey Hicks proved as mysterious as Mike suggested, a meeting might have interest.

She realised then that she had been a tiny bit bored. It had been some years since her last big contract. Was she becoming too attached to the comfortable life of a blameless citizen? Was she settling down and losing her spirit? That was a terrible thought. An image flashed into her mind – Mike Fanshawe taking her to a rugby match and lamenting the poor performance of a celebrated player. 'He's over the hill. Not the man he was. He's lost speed and lost power. He has no real appetite for the conflict any more. His tackling is half-hearted and ineffective'. Did she want to be like that? No. No. No.

A counter-attack: from her cautious self. If there was anything behind the Hicks approach then it might be a heavy, serious matter. Might she get drawn into something too big to handle? 'You have managed alright so far', said Mr Cautious (or was it Ms?) 'but if an assignment calls for skills you don't possess, are you young enough and determined enough to acquire them? And have you the psychological strength? There are forces in the spirit world that some witchdoctors can handle and others can't. Can you bend Astaroth to your will?' Another memory surfaced: some professor of psychology arguing that the ability to learn declined with age. 'A person who enters a field at thirty will never catch up with one who entered it at fifteen.' True or false, Nshila wondered.

Then more reassuring memories flashed up rapidly, like the single-second flashes that TV companies use as trailers for their up-coming films. They offered the big moments from past successes, successes that often came from her skill at marrying African and European witchcraft with modern technology. She remembered how a finding spell had been allied to images on his computer screen to lure Brad Pullinger to the killing ground. She saw again the grey desolation of Bodmin Moor and the fraudster Kevin Carruthers, walking in a daze towards the image of herself projected onto the mist – walking dead straight until he fell down a disused mine shaft. There was mental conditioning in that project, and text messages on a mobile phone, and immensely stressful spiritual effort to bi-locate herself and tempt the target. Science? Technology? Witchcraft? Psychology? Hard to say. But she had succeeded.

Of course, the preliminaries could be taken without any

commitment. She resolved to take the first step and see what followed. If it seemed, later, that she would need knowledge and skill far beyond her present competence, then she could walk away from the whole thing. Defeated, her cautious self retreated to it's lair. 'Don't kid yourself, woman', it muttered.

That first step was to research Jeffrey and guard against any discoveries that he had made, or might make, about the double life. It was a task for Snakesmith & Company, her first choice enquiry agents.

Their report arrived a week later. A bombshell. The man Jeffrey was some sort of apprentice spook, working for an obscure and unacknowledged branch of government. He had been traced to a dreary red-brick building in Horseferry Road that housed minor sections of the UK security services.

Nshila pressed the proprietor of the agency, 'Surely that building houses other organisations. It's a big place. Are you sure he doesn't work for some harmless business agency in the basement or wherever?'

'No, Ms Ileloka. The government departments have a separate lift to their own floors. Their space is entirely self-contained with no access to other parts of the building. The doorman was quite certain that Hicks uses the special elevator.'

The security services! Nshila wondered what had earned her the attention of people like that. She had done nothing in England that could affect national security. Her public image was that of an irreproachable citizen: a businesswoman: a taxpayer. She had no association with subversives or criminals. She had no penalty points on her driving licence.

Of all the unlikely scenarios, the least unlikely was that they had somehow connected her with witchcraft. Sustained digging along those lines would make the connection. For instance, Patrick Quinn had been appointed Professor of Sociology at a minor polytechnic. If they had talked to him they would have got wildly exaggerated stories about her powers – all based on that love potion business at school. Yes, he could have started a leak. A few years ago the school had held what was called a Gaudy; a prolonged party for old pupils. Patrick had bored lots of people with stories about being at school with a witchdoctor, and the extraordinary things she did. Come to that, they might even have turned up Mary Zonde herself, the target of that adolescent affair. Unlikely. Mary had gone back to her tribal area and become a teacher - walking to the river to fill water pots before going off to take school.

Why would they be interested in witchcraft?

Easy, Nshila thought. Picture a clever young graduate recruit wanting to get noticed. He makes a case to his superior:

'You know, Sir, an awful lot of effort goes into finding and using the most up-to-date technology. We spend nothing on research into the spiritual and the supernatural. Queen Elizabeth I had a top-class spymaster - Francis Walsingham – who used such methods all the time. Why do we ignore anything that is not technical and scientific?'

The imaginary superior is busy, under pressure, and wants to get rid of this keen young man. 'It's crazy and far-fetched. But put up a paper. We have done less likely things in the past.' Yes, Nshila thought, that's the way big bureaucratic organisations drift into ridiculous activities. They might be scouting around for supernatural capability and have picked up a lead. Jeffrey must be treated with caution.

What Nshila did not know was that some dark, devious operative within the civil service had already decided that Grant Toppley must die. Her imagined training experience for a wet-behind-the-ears recruit was credible but wrong.

'Nshila Ileloka?'

'That's me. You must be Jeffrey Hicks.'

Recognising Nshila in The Carpenters Joint was easy for Jeffrey. The place was almost full, but there were only three black women, and only one in the expected age group. Jeffrey asked the normal, 'What can I get you?'

'Vodka, please. No water. No ice. Just Vodka.'

Returning with the drinks, he commented on the noise level. It was high – as expected by Nshila, who had chosen the place deliberately. Noise is a protection, limiting the chance of eavesdropping and making it easy to deny things later. One could reasonably say, 'I must have misheard you' or 'I never said that at all. You got it wrong'. Even tape recordings would be hard to decipher.

The place itself had character. It picked up a historical connection with the woodworking trade, and the walls had pictures and diagrams about joining wood to wood. Scarf Joints were featured, and Mitre Joints and Bridle Joints and Dovetail Joints. Just above the table at which Nshila and Jeffrey sat was a display showing the preparation and assembling of a dovetail joint. On shelves and above the bar were old-fashioned woodworking tools. Larger display panels – one on each wall – showed wood-carvings from famous English buildings. The menu listed – amongst more usual items – Carpenters Casserole and an expensive liqueur called Joiners Juice. 'Don't touch it', Nshila warned.

The first exchanges were just ordinary politeness, focussed on Mike Fanshawe, the intermediary and point of contact. Jeffrey had tales of Mike's prowess on the rugby field and the appalling tuneless voice in which he sang rugby songs. Nshila offered memories of Mike in his mega-rich family home. Quite soon Jeffrey got down to business.

'Nshila, I asked Mike for an introduction because the company I work for is a marketing and public relations consultancy and we need to extend our capabilities.'

'Does that connect with me?' Nshila offered a neutral response and sent him off to the bar for Worcester sauce. It was a simple initiative-seizing gambit that usually worked – the demanding, hard-to-please woman.

'Our work is about influencing people', Jeffrey continued when he got back. 'Manipulating them if you want to use harsh words – though everybody does it. We think we might steal a march by investigating paranormal methods.'

'Won't you have a hard time distinguishing that from the nasty psychological gimmicks that advertisers use already.'

'Possibly, but what I want to explain is that one of our senior people has spent the last ten years on assignments in Africa. He used normal marketing techniques in the towns and got acceptable results. When it came to the rural areas, he found that he got nowhere at all if the witchdoctors were against him. They seemed to have the psychological scene sewn up. They know far more about mental influencing, it seems, than we do. It started us thinking.'

Nshila started a 'preparing to go' sequence : pushing her glass away, checking the contents of the handbag, fiddling with gloves and sitting back from the table as if about to rise. 'Stop right there, Jeffrey. Are you making the assumption that anybody from black Africa knows all about witchcraft. Is that why you wanted to meet me? I don't want any more of this.'

'No! No! I'm sorry. I apologise. I didn't mean to offend you. We seem to have gone too fast. Give me a chance.'

A successful wrong-footing move, the woman thought. Keep him off-balance and his prepared story might start to fall apart. She had the advantage, also, of knowing his background and being quite sure that whatever he told her was going to be less than the truth.

'Go on, then. But remember there's one strike against you.'

There was an interruption as a man passed dangerously close to the pair with two full pints of beer in each hand. A few drops fell on her boots and he muttered an apology. Jeffrey went on.

'I wanted to stand well with Colin Sandyman, my boss, so I picked up the lead and started trawling for educated people with an African background. It was a computer job. I called up the immigration records of people from your part of the world, and sorted for those who had got higher degrees from any UK university in the last ten years. There were five hundred names. Too many, I sorted again for people who had also achieved some distinction. The number got down to seventy. One of the distinctions I used was membership of the Institute of Directors.

So I'm not asking to meet you for no reason at all. I know you are a Director of The Rain Consultancy.'

He really had been scrabbling in the dark, Nshila realised. The likely outcome of such a trawl would be a list full of minor academics, doctors, nurses and social services staff with some sportsmen, pop stars and newsreaders thrown in. He had also given away that he was in the government service, since no private organisation could access such records. He would have done better to talk to the managers of African national football teams, who regularly employ witchdoctors to befuddle opposing goalkeepers.

It was a weak cover story, but revealed nothing about what it was covering. What was needed? Witchcraft? Psychological manipulation? A lead to one or more wanted individuals? Or might Jeffrey's outfit be looking for somebody able to deliver the ultimate solution? Nshila felt the subtle excitement that had overcome her in the past. Challenge – Difficulty – Life on the edge – Exploration – Achievement. Emotions that had driven her into dramatic actions - actions that were marginally justifiable in the tribal world but probably criminal in the UK.

'Let me get this clear. You have been sent out to interview seventy people – men and women – who originate from sub-Saharan Africa and are sufficiently intellectual to give an informed opinion about witchcraft. Is that right?'

'Yes. That's stage one. If I find anybody who has links into that scene then I have to follow up. This sounds crazy, but what would play best in the consultancy is that I turn up a genuine practising witchdoctor who will run a seminar for us and take a retainer as what we call a professional resource.'

There was no need for Nshila to manufacture a sceptical laugh or feign incredulity. They came naturally. 'It's not a subject I know anything about. There was a witchdoctor in my village, certainly, but I was just a child and hid myself whenever he appeared.' She made a mental apology to Kwaname, her tutor, and told Jeffrey to strike her name from his list of 'possibles'.

'It will be twelve down and fifty-eight to go. But are you

quite sure you can't offer me any lead at all? You must have plenty of friends from your own country. Could any of them be into that sort of thing?'

The talk was interrupted by a burst of noise from the other end of the bar. There was a football match showing and a goal had been scored. The bar was filled with the standard calls of 'off-side', and abuse of the referee. Nshila had time to think. Should she turn Jeffrey away and never know what lay behind the approach, or should she dangle one end of a string? She felt another of those arguments brewing up in her head – rather like that awful feeling she sometimes experienced in bed when she knew she was going to get muscle-cramp and could do nothing to stop it. But this time she stopped it, or rather the vodka stopped it for her. She had drunk just enough to immobilise the cautious self and give the floor to his opponent. 'You can't possibly slam the door on this one without knowing more. It's cowardly. It's gutless. What would Kwaname think of you?' The self reminded her of numerous growth opportunities that had been seized in spite of logic. It asked whether she had reached a plateau and was getting bored. It asked whether she no longer had the guts and determination to break new ground. It asked if she was growing old. It asked if she could not hack it any longer. It won.

To buy more time she sent Jeffrey off for another vodka (and get Worcester sauce in it this time). There was a crowd round the bar: getting served could well take ten minutes. She reviewed the scenario and asked whether it was quite as ridiculous as it seemed. Maybe not. She remembered the crazy things the secret services of the world had dreamt up in the past: the umbrellas tipped with curare; the pills containing delayed action poison so that the victim died elsewhere; the use of radioactive substances; the dolphins trained to place bombs under boats; the use of dowsers by the US army in Viet Nam. Hiring a witchdoctor made just as much sense.

Another side of her personality joined it. The fantasist and humorist who turned everything into a joke. How would she fare as a retained expert linked to the civil service? Where does an assassin rate, she wondered, in the civil service hierarchy? Would the retainer be substantial, or would it just be cash on the nail for every job completed? If serving for a long period, would she be in line for an MBE or a knighthood?

She had a vision of herself in retirement, living in a big mansion in the country, enjoying the respect of all the locals, opening church fetes and so on - nobody knowing that the status and wealth came from the discreet disposal of evil-doers. Dame Nshila Ileloka, maybe?

Jeffrey returned with the drinks.

'Jeffrey, I've thought about contacts, and one name comes to mind as an outside possibility. The name is Barney Caddick, and I don't even know him personally. I was at a party three weeks ago. I was talking with a man from the meteorological office about cloud formations, but four people beside us had very loud voices. I heard enough to realise that this man Barney was studying paranormal phenomena in an obscure department of London University. I don't know which or where, but I remember him saying that he didn't need a broomstick to get to work because it was only a short walk from his flat in Islington. Despite his name, Barney is black. The tribal marks on his face say "Congo" to me, but I can't be sure.'

Nothing more was said on that subject. The two talked about other subjects for another fifteen minutes and then parted. Nshila reflected on the encounter. What had she given away? Well, Jeffrey had talked with her for an hour and must have formed some opinions. He could renew contact if he wished. He might or might not have realised that this woman knew far more than she had disclosed. And he had the name of Barney Caddick to follow up.

What had she done herself? She had handed out one end of a paper-trail that might end up in profitable work. In less material terms, she had got a vision. A vision in which her profession – one commonly described as evil – was made over into a praise-worthy service to the state.

Chapter Four

A Professional

Nshila punched in her personal code number at the door of the Eastcheap building and took the lift to the fourth floor. She climbed the flight of stairs that had previously led to the caretaker's apartments, and now to The Rain Consultancy and her own private flat. Gillian Harker and Peter Grace had long gone, but Rasputin, her black cat and confidant, was present and welcoming as usual.

The flat was stark and simple. For her private space Nshila rejected the luxuries of western life and chose things that reminded her of childhood – despite its relative unhappiness. The walls were white emulsion, and the furnishings sparse – nothing that was not necessary – nothing that had ornamental value only. Chairs and tables and even her double bed relied on strips of hide instead of springs. There were cushions, but thin ones stuffed with horsehair. On the walls were six prints showing the formal dress of African women from her tribe and five neighbouring tribes. The concessions to modernity – cooker, refrigerator and so on were concealed. There was no radiator to be seen; not because Nshila could endure cold – she hated it – but because she had installed under-floor heating at great expense. The big contradiction was the bathroom. There, everything was totally modern and expensive. 'Never again', she had determined, 'am I going to walk to the river, bathe in cold water and carry several gallons back on my head.' She sat length-wise on the couch with her head on one end and her feet on the other.

She had returned from similar encounters before, and agonised over her performance. Had she given too much away? Had the excitement – and sometimes the humorous possibilities – prevailed over common sense? Rasputin, curled up on her lap, was oblivious to the problem.

What about that paper trail? Barney Caddick was a low-level contact point for people who wanted dubious or unlawful products or services. He was one of those who 'doesn't know, but knows a man who does.' He knew a man who could carry the message one step higher. If a request seemed to him to be connected with smuggled alcohol then he knew that the next person up the ladder would be Madeleine Cookson. If the request were about industrial espionage then the next person would be Harry Taylor. If it were to do with the supernatural or witchcraft then the name would be Neil Crichton. Barney got small retainers from a large number of people and the occasional big bonus if his leads proved valuable. He didn't know that one of his retainers came from Nshila and that some of the messages finally reaching her were to do with assassination. She concluded that there was little risk. The number of intermediaries, and the subtle language used, gave adequate security.

But how would things play if the organisation behind Jeffrey Hicks was serious, and committed, and really wanted somebody dead, and managed to identify her as capable? That lifted the lid on all her old dilemmas. Did she regret the assignments in which she had caused death? Surely it ought to fill her life with guilt, remorse and misery? Why were they absent? Possibly because the first one had been a tribal matter of which all her associates approved. Something a person has done once has less significance if one is asked to do it again, and the others had all been thoroughly evil people whose death improved the world. Killing a few evil-doers was surely nothing compared with the politicians who sent soldiers to war or industrialists who overlooked safety risks in order to maximise profits. But why had she done it? Why might she do it again? Was it money? No. She could enjoy a good life style from her legitimate activities: only in one case had the money been important, and that was to escape from the life of a penniless student. Why, then? Perhaps it was the risk. There are many people, she told herself, who are compulsive risk-takers and only feel truly alive when they are in danger. And there was the knowledge that in some sense her

23

qualities were unique. Very few people had her knowledge of African witchcraft and also some mastery of western technology. There were things that she could do which nobody else could do. Amongst them was the ability to kill by methods that were deemed impossible and could therefore not be prosecuted.

Unique. The word and the images that went with it took over her mind: she thought back over her life while the television – muted – finished a news programme and launched a soap opera. Was she unique? If so, how did she become so? Where did she learn the different skills? Surely it started with old Kwaname and the witchcraft she learnt from him in the hut under the baobab tree. But how did that happen? The first encounter was accidental, the hut being the only possible refuge as she fled from a vengeful and violent half-brother. But how about his acceptance of her, slow as it was? He had no duty to let her frequent his hut and stand by him and watch him at work. There must have been some quality in her that attracted him.

Did the roots of her adventurous spirit lie there? Kwaname had been a witchdoctor of the old school, taught by his father in a traditional, conventional way and not too bothered about why things happened provided he got what he wanted. Nshila remembered times when it had seemed to her that if you made 'this' happen then there was no reason why you could not make 'that' happen, too. Once or twice she had experimented successfully, and the buzz it gave her was terrific. In modern terms she had been at the cutting edge. What was the current term? Yes, 'thinking the unthinkable'. Most people would see that as exciting, even if they had no way to execute the thought. But why did she also find some of her adventures amusing. Why did certain prospects strike her as extremely funny? Could it be that they were sometimes outrageous and bizarre – things that ordinary people would never imagine because they were so extreme and on such a grand scale? Like some of the big hoaxes of history. She had read with pleasure the story of Piltdown Man; how Professor Dawson had deceived the archaeological world for many years by falsifying the bones found in a dig.

She had also once travelled by train to Hastings and passed through the Mountfield tunnel – now single-tracked because the original contractor had lined it with fewer layers of brick than were specified. When the deception was discovered, there was no option but to make the tunnel narrower by putting additional layers of brick on the inside. That made it necessary to build special coaches for the Hastings line only. Quite an achievement to create a whole train set by your own efforts! Public money wasted? Shareholders money wasted? Huge numbers of people put to unnecessary work? All true. But surely it was funny as well?

Whatever the history, whatever the reasons, she was qualified as a professional assassin and realised that if Jeffrey's people came through with an assignment, she might be tempted to accept it. She still slept soundly.

Chapter Five

Friendly Policemen

In mid-afternoon of the day Nshila met Jeffrey Hicks, a meeting was held more than a hundred miles away in the Georgian building – once a brewery – that housed the headquarters of The Inner Marches Constabulary. It stood beside a river not far from the town centre and had been converted into offices when the family owning the brewery had sold up in the 1960's. The developer doing the conversion had gone bankrupt and the local police force had bought it. At that time they were a 'town' force in the traditional sense and it was their only building. Later on, amalgamation with ten other forces produced The Inner Marches. The new organisation seized the brewery as headquarters and the local police station was set up in a modern, rather hideous building close to the railway station.

Gerald Woodchurch, the Chief Constable, had abandoned his right to the most prestigious office because the corner one, slightly smaller, had a picture window offering a view across the river to the playground he had used as a boy. It seemed a long time ago, but he was young to be a Chief Constable. It was only thirty years since the boy of ten had worked up the swing to maximum height and thrown himself forward, to land on his feet, running fast, and cannon into a pram-wheeling woman. He had joined the police at eighteen, risen to sergeant locally and then done ten years in the Metropolitan Police. Moving quite rapidly through the ranks, he had reached Chief Superintendent and passed the interviews and examinations needed to become eligible for a Chief Officer post. The first he was offered was as ACC here in his hometown. He had accepted immediately and had now moved up to the top spot.

The playground he looked at was in the same place as ever, but swings, seesaws, roundabouts and slides were all newer and safer designs. Beside each was a notice describing the safe way to use it and prohibiting most of the things he and his friends had done.

There was a knock on the door, and three of his senior staff entered. Gerald took his seat at the mahogany conference table. It was big for four people, adequate for six and small for eight. For any larger meetings Gerald had to migrate to the old Board Room – panelled in dark oak and poorly lit – where the be-whiskered Managing Director of the brewery (portrait still on the wall) had sat in state. Gerald's own room was light and airy. The walls were decorated with water-colours of famous golf-courses and with group photographs from programmes Gerald had attended at The Police Staff College. In one wall was the door to the ultimate prestige symbol – his own washroom and changing room.

The meeting had been called to discuss the police image. The mood of the times was to demand more and more from the public services but to provide little extra in the way of resources. More than that, there was pressure to meet 'targets' thought by government to be indicators of success. Since these were precisely defined, and more realistic indicators could never be equally precise, much police effort went into meeting the targets, or creating the appearance of having done so. The effort going into other work – like providing a presence on the street – suffered. Additionally there had been one or two recent cases in which a person arrested and accused of a crime had been acquitted for technical reasons. Worse still, a few people convicted of a crime had later been proved innocent. There was strong public feeling that, whatever the police were doing, it was not what was needed.

'Good afternoon', Gerald began. 'I wanted this meeting because you, Audrey, have put up this proposal for police involvement in the Three Counties Show. You are not talking about the usual law-enforcement presence, but about active participation as exhibitors, administrators, sponsors and so on. It's a novel idea, and there are several arguments against it, particularly financial ones, but we desperately need to do something about our public image and I want to hear more from you.'

'Sir', Audrey Canning began, 'I don't need to tell you what a big event this show has become in recent years. It is no longer restricted to agriculture-related activities concerning one section of the community only. It has grown to include commercial activities in general, and of course that includes the leisure industry. Now it has decided to become family-friendly and provide entertainment for all ages. If we put on displays by motor-cyclists, dog handlers, and safety experts we could get a lot of attention. We might stage a murder mystery at The Rainbows End Hotel. It could be staffed by senior detectives and offer a huge prize to whoever identified the murderer. We might do something in partnership with the Fire Service and the Ambulance Service and the Hospitals, to show how a major emergency is handled.'

Stan Trautmann voiced the inevitable doubt. 'The expense is always the worry. I like the idea well enough, but there will be plenty of people saying that the money would be better spent putting policemen on the streets. Another big problem is the weather; there have been a few years when the show was ruined by the weather. We might get little benefit for our money.'

No final decision was taken, but Audrey was given permission to use two officers for one week on planning activity. So Bill Waterhouse and Claude Mason were told, amongst other things, to find out about weather prediction; how accurate was a detailed, local forecast likely to be, to what extent did accuracy decline as the time before the event lengthened, and were there really significant differences between nearby places because of hills and valleys and expanses of water? What about soil and drainage? How long did showers typically last at given times of year? They started off enquiring from the meteorological office and got answers so vague, and qualified as to be meaningless. Then they became aware that independent agencies existed and got the address of The Rain Consultancy. They gifted themselves

28

a day out in London, and greatly enjoyed it. A few days later they told their story in the drab, lime green environment of the police canteen, with its usual smell of fried food and stale cabbage.

'The place called The Rain Consultancy was great. It's quite hard to find, of course – a small old building tucked between modern tower blocks in Eastcheap. The lift only takes you to the fourth floor and then you climb a narrow staircase lined with the most beautiful weather pictures – sunsets and thunderstorms and cloud formations and tornadoes and rainbows and so on. They have a polished oak door and a bell-pull. When you pull it you don't get an electronic tinkle, but a loud clanging sound like an old cow bell. The door was opened by a dark, tough-looking type who looked more suited to a Saturday night punch up than a city office. The boss woman was another story.'

Bill and Claude had different views about Nshila. Bill described her only in physical terms – slender, taller than most women, ebony black skin, striking, smartly dressed, and so on. Claude agreed with all that, but took more notice of the intelligence she displayed.

'She was very quick to understand and asked penetrating questions. When she offered an opinion it was clear and positive. It was a good thing we had done our homework. We had specialised maps of the show location, so we could discuss the possible effects on the weather of local geographical features, and the way the geology affected drainage. It was not just a matter of 'Will it rain or not?' We were concerned with the probabilities of 'how heavy' and 'how long' and the degree of inconvenience that might be caused. We gained a lot of useful knowledge. She was full of hints, for instance, of how we might make a heavy shower into something of interest instead of just an annoyance. We got on really well with her. We ended up asking her advice about where to lunch.'

Bill Waterhouse took up the story. 'Some of the places she suggested were way outside the range of our subsistence allowance. We were looking a bit disappointed when she came out with one of those offers you can't refuse.

'She suggested taking us to lunch at The Institute of Directors. She had no appointments for the afternoon and found it interesting to have policemen as clients, and if we felt bad about being guests then we could pay for the wine.'

Bill and Claude described the downstairs dining room at the IOD, making much of the fact that it had been converted from the old gentleman's lavatory and retained some of the décor. They told of what they had eaten and drunk, and how much it had all cost, and related some of the stories Nshila had told her about her childhood. What they never told any of their colleagues was that they had become rather indiscreet about their big current worry, saying more than was wise about Maud Franklin, their boss.

Inspector Franklin was their immediate superior, and in charge of other officers as well. She was known for taking full credit for every success achieved by her staff and ensuring that they were blamed for any failure. She was seen as clever, inhuman and manipulative. One of her case reports had been a real knife-in-the-back job for Claude, who was known to have a minor drink problem and made a mistake on an observation job. A group of people had moved very fast from a house into a car and he had believed the main target to be still in the house. Maud had discovered that Claude's observation point had been directly opposite a pub and had managed to suggest that perhaps Claude had been inside rather than outside. She was believed to have a dossier on every person in the station, to be intensely ambitious, and capable of climbing over friend and foe alike to join the elite group of female Chief Constables. Having some money of her own made her less liked than ever. She had a small flat in London as well as her modest local house, and she was reputed to have a computer there on which she stored masses of data about colleagues, superiors, and alternative career paths for herself.

They had slight feelings of guilt, Bill and Claude, because they had exposed some of the political nastiness of the police to an outsider. But they comforted themselves with the reflection

30

that similar things happened in all big organisations. What they did not know, and never got to know, was that they had described the type of malicious underhand operator that Nshila most hated. They had left her thinking how much enjoyment she would get from destroying Maud Franklin, if she ever got the chance.

Chapter Six

A Supernatural Servant

The modern businesswoman is concerned to keep up-to-date. The world changes so fast that one has barely had time to master a skill before it is superseded. Awareness of this was one of the many benefits Nshila had gained from the Open University. It assumed extra importance now, when a major contract might be in the pipeline. She was still telling herself that it might not materialise, and that, if it did, she might not accept it. But suppose it did materialise, and suppose she did accept it, were she, and her supportive organisation prepared? Was it time for an overhaul? Almost two years had passed since her last major contract, and in that she had relied on very traditional methods. She had not been innovative.

Some people have special places or activities that stimulate their thinking and through which ideas come to them. Perhaps more people identify the bath as their special place than any other. Nshila had several such places and activities, one of which was walking through the City of London, with its many historical connections. She left the office, crossed the road and walked down to the Monument. Should she climb it? Years had passed since she had done so. Well, it was a challenge. How much the view had been curtailed since the structure was finished! High-rise buildings in all directions, inconceivable at that time. She walked up St Mary at Hill, crossed Eastcheap again and walked up Rood Lane into Fenchurch Street. The station, she thought: visit the station. Up the stairs she climbed, to sit down on a deserted platform, the place being silent and empty in the middle of the day. One train stood at a platform, ready for the evening commuters. A modern train. What was the first train to use this place, she wondered. Some early steam train, recognisably descended from George Stephenson's Rocket? On to the end of Fenchurch Street to gaze on Aldgate Pump. How long since anyone drew water from it? The distance from here to her office was about the same as the distance from her village to the river. What astonished glances she would draw if she filled a large jar with water and carried it back on her head! Down Minories to Tower Hill and the Tower itself: William the Conqueror – his little contribution to history! Not much use as a military defence these days.

It all changes, she reflected. New technology alters what it is possible to do, and changing fashions alter what people want you to do. Go on as you always did, and quite soon your business will collapse. It's no use trying to make money by running stage coaches once the railway has arrived. Even if your product or service still has merit, customers will want the emotional satisfaction of something that is 'modern' and 'state-of-the art'. You have to keep up to date. Whether you are a poet or a hairdresser or a dentist or an assassin, the message is the same. But the assassin has special problems because of the need for secrecy. What are the others doing? You don't know.

The Open University taught students to examine the markets. How big was the market? What share was taken by the major firms? What were their strengths and weaknesses? What new products, and new technology were around? What lines of research were firms pursuing? Such questions were not easily answered for an assassin.

A manufacturing firm, learning that a competitor has launched a new product, can buy it in the shops and analyse it and imitate it, or improve on it. A cruise ship operator can book a cruise on a competitors ship and assess the service offered. Can an assassin find a body killed by a competitor and figure a better way in which it might have been done? There is no trade association. Search the bookshelves for a trade magazine, and nothing will be found. There is little communication between practitioners. There is nothing equivalent to the medical world in which several doctors form a group practice.

So 'networking' was inadequate as a way for an assassin

to keep up to date. Progress had to come from development of existing resources, or experiment and adaptation, or literary research. How had she made progress before, Nshila wondered? She reflected on major gains from studying ancient texts in the British Library – in the wonderful old circular reading room where Karl Marx and other famous men had studied. She had loved the experience of putting in a request for a book, and waiting in aristocratic leisure till a flunkey brought it. Good ideas had abounded in the Grand Grimoire, though interpretation and adaptation were required. Sometimes the text was hard to understand, and sometimes materials were prescribed that were now unobtainable.

Another technique that had helped her was comparison of what she had learnt as a child and what she had discovered of historic witchcraft in England. It had become apparent to her that there were similarities – that certain concepts were universal. The manner in which they were exploited in different countries and different ages showed huge variation, but the underlying belief was constant. Sometimes she could remember techniques that had brought only partial success in the tribal environment but, applied in a different manner in mediaeval England, appeared to have worked well.

'That's enough reflective analysis.' Some inner discipline issued the command. The big steps forward in her life had always been associated with a practical challenge. That was what she now needed. If she placed herself in a situation where new skills were demanded, then new skills she would find. Nothing ever energised her learning process like attacking a current difficulty. But there was no such project available.

'Watch it, Lady! You don't want to be the next headline, do you?'

Nshila had stopped dead two feet off the pavement in Crutched Friars and a newsvendor had pulled her back as an enraged taxi swerved past. How could she have been so blind? An obvious practice exercise was staring her in the face - Maud Franklin! She could focus on that woman, learn her habits, and put a few neat spokes in her wheel. She would practice her skills, get back in the groove, and be up to speed if the Jeffrey Hicks people came through with serious work. The idea was specially attractive because there was no direct connection between her and Maud. They had not met. Each was unaware of the other. Maud was unaware that Nshila even existed and Nshila's knowledge came through a channel that would never be discovered.

She would start by using Zach Kawero's hacking abilities to confirm that Franklin really was making use of discreditable knowledge to damage the careers of others and promote her own. Was she an organisational blackmailer? What nasty records existed on that database in her London flat?

The interview with Zach did not go the way she had planned.

'Zach, I want you to get inside the PC of a woman called Maud Franklin and install some sort of bug that will give me total access to everything she does.'

His response surprised her.

'Nshila, I can't do it. There are laws now that carry harsh penalties for that sort of thing. There have even been successful prosecutions. One hacker got five years. And this woman, you tell me, is a police officer. It's too dangerous.'

It was a shock. People seldom refused to do what she asked. Socially, it was because she was an impressive woman, with an easy, friendly manner. At work it was because she always explained the reasoning behind her request. Her hearers felt included. And there was something in the way she asked that boosted the ego of any hearer: some subliminal message that said 'Only you can do it to the standard I need'. She responded sharply to the refusal.

'What on earth are you talking about? Surely some of the things you have done for me in the past were dodgy enough? What's different?'

'Most of those were directed against organisations, with complex systems in which thousands of transactions took place and there were ways of disguising what I was doing. It was

35

criminal but the chances of detection were low. At the individual level, such activities are more exposed. I don't like the idea.'

'But would you be able to do it? Is it possible?'

'Yes.'

'Then do it. You'll be paid well enough.'

'No. I won't. This one is just too much to ask. I've done a whole range of things for you, Nshila, but we've reached the limit. Sorry, but No.'

She dropped the subject, and talked about events in the day's news. But she didn't intend to accept this refusal and determined that Zach was going to be brought into line. How? Her mind responded to the stimulus with alacrity. She would use The Companion to persuade him. This was a piece of witchcraft she knew well as theory but had never tried out in practice. She felt excitement building up.

In the hut under the baobab tree Kwname had sometimes attached an unseen companion to his enemy. If Kwaname burnt the right herbs and spoke the right words, and directed the spirit correctly to the target then that target had a most unpleasant experience. Every moment of the day he sensed a malignant presence just behind his shoulder, with the faintest smell and the faintest whisper of sound. When he turned his head there was nothing there: when he turned back the presence had returned. Nobody else could see anything. The victim had, all the time, a slight ache in all his bones and a feeling of sickness. That had been the fate of Enoch Mutale, the rapist. He had blundered around the village for three days, constantly looking over his shoulder and screaming 'take it away'. He had finally killed himself. Zach was a bit of a loner: The Companion was going to be alongside him!

Using The Companion required the target to be identified. Before parting with Zach, Nshila went to her bedroom and took a large ring from her jewel case. The stone had fallen out a few days before and it had a rough, sharp edge. As she said farewell to Zach she put her arm across his shoulders. Moving it away, she dragged her hand across his neck just enough to

36

leave a small cut. She apologised profusely and exclaimed at the missing stone as if she had just noticed its absence. Her last words to Zach were:

'I think you're going to have a visitor, early tomorrow. I hope you like him.' Then she returned to her fastness on the top floor to prepare the details.

Some special materials were needed, not found in their natural state in England. But one advantage of western civilisation is that supermarkets and pharmacies can provide every sort of fruit and spice and vegetable and drug. If one wants the seeds of an obscure South American tree, one can probably find them used as an ingredient in a face cream or a patent cure for arthritis. Three hours research work on the internet and one hours shopping were enough to obtain them. She called up the Specspell database on her PC and printed out the instructions for The Companion. It was a shock to realise that she had quite forgotten some of the details. If she had tried to work the trick from memory alone, she would have failed. It was true – she was a bit like that rugby player – losing touch. Something else also nagged at her mind. Surely there was more to The Companion than she had written into Specspell? When had she written it? Had she been under pressure and omitted details? Surely she had seen Kwaname do quite elaborate things with it? And yet, could she trust memories of events she had witnessed long ago as a young girl? It worried her. She went out to her roof garden, remembering a few school reports that had said 'Must try harder'.

The roof garden of the Eastcheap flat was not large. Space was lost to a shed-like structure enclosing the water tank that supplied the building and to machinery associated with the lift. There was also a smaller shed for tools and emergency equipment. Nshila had acquired keys to both sheds and sometimes used the smaller for minor witchcraft activities. It had little resemblance to the hut under the baobab tree, but on a dark night, lit by a few candles and with the walls bearing such symbols as she had brought with her from Africa, it was spooky enough. It certainly gave a feeing of isolation and secrecy. One feature that did duplicate the hut was an annoying number of draughts, that crept insistently through small holes. In Africa these were warm draughts: in England they were cold. Nshila reflected that in the old days she would not have had to work wrapped up in a thick cardigan from Marks and Spencers. About midnight she burnt the herbs, smeared the ashes over a drawing of Zach's new scar, raised her arms in the air and called on the spirit. Quietly, she called at first; hardly more than a whisper, then a little louder each time until she reached an impressive scream. As it faded, she took an old plastic knitting needle and stabbed it through the pictured scar. 'Let's see how you like that, Zach.' As she removed the needle, the sleeve of her cardigan caught one of the dishes that held her ingredients and knocked it to the floor. No matter. The job was done.

Then the doubts came creeping in. Was short-term anger and impetuous action the right way for a witchdoctor to behave? In the tribal context he was a highly responsible member of the tribe and whatever action he took was expected to benefit the community as a whole – even when it meant getting rid of somebody. Such decisions are not taken lightly. Another worry was whether it would work. After all, she had no guarantee that a spirit that had worked in Africa was going to hear and respond in London WC1. She might have remembered some details of the spell wrongly. If the spirit did hear and obey, how would it get on in the ant-like world of London? Would it find the target? Worse still, cases were known in which an incorrect spell had caused the curse to rebound upon the curser. However, nothing nasty happened in the next hour. She felt completely alone and comfortable (Rasputin being out on some feline adventure). She went to bed and slept well.

For three hours. Then she woke in a panic. Her earlier worries had been about the spell not working; she had never considered that it might work too well and that Zach might be so disoriented that he had a fatal accident. He might even be driven to suicide like Enoch Mutale. Was it possible? Yes. Unlikely, but possible, Zach was African, susceptible to witchcraft. She must act immediately.

Turn on the PC. Panic. Does it always take this long to boot up? Has something gone wrong with it? Have I lost the database? No, it's just the protective software – firewall and anti-spam etc. which is barely noticed at normal times but takes an age when one is in a hurry.

Access the spell for calling off The Companion and print it out. Read it. Panic. One of the items necessary for the spell could be the very one that got spilt on the floor.

Up to the shed. Which is the missing item? Panic. It's the one on the floor and the draught has blown it away. No chance of scooping it up. No chance of working the spell. Panic. What will happen to Zach? The only alternative – get to him personally and tell all. If he knows what is happening he will find the strength to endure it till the calling off can be fixed. How to reach him? No tubes this early, no buses, much too far to walk or run (Eastcheap to South Kensington). The car was in the garage down by the river, no attendant till 5.30am.

Idea. Local residents with permanent parking spaces have a special code that will get them into the garage when it is unstaffed. Never used before. Panic. Where is it? Where might it have been written down? Probably last year's diary. Where's that? Found in the drawer of the bedside table. Clothes. Anything will do. Down the stairs. Down in the lift. Out of the building. Down the side streets to the garage. Panic. Will the combination have been changed? One. Three. Four. Two. Five. Nothing. No movement. Panic. Look more closely at the key pad – hard to read in the dim light. Hope. The numbers go bottom to top and not top to bottom. One. Three. Four. Two. Five. A pause, a clunk, the sound of electric motors and the door moves slowly upwards.

Mobile at last. Out of Lower Thames Street into Upper Thames Street. Traffic lights red at the Queen Street/ Southwark Bridge junction. Panic. Forget them, girl, this is an emergency. Don't die, Zach. Don't die. I never meant real harm. Up to seventy under Blackfriars Bridge and along the Embankment to Westminster Bridge. Round Parliament Square, missing a milk van by inches. Pigeons scattered in all directions: three of them leave it too late.

Into Victoria Street. Panic. Blue lights flashing and something huge stationary on the left-hand side. Surely they can't have intercepted that quickly? No. It's an articulated lorry from Poland that the police have stopped. Slow down and drive cautiously past. Eaton Square. Belgrave Road. Pont Street. Beauchamp Place and out into Brompton Road. Was that a postman jumping and swearing? Thurloe Place. Cromwell Place. Harrington Road. Left into Reece Mews where Zach owned the upper floor of a mews house. Double park and rush up the stairs. Don't be dead, Zach. Don't be dead.

Nshila had a key to Zach's flat – borrowed long ago for some meeting and forgotten. She opened the door a crack and listened.

'No! No! Please! Never! Ah!' Words or just inarticulate sounds? The cries of a terrified person? Muffled and incoherent they certainly were, but the fear came through. She was across the main room instantly to see a blanket-covered figure striving to dig itself further into the crack between the bed and the wall. It was trying to escape from something, but the something was invisible. The Companion seemed to have exceeded his reputation. Even if she explained things to Zach, the thing was going to be hard to bear.

Salvation! From God? From the spirit world? From her own mind, working subconsciously on the problem? On a table were the terrible black cigars that Zach smoked. Nshila lit one, drew on it to get a bright glow, and stabbed it onto the scratch that she had made on Zach's neck.

Zach screamed. Loudly. Several times. But she kept the cigar in place till she was sure the mark would have been burnt out.

It worked. She took the cigar off and saw only a spot of burnt flesh about the size of a pound coin. The mark had gone.

The spirit could no longer identify the target. Zach's screams subsided, his breathing gradually went back to normal and he slept.

Nshila sat there for fifteen minutes, cradling his head and shoulders in her arms like a girl comforting her wounded lover. Luckily, nobody investigated the noise or the open door. She also found some ointment in the bathroom cupboard and made an attempt to dress the burn. Finally he stirred.

'Nshila?'

She said nothing. It would take him a few minutes to make sense of what had happened.

'Did you send that Thing?'

'Zach, I'm terribly sorry. I was experimenting, and I was angry with you. I didn't think. It's gone, Zach. Finished. It can't hurt you.'

'It's had a good try.'

'I promise you I'll never do anything magical against you again. Not ever. Total immunity, that's what you've got. Lucky man.'

He thought for a while.

'You're here, Nshila.'

'I had to come. When I realised what might happen it was just too awful. I could not think of anything but getting here as soon as possible.'

'Why did you have to brand me with the cigar?'

'I didn't know how to call the Thing off. Then I thought that it only knows who to go for because of the mark. Get rid of the mark and the Thing can't recognise you, I thought. And it worked.'

'I always knew you were dangerous. If you are going to play with things you can't control, you are totally lethal.'

'I need a bit more personal discipline, don't I? But you are safe, Zach. It could have been worse.'

'Not a lot.'

It took a while for the two of them to calm down. Zach was obviously shocked that Nshila could have been so callous and

41

careless. He also noticed how distressed she was. It was clear that she cared about him.

Eventually they decided that they needed food and migrated to an early breakfast place near Victoria station. Nshila said nothing about the cause of the quarrel and did not really know how to raise it. Zach did it for her.

'You said you were really mad at me. Was it because I wouldn't hack into that computer for you?'

'Yes. That and your foul cigars.'

'It wasn't necessary. On my way home from your place I was worried about refusing, and I figured out a way to safeguard myself. Provided she is networked to a few other computers, I can cover myself adequately. I am pretty sure it will work – certain if she uses the type of database favoured by the police. It's a variation of one widely used in government and I know it well.'

'You mean you'll do it? After all this trauma?'

'Yes. Now that I've thought it through I am keen to try. I love breaking new ground. The experience may pay off in some later project. That often happens.'

'Let's just hope that your idea of experimenting will be safer than mine.'

The end of the mad incident saw the two still friends, and Zach eager to start the hacking task on Maud Franklin's PC. But he asked and got double his usual fee.

Chapter Seven

The Hand Of Glory

After Zach agreed to an attack on Maud Franklins PC, Nshila thought she could sit back and wait for the results. She expected Zach would send Maud some harmless-looking message which would install a recording and transmitting code so that her every electronic move would be known in Eastcheap. She was surprised when he reported a problem.

'What do you mean, Zach? She is bound to have an internet connection and an e-mail address. Just get on with the job, and send in your ferret. This is a pro-bono job and I don't want it to take forever.'

'I could do that, but I could do a better job, more secure, more reliable and less risky, if I could have access to the machine itself. I want to have thirty minutes undisturbed in her apartment. Can you fix it?'

'So we have to commit some sordid little crime like "breaking and entering", do we?'

'Considering what you did to me a few days ago, I don't think you can lecture me about minor crime. Anyway, you weren't worried when you expected me to do it all on my own.'

'Nobody could prove that I did anything at all. There was nothing to see. You had a bad dream. I happened to stop by your house to bring you a message, and woke you up.'

'Legal – moral – good - bad. You know what I mean. You can help me if you want to, and I promise you we'll get better results my way.'

Another problem! Something else to which she had no immediate solution. She had embarked on the project partly as examination of her skills and an attempt to extend them. The plan was good. But now she had to keep Maud absent or unconscious for thirty minutes if she was to make the next step. How?

43

Sleeping spells! She was well aware that they are common in primitive societies. She recalled some from that fine old book The Golden Bough by Sir James Fraser. In the passage concerning theft, he recounts how an intending thief will plant some object associated with sleep in the hut of his intended victim. It might, for instance, be the root of a plant that, when eaten or smoked, produces hallucination, trance, drowsiness and sleep. If the spell works, the thief will be able to enter the house, rummage around, take what he wants, and leave the victim still sound asleep.

Great, she thought. But turning up the references revealed that every one was culture-specific and hardly appropriate for white police officers in England.

There was another book. The Ingoldsby Legends. Where had she read that weird book, and what had brought it to mind? It somehow connected with the east coast of England and the sea. Where could it have been? Answer: visiting her brother in Margate. Whenever she went there he arranged accommodation in a local Bed and Breakfast place that had a retainer from the school. She had been there once in the evening and wanted a book to read. The landlady had dug up the work of R.M.Barham, who had been well known in Kent in the nineteenth century and had written some rather nasty stories based on local superstitions.

One of the best concerned The Hand of Glory. It was a sleeping spell and it was as culture specific to the UK as anything could be. Kent. The Garden of England. Apparently all the practitioner need do was chop a hand off the corpse of somebody who had been hung for murder. Then a candle had to be fixed to the end of the thumb and the four fingers. The practitioner knocked on the door at dead of night and spoke:

> *'Open, lock, to the dead man's knock*
> *Fly bolt and bar and band.*
> *Nor move not swerve, joint muscle or nerve*
> *At the spell of the dead man's hand.'*

Immediately, according to Reverend Barham (who was a

clergyman) every lock in the house falls open, bolts slide back, bars are raised, and every living thing in the house is paralysed. Nothing can move and dead silence falls. Well, thought Nshila, that should be enough to fix Maud Franklin.

There were problems, of course, but using The Companion and getting away with it had left her in a risk-taking mood.

First of all, the hand of somebody hung for murder. The UK had no death penalty, and even if it had, the method of execution would not be hanging. The perfect item was unavailable.

She thought back to her time at the Open University and the session on problem solving techniques. One of them was called 'brainstorming'. Write down every idea, however ridiculous, and then re-examine them. It may cause cross-fertilisation and a truly credible idea will emerge. One evening, when Gillian and Peter had left work, she cleared the big electronic whiteboard in the office – the one for weather maps – and started a list.

1) Trace the grave of the last person to be hung in the UK (sometime in the 1950's?). Steal a skeleton hand.
2) Steal and import a hand from a country where they still hang murderers.
3) Find a murderer who has served his sentence and been released. Hang him and cut off a hand.
4) Find an incompetent doctor. Hang him and cut off his hand.
5) Find a recently dead actor or actress who has played, say, Macbeth or Othello or Richard the Third. Rob the grave.
6) Burgle a waxworks. Steal a hand of a waxen murderer.

It didn't look promising. What degree of conformity was required by the spell. Did it really require the hand of a hanged murderer, or were those words just the natural form of expression when the spell was recorded? Did Barham choose the words because in his time, murderers could easily be found hanging on the local gallows? If the words did not have to be taken literally, then what was the spirit behind them? Would the spell work if the hand came from a person who had committed murder and been convicted and executed by another means? Would it work if he had been convicted but not executed? Would it work if he had not been convicted? Would it work if he had not murdered, but committed some other appalling crime?

Of her list of six possibilities only Option Two looked to have the faintest chance of success. She found an internet site that provided recent data of executions world-wide, and the methods used. She was surprised to find that hanging was still Number One, and with the total standing at 319, getting a hand seem faintly possible. But then she saw that seven of the eleven countries that hung people had scored below ten in the year described. Her chances in Malaysia, for instance, were terrible. They had hung just one person, and might easily hang nobody in the current year. The USA had killed 52, but had used lethal injection in all cases. She glanced briefly at beheading (Saudi Arabia – 39) on the grounds that the executioner need only make one more stroke to provide a hand, thus eliminating one stage of the acquisition process. (Black humour, Rasputin. Both you and I can appreciate the double entendre!) But that would not be a literal interpretation of the spell.

There was one genuine possibility. Pakistan had hung 58 people in the year concerned. There was frequent traffic between England and Pakistan and a few travellers must be criminals. Pakistani residents in UK were known to bring in illegal relatives from time to time. A dead hand was surely a lot easier than a whole live body? And Pakistan apparently had a great many candidates on death row. The odds were getting better.

But that would be a long-term project. Dealing with Maud Franklin was immediate, but not important enough to justify major effort. In fact, the effectiveness of the spell was not vital. She could safely use substitute materials. If the spell worked, that would be fine. But if not, and Maud, awake, came to answer the knock on the door, then she would find nothing much worse than children produce on Halloween. That was no crime.

The finding of any old hand was quicker than expected and produced a good result. She bribed a medical student whose hospital had a link with the prison, Wormwood Scrubs. Prisoners sometimes died in prison, and those who felt remorse for their crimes sometimes bequeathed their bodies to the hospital for teaching purposes. The bribed student provided a hand belonging to a prisoner who was no murderer but had nevertheless killed somebody – in a traffic accident twenty years ago. The hand of a hanged murderer it was not. Yet it was better, Nshila thought, than a hand with no provenance at all.

The next step, fixing the candles onto the thumb and four fingers, was tough. The ordinary candle is about the same diameter as a human finger. How can it be attached so firmly that one can hold the hand upright and the candle will stay in place? The first thing Nshila tried was melting the bottom of the candle so that the wax dripped down over the top of a finger. That way she got splashes of wax down her leather boots and the candle fell off the finger. The next trial was a splint. A stick tied to both finger and candle. That was a delicate and time-consuming business, and it was hard to get the knots sufficiently tight. It worked for a time – until the flame of the candle burnt the string and the candle fell off. Finally she found some of the neat silver-coloured tubes that are used to pack single high quality cigars. What were they here for? An intended present for a client that she had forgotten all about. Had she triumphed? Not quite. She was off on a clandestine adventure and must carry the Hand of Glory concealed. A man could put it in a briefcase but it was too long for a woman's handbag. Nshila bought an artwork case; one of those things a would-be model uses to carry a portfolio of photographs.

Disaster nearly overtook her in rehearsal. She was up in the shed on the roof with the hand, ready to run through the ritual once more. It was early evening, not long after people left work. She lit the candles and recited the spell. There was a sound, immediate, clear and surprisingly loud. It was a sharp click and came from behind the door that concealed the water tank and the lift mechanism. Startled, she blew out the candles and went to investigate. There was a red light on the lift mechanism and the safety switch was in the position labelled 'Emergency cut-out'. Some force had triggered it. Well, it was a spell to open locks and the switch was some sort of lock. No great surprise.

She re-set the switch, but in case the lift did something stupid again she walked down the stairs. On the second floor she met two people coming up. Unexpected people, Japanese tourists loaded with cameras. What on earth were they doing here? Perhaps a friend had asked them to meet them at the office after work. There was a brief exchange of politeness.

'Excuse me, please. This lift is not working? It is for maintenance, perhaps? We pressed the button downstairs but there is no response.'

'Oh? Has it gone wrong?' She went to the lift, pressed the button, and the doors slid open normally. 'There you go. Maybe it has a mind of it's own sometimes. Or somebody cast a spell on it.'

'Thank you, Madam. Thank you very much.'

The operation at Maud Franklins place was tricky. She had told Zach nothing about how she was going to fix things, only that if he went to the apartment at a particular time he would find the door open and Maud sleeping. And she would not wake up, Zach was told, however long he took. She had also told him, 'On no account do you go into the bathroom.' Why was that so important? Because to keep the spell in operation the hand must be on the premises, fully lit, all the time. She aimed to get there before Zach and sit in the bathroom with the hand.

Entry to the building was easy. She had a piece of plastic in case witchcraft failed, and climbed one flight of stairs to Maud's door. Now it got harder, because other tenants might come by. She turned the corridor light off so that darkness would cause anybody to exclaim in annoyance and provide warning. She lit the candles. Then came the big surprise. The door was already ajar. There was a narrow gap between the door and the jamb: when she pushed, it swung open easily.

She resisted the temptation to walk in straight away. The spell was about keeping people asleep, not merely opening doors. So she muttered the words. She muttered in a slow meaningful, theatrical manner, seeking for high dramatic effect. Then she entered, found the bathroom, stuck the hand on top of the lavatory cistern and went to find the sleeping – hopefully – Maud.

Asleep! More than that. She lay on her bed in her daytime slip, snoring heavily. One high-heeled shoe was on her foot, and one lying beside the bed. She stank of whisky and stale cigarette smoke. She had clearly been to a party and was out for a long time. Maybe it was one of those heavy-drinking sessions that detectives go in for after a hard day detecting. Maybe she had made an arrest. Maybe she had tried to show her staff that she was one of the boys and could match their consumption. Whatever the reason, she was unconscious. Bathos. A colossal let-down.

Slightly depressed, Nshila went back to the bathroom. Zach arrived on schedule and was to be heard working at her PC. Nshila wedged the hand upright between two jars of face cream on top of the bathroom cabinet and sat on the toilet seat. Marvellous! Maud was of those people who do the crossword puzzle in the bathroom. Here it was.

5 Down. 'A bad end in a bad place (5,2,7)'. A police officer should have been able to do that. Death in Custody.

13 Across. 'Contradictory musical instrument in US (6,3,4).' Little Big Horn.

Zach took about twenty minutes and left. Nshila left too. She nearly took the paper with her, being stuck on 17 Down; 'Assemble and fire (5,4)'. Just in time she realised that the absence would be suspicious. But as she replaced it on the edge of the bath she saw her own completed clues. Which was worse – a missing paper or two clues completed in the hand of a stranger? No contest, she tucked the paper under her arm and left.

On the way home she diverted to the hospital that had provided the hand. She cleaned it off and threw it through an open window of the dissecting room. As it landed with a flat, squashy sound, her subconscious provided the answer to 17 Down. 'Screw-guns' – as in Kipling's poem.

Back home, she reviewed the adventure. On the down side, she knew nothing more about the effectiveness of the spell with substitute materials. The door had been open before a candle had been lit or the ritual spoken. Her victim had been insensible from drink. But without the spell, would she have woken up? Would she have sensed intruders and pulled herself back to consciousness? As regards the lift mechanism as she left Eastcheap, there was a clear time sequence connecting the charm and the event. That was better.

Could there have been a psychological side to it? Would she have made the attempt without belief in the spell? Did it operate on the person who cast it rather than upon anyone else? Or did it, in some way, operate in advance, and without it Maud would not have come home drunk and failed to shut the door? The trouble with witchcraft, as usual, was lack of certainty. But that was also a strength, because if a crime can't be proved, then nobody can be convicted for it.

What Nshila did do, a few days later, was to advertise – secretly – her need for an experienced Pakistani criminal able to locate a treasure currently in Pakistan, steal it, and carry it to London.

Operationally, the event was a huge success. Everything that was on her PC at the time of the theft transferred through to Eastcheap, and Zach's program gave regular updates. These hardly proved necessary, because the existing material was astonishing. Maud had files on almost every person who might help or hinder her on her march to the top. Typical of these were younger Chief Officers who might see her as suitable for accelerated promotion, and officers one rank above her who might get her a Chief Inspector post. She had data on people who she saw as rivals. She had a time chart showing the ages of present Chief Constables and the dates on which they would retire. She had six alternative progression charts showing where she would be, and at what rank, at various future dates. One of these time-lines showed her as Commissioner of the Metropolitan Police in 15 years time.

What sort of data was it? Crudely, blackmail material. It would allow her to extract favours by subtle hints of exposure. It included a few notes about how she had used the knowledge already. Five police officers had had their careers abruptly cut short because misdemeanours from their past had become known. Two of these men had been divorced by their wives. All this was clinically recorded, with no hints of remorse. Maud was clearly a ruthless woman. One entry especially caught Nshila's eye because she had met the man once at a reception at Mike's family home. She had liked him. Maud had written;

Hunterman. Charles. Chief Superintendent in Blankshire Constabulary, currently in charge at Meggaport. Higher Education; Nil. Vast experience in CID with numerous commendations. Queens Police Medal. Generally considered as dictatorial and hard to approach but extremely loyal when anybody is in trouble. Slow to accept new ideas and likely to favour staff who share his ideals about 'old-fashioned coppering'. Would have to be approached with great care over a long period

Generally believed to have framed George Watchmaker for the break-in at Meggaport hospital when a huge quantity of valuable drugs were stolen, appearing later on the black market. Has been heard to make comments like, 'George Watchmaker is a villain through and through. If he didn't do this, it was only because he was busy on another job elsewhere. Prison is the right place for him.' The conviction was obtained with the help of a confession extracted forcibly from Gilbert Gall.

The comments about James Milverton were equally critical.

ACC in Borders and Coast Constabulary. Young and extremely ambitious. University Degree in Sociology. Detractors claim that he raced through the ranks because everybody wanted to get rid of him and promotion was the quickest way. A surprise choice by the Police Authority of Borders and Coast, probably made because they wanted to project a modern image. Milverton will accept any proposal likely to make him look good in the public eye.

As a Chief Superintendent, Milverton influenced the award of a computer installation project. It went to a company owned by the family which his wife came from, and where she was still a director. He cleverly concealed these facts, and it seems that nobody else knows. The company quote was not the lowest, and the work poor. Failures were common and rectification slow.

The database was very extensive, and confirmed that she was indeed a very devious person. Should Nshila act on all this information? If so, how? She soon concluded her Detective Sergeant friends deserved help.

It was Zach Kawero who did the job. Selected pieces from her database started turning up as attachments to internal police e-mails. They gave away the minimum number of secrets, but made it quite obvious that somebody, somewhere, was spying on colleagues with the intention of climbing over them. The investigators narrowed down the search by deciding who could have been aware of the things disclosed. That would not have been decisive, but there was internal evidence also. The wording included certain phrases that were almost 'signatures' in Maud's day-to-day conversation, and the text displayed attitudes that she was known to hold.

Was that proof? Of course not. But in a big organisation proof is a flexible concept. The word goes out that so-and-so is no longer on the fast track. Little is said, but the opportunities are given to other people, access becomes limited, information is revealed to others but not to the person concerned. In a variety of ways the message is made clear, 'You are going nowhere in this organisation'.

Surely that is illegal? Maybe. In today's society it is possible to bring a case for discrimination against the employer. Maud could have acted. But she knew what the result would be.

For every instance of discrimination that she cited, there would be an explanation that attributed the event to some totally different, and quite legitimate, cause. Nobody can lie better than a policeman when the going is tough.

Maud soon left the police. She applied for, and got, an advisory job with a police force in Central Africa. Amazingly, it was in Nshila's country of origin. 'Bad deal for the nation', Nshila thought. 'You have lost me and gained Maud.'

Chapter Eight

The Client Surfaces

The Companion and The Hand of Glory had each contributed to an operational success, but Nshila recognised that her degree of control had been poor. Events had not run according to plan. It worried her. And then her cautious self got started. 'See? You don't have the skill you thought you had. Take on a big contract – like this Hicks thing might be – and you're sure to foul up. Leave it alone'.

'It's daft to decide this early', said her risk-taking self. 'There's been no message at all, yet. Keep your mind open'.

The wait was short. Two days after the Hand of Glory adventure there was a message from Jessop in the usual section of a certain trade magazine. 'Catalyst has made contact with Courier'.

Nshila had a 'supply chain' through which contacts were filtered. Any customer who might require her services was passed from one contact to another, with the project being slightly better defined at each stage. Anything unsuitable was quickly killed. Barney Caddick was a very early contact. A prospective client might ask Barney whether anything could be done about a person who was proving inconvenient. Barney was tasked to establish just what was needed. Could the person be bought off? Could he be persuaded to give up by a visit from some thugs? In either case the client would be referred to another specialist – not an assassin. If permanent removal seemed necessary and possible, then the news reached Jessop, who had direct contact with Nshila. Anything Jessop passed on would have passed four critical tests.

Somebody (the client) wanted somebody else (the target) dead.

The target was widely regarded as an evil man or woman.

The client was able to pay the fee.

The identity of the contractor to be approached would be safeguarded.

Not many contracts were accepted. Nshila's attitude went back to the death of the cattle thief and the respect shown to her by the tribe. Subconsciously, she wanted approval. In the UK, she knew, that would never be official. Nevertheless, she wanted to feel that if people knew the full truth they would be on her side. Several times she had explained things to Rasputin. 'There are people around, Ras, who will do anything at all for money. Practitioners who would knock off Albert Schweitzer or Mother Theresa or Nelson Mandela or even St Francis of Assissi. That's not my style. I want to be sure that the world will be a better place when my target is dead.'

When Jessop provided details, it was obvious that Jeffrey Hicks, or his employers, were the client. That was apparent because the first person who had been approached was Barney, and the person making the approach, though calling himself Michael Morgan, fitted the description of Jeffrey Hicks. The knowledge also put a gloss on what Jessop said next.

'I decided to pass this on, Nshila, but I have doubts about it. The client has not named the target, nor even spoken openly about assassination. The words used are "relocated" and "moved on" as if it was a matter of pushing some obstacle aside. The information comes originally from a philanthropist who runs voluntary youth clubs and is mad keen on developing people through sport. He is very successful, and several boys and girls from his clubs have reached national level in a variety of sports He is into football and rugby and cricket and skiing and shooting. You name it, and he has contacts who will help him. But he does not manage his enterprises himself in a day-to-day manner. He hires others to do it, and some are better than others. The weaker ones have allowed a very unscrupulous man – the target - to gain influence in the clubs. This man has great personal charm and a very good sporting record. He is alleged to be a corrupter of youth, who gains the confidence of young people and leads them into binge drinking and smoking and drugs.'

'Really, Jessop, if everybody who led youngsters astray was knocked off, there would be a great many bodies. These are very common hazards.'

'Quite true, but the client says that during the past year six youngsters, all girls, have disappeared. Normal means of tracing them have failed and the client believes, for reasons he won't reveal, that they have been sold into prostitution overseas. The story invites a huge number of questions, but nothing more is going to be offered now. Apparently much more will be forthcoming at a meeting with your representative.'

'Well, perhaps it's good enough to warrant a meeting. Set it up, will you? Remember that I am not to be identified as the principal. The client must be told that he will meet a representative.'

Her decision was influenced, though she tried to persuade herself otherwise, by the new vision of government as a source of business. The client, as described, was obviously an invention designed to explain the detailed knowledge of the target. In reality, the service was sought by devious civil servants in Horseferry Road.

Meetings were normally scheduled for public places, out of doors. The Embankment Gardens had been used, and Green Park and the Zoo and Lords. (Once, at the zoo, the meeting was interrupted by an escaped ape, and once at Lords by a streaker.) This time the security services were involved. If they were aware of the meeting place, they would probably have directional microphones aimed from hundreds of yards away. Zach was therefore required to provide an electronic jamming gizmo. It was not foolproof in the long term, but Nshila never allowed such a meeting to last longer than an hour, and that was not long enough for any expert to circumvent it. The gizmo also had an additional function which enabled her, by pressing a button, to destroy any tape-recording that had been made of an encounter. The ticket office of The London Eye was appointed as the meeting place.

Nshila enjoyed disguise, employing an old friend from LSE who had given up her economics course and somehow got into RADA. A precarious existence as a bit-part actor was augmented by work as a make-up artist. She had given Nshila some striking images in the past – images that could be lived up to only with concentration and thus provided their own challenge.

'What would you like to be, Nshila? I had a nice contract from a Pantomime company last Christmas and I can do you a wonderful washerwoman image. Do you fancy Widow Twanky? Or would 'principal boy' be better? I can't see you as one of the brokers men or either part of the horse!'

'Not Widow Twanky, Gemma, and not the Old Woman who lived in a Shoe. For this interview I have to look responsible and respectable and a little imposing. The real me would be fine, except that I can't afford recognition. Make me a few years older and a little bit more solid – as if I was just starting a middle-aged spread and dressing to conceal it.'

Nshila came out looking like a high-ranking Foreign Office official – similar to the heroine of the musical *Call me Madam* but a little bit older. Gemma gave her some age lines, and some laughter lines and made her slightly fuller in the face. A smartly tailored suit in charcoal grey was matched with flat but stylish Italian shoes in the same colour. It all said 'Don't mess with this woman'.

She had subconsciously assumed that the contact would be a mature male. It knocked her over when a tiny Dresden Doll approached and said, 'The tide is just turning, isn't it?' The top of her elaborate hairstyle reached only to Nshila's chin, despite impossibly high heels. She was one of those girls who makes you wonder how God managed to squeeze all the necessary parts into so small a frame. And she spoke the purest upper-class English. How did she get through the selection process, Nshila wondered. Surely the days of recruiting relatives of senior officers were long gone? Surely it was now mandatory to search out graduates from minor universities with strong regional accents? But perhaps she was so brilliant intellectually that they could not ignore her. Or perhaps seductive skill was a qualification. As bait for a honey trap this creature would be ideal. Nshila felt slightly annoyed at this competition in the 'most attractive woman' competition. Yes, she had chosen the older, experienced woman image, but would she have done so if she had known what her contact would be like?

The doll obligingly paid for the tickets and the London Eye bore the pair slowly upwards. Little time was spent on the preliminaries. Nshila opened up aggressively – still slightly resentful about being up-staged.

'My principal has doubts about what your people have said so far. You seem to have got the idea that he can somehow spirit away whatever individuals you dislike – almost as if he was a professional assassin. That's rubbish. For the record, hear me telling you right now that my principal carries out legitimate investigative work and to suggest that he kills people is ridiculous.'

'I'll report what you say.'

'Even if he was what you imagine, nobody would accept a contract on the story that has reached us. It's so full of holes that you can't see the string. Plus the fact that we don't know who you are or where you come from.'

'I understand.'

Nshila was annoyed by the brief responses. Was this woman paying proper attention? She seemed to be concentrating on the scenery more than the conversation. The annoyance must have come through, for the Dresden Doll turned from the window and apologised. The wheel had been lifting their pod above local buildings and started to reveal the wider view.

'I'm sorry. I've never been in The Eye before and the view just grabbed me. You were saying that your principal was suspicious about our approach, I think.'

'I certainly was.'

The Dresden Doll had a ready answer. 'That's reasonable. But we had doubts, too. We saw no reason to give away too much too early. It's a bit different if you, personally, have direct access to somebody who can do the job. That's true, I believe?'

'Yes.' Nshila was willing to admit that much.

'About us, you need only know that we are a small and very specialised department in a government security organisation. About what we want, and why we want it, well, things will be a lot clearer when I tell you that the target is Grant Toppley.'

She was right, Nshila thought. Most people knew of Grant Toppley, and knew that one of his more legitimate interests was sports, and sports clubs. Fewer people knew that these interests covered others less reputable.

Grant Toppley. A very nasty piece of work who was almost untouchable by normal sanctions. He was rich and well-connected. He was a member of parliament, maintaining a precarious membership of the conservative party, whilst holding views that were dramatically different and a long, long way to the right. Several attempts had been made to expel him, but his constituency was a reactionary hotbed, and he controlled it by violence and bribery. He was effectively the Godfather. Nshila felt that some degree of mutual understanding now existed. After she had thought it over, she responded.

'As you say, that tells nearly all. If there was a national referendum today asking whether he should live or die, I suppose it would be seven-to-one on death.'

Her companion did not totally agree. 'But not amongst gullible young people,' she said. 'He has such a way with him that they regard all warnings as prejudiced and biased and discriminatory. They seem to think that he has somehow been misjudged by 'the establishment', which they hate, and deserves their admiration.'

She followed on straight away, apparently now focussed on work rather than the view.

'There's one question you will surely be wanting to ask me. "Why can't Grant be prosecuted for some of the crimes he is known to have committed, and locked up for a good long time?"'

'Yes. I want an answer to that one, and also an explanation of

59

why your department thinks it can get away with an assassination. If you are a genuine part of the government service you ought to be upholders of the legal process.'

'Look, we both know that this conversation is totally deniable, so let's be realistic. Grant has so many people in his pocket, and such huge financial resources that the legal route will get us nowhere. Witnesses will be suborned; lawyers will produce technicalities, newspaper editors will write about persecution. It will be far better if he can be quietly disposed of.'

Nshila wanted spades to be called spades. 'Are you telling me that your department is above the law?'

'That's a crude statement. But in certain very limited cases, discreet termination will be allowed to pass unnoticed. There are people in government who feel the law has become heavily biased in favour of wrong-doers and against their victims. These people look with favour on unilateral action. We are open to attack by high-minded people on the extreme left, and that does force us to be extra careful, but we can cope with it. We have evidence that Grant is seriously into white slavery, and the most permanent way of stopping him is death. We will show you our evidence if your principal will consider the job seriously. That's the full story.'

Nshila detected a mis-match between what she was being told now, and her earlier information. 'In previous contacts your people suggested that your target was primarily into drug distribution, using his contacts in sports clubs to make addicts of young people. You have not said anything about that.'

'It's true, but there are other villains who do as much and don't qualify for such special action. Selling young girls as prostitutes overseas is crime in a different league. Don't you agree?'

A nod of the head showed agreement from Nshila, who passed on to another problem. 'Grant Toppley is a high profile target. He is probably well protected. The assignment could be difficult and dangerous.'

There the conversation paused for a few moments. The

car was moving towards the highest point of its cycle, offering views of London that were impossible to ignore. Yet Nshila was disappointed by the way the high, modern buildings grabbed the eye. It was quite hard to see into the canyon-like streets between them, and architectural gems of yesteryear – like the Wren Churches - were almost lost. The doll, unveiling another surprise, showed herself to be historically knowledgeable.

'Did you know that after the Great Fire of London there was a plan to re-build the place in nice neat rows and squares? How dreary it would have been. I'm glad the plan got ditched and re-building followed the old lines. Much more romantic.'

'No. I never heard that.' Nshila continued looking down, and reflected how totally different ordinary things appeared from this perspective. The flight path into the airport of her home country went over a major game park. She remembered peering through the windows, hoping to see a giraffe nibbling at a treetop, but always being disappointed. They might have been there, but the shape was so different from above that she could not recognise them.

The river, of course, was a different matter. The Thames may be unimpressive compared to the Zambesi, but running through London – coming out of one horizon and flowing right through to the opposite one – it was magnificent. And there was still traffic on it, even in this age of air travel and juggernauts. Pleasure boats, and commercial boats, and strings of barges, all throwing up bow waves and leaving wakes behind them. She wondered where they were all going. There were restaurant ships moored at the bank; what business deals were happening on them, or what romances starting and ending on their decks.

The next car contained a small party of schoolchildren, some of whom were waving at them, the way happy children are apt to wave at strangers. What did they see, Nshila wondered? Perhaps an important foreigner being shown the sights by a British exporter – who had chosen their smartest saleswoman.

The Dresden Doll was speaking again. 'I suppose you are going to ask why we don't do the job ourselves.'

Nshila smiled. 'I didn't have that in mind, but I would certainly like to know. Tell me.'

'We have only one suitable person on our staff and he is on an assignment in Cambodia. Another factor is that we have heard rumours that your principal might – just might – have paranormal skills that could cause death through non-physical means. That would be a huge advantage for us. Methods of that type, witchcraft for instance, are not recognised by law and the act could never be proved.'

Nshila thought things were going too fast. She still needed answers. 'If the number of girls who have disappeared is low, and you don't have enough evidence to follow the usual route, how have you come to develop such a clear picture about Toppley's activities?'

The Dresden Doll put her hands to her temples for a moment, wondering how to condense months of research into a short, convincing answer.

'Because there's a pattern to this sort of operation. It's been done before in other countries and may even have been done here. It has to be set up so that there are backers, and buyers, and transport and all the necessary infra-structure. That includes medical staff to ensure that 'the product' arrives in good shape. Our opposite numbers in Belgium have given us details of a ring they have just smashed. We think that the people missing so far may have been passed through the Belgian system. We think that Toppley has worked with them to see how things are done before branching out on his own. He has been going through all the necessary preliminary actions; making contacts, securing premises, laying out money and so on.'

'You are starting to make sense.' Nshila felt she better understood, now, the reasons for dealing drastically with Toppley. Her would-be client pressed on with the build-up.

'I've left out one of the nastiest parts. We believe some girls have been 'handed down' like outgrown clothing. There are probably compensations for being the most favoured woman of a mega-rich Arab, but what happens if he gets tired of you?

We have heard of girls being passed into the hands of second or third users. It's like what happens to a second-hand car when it can't be put on a high-price forecourt any more. It disappears into 'the trade'.'

The car had reached the bottom again. As they stepped out, Nshila offered a formal response.

'My principal will want time to consider. He has recently been inclined to reject contracts because he isn't satisfied the target is evil enough. You may well think that a peculiar position, but it's a fact. He needs a lot of convincing, and insists on researching the target himself. My own belief is that something has turned up about a previous victim and that it makes him regret what he did. There could also be problems about the crime being only in the preparation stage, and about the witchcraft requirement. You'll hear from us within two weeks.'

She went back to Eastcheap very pleased. These people have a real need, and they want me badly. The target appears so far to be worthy. For the moment, doubts about her competence disappeared. She would rise to the challenge somehow.

The emotional high took a different turn as she opened the office door and heard an excited female voice.

'Nshila! Listen! You know we gave the Mayor of Borobroughton a GO for the centenary fete of their local hero?' Gillian Harker was bouncing with glee.

'Yes. It was a very dodgy decision; indications for good and bad weather almost equal. You persuaded me to take a risk because of your reliable local contacts. And you were right, I remember now. The rain cleared around dawn and they had a fine bright day with temperatures in the eighties.'

'Yes, I was right. We have just had a fulsome letter of thanks from the principal organiser, and the news that he is taking a new job as Celebrations Officer for the whole of Scotland. We'll get stacks of prediction business for events from John-O-Groats down to Gretna Green. It's marvellous.'

Gillian rattled on. 'And Peter has news, too. Tell her, Peter.'

'It is not about business, Nshila, quite different. My probation has ended. They are short of staff, and decided on early release for a few chosen probationers. I qualify because I have a steady job. Your reputation helped, too.'

Nshila replied in employer mode. 'Does that mean that they can't haul you back to prison without trial when you beat up the postman, or something. Can I see you as a fixture here?'

'Yes. Yes. Yes. If I commit any crime at all from now on, they have to go through the whole business of arrest and trial all over again.'

So there had to be a long and expensive celebration. The big let-down came when Nshila was finally alone in her flat and saw the light blinking on the answering machine. It was Masuko in Margate asking for an immediate call back.

'Nshila, I'm so sorry about this, but your mother is dead.' Masuko was the one who maintained contact with the village they both came from. He sent money regularly to his mother, and as the business grew Nshila had begun giving him money to send to hers. Whether it did the mothers any real good remained a mystery. Possibly their father squandered the lot. But Masuko and Nshila felt they had a duty.

She had never been close to her mother. As the youngest wife, with only a girl child, her mother had devoted a lot of time to safeguarding her own status; she had been too insecure to lavish love on her child. But a mother is still special. Nshila cried for her mother, and fell asleep in her chair.

The next morning she was still pretty mixed up. She felt a need to visit Masuko. She felt, too the need for a short holiday. Bur where to, and with whom?

Chapter Nine

Time Out

Mike Fanshawe was searching his flat for a data stick that he needed at work. He had taken it from a laptop, he knew, and probably put it in a pocket. Which suit had he been wearing? The one that had gone to the cleaners? This was a bad moment for the phone to ring.

'Why such an early call, Nshila? I am just off to work.'

'I caught you in time then, Mike. I've had this inspirational idea and I've got to try it out on you. Have you got ten minutes?'

'Ten, yes. If it goes on longer I shall have to call you back.'

'I need relaxation, Mike. I've worked myself into a state recently and had a few near misses. I want a break, and you are my first choice for company.'

'When and where, Nshila, and for how long? I have commitments right now which I can't really break.'

Mike hardly expected this mild protest to stop her. As his searching hand closed on the data stick – in the pocket of a third suit - he imagined her typical behaviour in this sort of impatient mood. Probably standing in front of her wardrobe with the phone wedged between neck and shoulder while she decided what to wear. He was right. His intervention made no impact.

'I want a long weekend walking, Mike. Dawn to dusk in the fresh air with never a thought of work.'

'Walking isn't my first choice. Can't you make it hang-gliding?'

Once again, no impact. He might not have spoken.

'It will be East Kent. We are going to start from Margate, where my brother teaches, walk down the Kent coast and into Sussex. We'll visit some of the Cinque Ports, and look out over

65

The Channel from the White Cliffs. We'll cross Romney Marsh and talk to the sheep. We'll spend the last night at The Mermaid in Rye and have a really expensive dinner.'

Mike was not surprised by the location she had chosen. He knew of the brother in Margate and he knew that Nshila found the history of England fascinating. She had become enthusiastic about her adopted country and was forever retailing odd events from the past that the ordinary Englishman had never known or had known and forgotten. The Kent coast meant invading Romans, and Saxon raiders, and French raiders and threats from Napoleon and Hitler. Not to mention William the Conqueror. He saw himself being dragged to the replica Viking ship at Ramsgate, Martello Towers and the Royal Military Canal. But he could win something for himself, too.

'You sound determined. It's a deal, but with two conditions. We're in the middle of a share floatation, so it can't be next weekend, but the one after. And I want a favour in return.'

'Groan, groan. Some of the favours you ask are ghastly.'

'In six weeks time I have to go to a party at the House of Commons given by my local MP. My family have a lot of influence in our area and we were involved in his election campaign. He has re-married and wants to flaunt his trophy. I can't avoid going, and I need support.'

The phone made meaningless sounds for a few moments before Nshila's voice came through again.

'Sorry about that. Rasputin ran under my feet and I dropped my best dress on the floor. What you said sounds utterly grim.'

'It will be, for you. Most of the guests will talk in loud braying accents about their dogs and their horses and future social engagements. The women will be dressed to show how much money they have, and how little taste. If I went on my own I would fit in seamlessly, because I was born into that world. I can bray for Britain if I have to. But deep down I would hate it. If you come, it will alter the whole chemistry. They won't know how to treat you, and most of them will be confused. Some of them will get right up your nose, and your one-line put-downs can be hilarious.'

'So you want to parade me like an animal in the zoo, and see how the punters react. You're a manipulative sod, Mike. But walk for me, and I'll talk for you.'

They often made similar bargains. This time Nshila asserted herself by hiring a chauffeur-driven car for the journey to Margate, and booking another one for the return journey from Rye. Lunch-time on the outward journey found them at Chilham, taking a relaxed meal at a hotel in the famous old square. Mike took advantage of the moment to ask about Nshila's need for a holiday.

'Is it some sort of worry that I could help with?'

She had to be careful. Mike was a good friend and entitled to be concerned for her. But he knew nothing of her secret life.

'Just two things that I need time and peace to think over, Mike. A man who I might or might not do business with, depending upon his record, and doubts about my ability to carry off an assignment I have been offered.'

She laughed within herself at her phrase 'doing business with'. It would cover assassination, she supposed.

'Do I know the man? I might have knowledge that helps you.'

'You might, Mike. But I won't name him because I have no proper evidence for what I think. I might prejudice you unfairly against him.'

'OK. But on the other matter, I don't believe you need to worry. You are a very resourceful woman and I've never known you fail to rise to a challenge. You may have doubts beforehand, but when the moment of truth arrives you always prove capable. I wonder sometimes how you do it.'

'Thanks, Mike. You're always a help to me.'

They arrived at St Finnegan's and found Masuko in a happy, excited state. He had just been told of a double promotion. From the next school term he was to be Head of Science and a Housemaster. He decreed that the two should be his guests for dinner at the smartest local restaurant. He had also booked rooms at a hotel, saying that there was no point in walking anywhere that day.

So the two were given a tea of crumpets, scones, jam and cream, in the schools 'hospitality area'. Then they waited in Masuko's rooms while he taught the last lesson of the day and supervised 'prep'. Before he left them, he threw a large book at Nshila and said, 'This belongs to Mrs Holland, who runs the B&B place. You borrowed it, and left it here by accident. You don't need to apologise to Mrs Holland. I've done it for you.'

Nshila grabbed the book with delight. It was The Ingoldsby Legends in which she had read about The Hand of Glory. Perhaps there would be other inspirational leads. Mike found plenty to interest him in the school-related literature that covered every flat surface in the room. St Finnegan's was a school of the same basic type as Eton, and he was pleased to find that some things had not changed. In the chemistry book there was still an experiment that he remembered from his 'A' level year, and a book about history which still said that his side had won at Agincourt and lost at Austerlitz. Some things, he thought, the revisionists had not managed to alter. His reading was interrupted by Nshila.

'Change of plan, Mike. Tomorrow morning we are going to re-trace the route of Smuggler Bill as he fled from Exciseman Gill and the Horse from Hell. Go down now to the school library and look for the local ordnance survey map.'

Mike had two sisters. He knew how impulsive and illogical women could be. Having strange ideas thrown out without warning was not a new experience. He looked up from his study of school literature but made no move.

'Hang on a moment. Who are these people and what have they got to do with us, and why must we re-trace their journey?'

'Look, The Ingoldsby Legends was published in 1889 and it's a collection of stories written by a local clergyman. They are either humorous, or weird, or frightening or all three together. Smuggler Bill got chased by an exciseman. He looked to be getting away because he had the better horse, his 'dapple-grey steed'. Then the devil turned up on a supernatural horse. He offered to lend it to the exciseman in return for his soul. The exciseman accepted, and caught up with Smuggler Bill. Then the two horses and two riders leapt over a cliff as the smuggler tried to escape. In the morning, people found the bodies of two men at the foot of the cliff, but only one horse. It's a great story.'

Nshila was lying back in her brother's huge leather armchair, with her shoes off. She obviously had no intention of running errands herself. 'Go on. Do it!'

'What's got you so excited about a daft legend like that?'

'The lively, colloquial style. I suppose you could call it slang. It's hardly poetry, maybe doggerel. And it's full of romantic local place names; some of them must be in use today. I want to go up Reculver Cliffs where they watched for the blue answering light on the skiff. I want to see the places through which the smugglers ran when they were scattered by the Custom-house officers; Fordwich Level and Sandwich Flat and Sturry and Rushbourne Lane. Smuggler Bill himself went down Chislett Lane to Up-Street, and Sarre Bridge and Monckton Hill and Minster Level. He was aiming for his hide-out at Manston Cave, which was "a mile to the north of the Ramsgate Road". You can just feel the excited metre in that line.'

Mike got up and moved to the door. Turning back, he made a final protest. 'We'll never find all those places, even if the names are still in use.'

'Maybe we will, maybe we won't. We have to try. Just get the map, it will give us a start for the project.'

The subject came up again over dinner, but this time Masuko was present. He had heard enough to suspect that his sister was into some new and dubious escapade. As soon as they were seated in the restaurant and had placed their orders, he started the elder brother act.

'You ought not to read that book, sister. It has some pretty nasty stuff in it. One of the boys borrowed it from my study last term and had nightmares for a week.'

'I'm not a feeble-minded schoolboy.'

69

'No, but you are just as vulnerable. I know you got mixed up with old Kwaname, back at home in the village. Once you have meddled with supernatural things, they can creep up on you again. And I don't suppose you have changed. You were always a nosy, inquisitive child, knowing more than was good for you. I have told you often enough to abandon all that stuff, but you seldom take any notice.' Nshila tried to shut him up. Mike kept quiet, having no wish to interfere in a sibling argument. But obviously something had been given away, and Nshila did not like it. Well, Mike thought, she ought not to have gone over the top about Smuggler Bill and his misfortunes.

Masuko abandoned his attack and filled the conversational gap with stories of school events. He pointed to two men who were seated in an alcove close to the bar, both teachers at St Finnegan's, and explained that the common room had so far failed to decide whether they were a gay couple. Masuko was enjoying the company of his visitors, and during the main course he mounted his favourite scientific hobby-horse.

'Of course, the supernatural stuff that society has toyed with down the ages is total rubbish. My work here hardly challenges me as a scientist, so I study extensively. I read the scientific press, I have gained some understanding of what quantum physics is all about. The top people are working on the idea that the basic components of matter are somehow all connected to each other and that an event in one place can have a consequence in a quite different place. They have also found some evidence that things which have once been in contact with each other retain a connection. If such things prove to be true, then many magical events would turn out to be natural after all. The magicians and shamans and priests and witchdoctors would be seen as people who made mysteries where none existed.'

The wine made Nshila less able to hide her feelings, and she got visibly annoyed. The argument became complicated. Mike lost it completely when they got talking about something called Schrodingers Cat. It seemed to be an imaginary experiment, centred upon what might or might not have been proved by

70

whether the imaginary cat lived or died. He got the impression that Nshila was winning more points that she was losing.

Then the argument was interrupted by the arrival of the local rugby team and a dispute with the management. A booking had been made, apparently, but the team had spent too long drinking and arrived an hour late. The proprietor wanted to turn them away, but the presence of fifteen large men was hard to resist. There was the money, too. He disappeared into the kitchen and persuaded the chef to do overtime. The rugby team sat down and the noise level escalated. Mike found it hard to follow Nshila's last shots in the argument.

'Brother, your whole case rests on the pig-headed belief of Western science that you will eventually be able to explain everything. Right now, you have a partial theory from which you can get no practical results. You seem to be saying that all matter is interconnected and an action in one place can have influence in another. Well, old Kwaname made an image of Morgan MacMillan and squashed it with his door stop. A few days later Morgan was trampled by an elephant. It's called sympathetic magic. It was effective. It worked. Can you scientists work the same trick? When you can, I'll listen to you. The shamans and priests and witchdoctors say that a connection exists between Action A and Consequence B. They don't bother with the nature of the connection: they don't bother about the 'why' because they can control the 'how'. Next thing, you will be suggesting I can't drive properly because I don't understand the internal combustion engine.'

Mike had a headache the next morning. Nshila had none. Life was not fair.

Over breakfast he tried to reassure Nshila about her indiscretions. 'If I heard anything last night that you want me to forget, consider it done. Think of my memory as a computer that has been entered by a virus and the protection program zaps it. Gone! No trace!'

'Don't worry too much, Mike. I can live with what happened. If you had an elder brother you would know what a

71

pain they can be.'

Tracing the steps of Smuggler Bill was only partially successful. They found some of the place names but not all. Of those found, a number had been built over and become down-market housing estates. If they had got as far as Manston, which they didn't, they would have found that Smuggler Bill's cave had been buried deep under the concrete of Manston Airport. The one big success was early lunch at a pub called The Hellish Horse. It obviously commemorated the lines from the poem in which Smuggler Bill fires his pistol at the pursuing horse.

> *'The trigger he touched, and the welkin rang*
> *To the sound of the weapon, it made such a bang;*
> *Smuggler Bill ne'er missed his aim,*
> *The shot told true on the Dun – but there came*
> *From the hole where it entered, - not blood, - but flame.'*

The horse on the inn sign was galloping past bright green trees. There was flame coming out of its nostrils and Exciseman Gill was clinging to its mane with an expression of terror. In the chest of the horse was a large hole from which a bolt of flame shot out a good two foot.

The beer was excellent local stuff. The bread was fresh and crusty. The cheese had flavour.

There was a map on the wall of the pub, from which they learnt that they could walk from Sarre, where the pub was, to Sandwich down the old sea bed, now called the Wantsum Channel. It was really interesting to learn that in Roman times Thanet was truly an island and that if one were sailing from the channel into the Thames one would pass west of it, not east. The map made it clear why the Roman forts of Reculver and Richborough stand in such odd places. They are guarding the ends of a channel that no longer exists. Apparently it was possible, as late as the fifteenth century, to sail right up to Canterbury. It made St Augustine's choice a bit more obvious.

Mike rapidly consumed two pints of beer, and failed to

notice that Nshila was more abstemious, drinking only tonic water with ice and lemon and eating about half a cress-and-cucumber sandwich. So the pace at which she set off southwards almost defeated him. He knew that she did the London Marathon every year, and used to think 'Oh! How interesting!' He had not expected such Amazonian behaviour on a holiday walk. The whole afternoon was a struggle for him and he was grateful to hit the main road from Ramsgate to Sandwich and find that the last few miles were flat. Nshila moaned about the dreariness of the road and the passing traffic. Mike was glad not to be climbing stiles or avoiding cow dung. They found a decent hotel in Sandwich but even then the woman remained active. It seemed to her the best way of shutting out the dilemmas left behind in Eastcheap. After dinner, she insisted on walking seawards down the river towards the sea. The Stour twists and winds like a mad snake at that point, and although the sea is quite close on the right, one is constantly frustrated by a new bend to the left.

The next morning was taken up by the long walk to Deal. Passing Royal St Georges golf club, Mike gained modest revenge for the previous day by boring his companion with lengthy descriptions of rounds he had played there, especially his chip from the bunker at the fourth hole and his birdie at the hole called The Maiden. They also gazed out at the barely visible Goodwin Sands. Mike had once seen a chart showing all the shipwrecks that had taken place there over the centuries. Nshila was fascinated by the stories he could tell. The centuries-long relationship between England and the sea had never struck her so forcibly before. She had not seen the sea herself, of course, till she was eighteen years old.

Deal struck them as a strange little town. Surely any seaside town should have a long pier, covered with amusement arcades? Deal had a long one, they found, but entirely devoted to fishing. The devotees were lined up all along it with baskets of horrible wriggly things that they used as bait. Looking back from the end of the pier, they agreed that Deal looked almost French.

In the afternoon they walked over the white cliffs to Dover, and diverted en-route to St Margarets Bay. The day was fine and they could see the French coast clearly. They marvelled how two countries can be so different despite being geographically so close. Nshila got to talking about cultural differences, and Mike asked whether she had found the cultural adjustments of her life hard to cope with.

'Yes and no, Mike. I found it tough moving from the village to the school, and nothing in my life has been worse than emerging from Heathrow terminal at 6.00am on a November day in England. But it's a bit like swimming in a cold sea. Do you remember having to do that?'

'Don't I just! It was during a school trip in the Easter holidays. We were taken to a rocky shore where several natural hollows in the rocks were large enough to form swimming pools. Once one boy had dared to go in, we all felt we had to follow. I was paralysed by the cold.'

'Well, culture shocks are similar. You dive in, and your entire system shrieks in protest. Next, you find you simply have to act positively in order to survive. A few moments later you think "Good Heavens! I've done it!" And the rest does not feel so awful. The people who learn nothing and gain nothing are the ones who won't take the plunge.'

'Is that where you got your mad urge to experiment? I mean, the fact that as soon as you know something can be done at all, you want to do it yourself?'

'It's the other way round. The psychological urge to try new things leads to the experience. It's some sort of virtuous circle – or treacherous circle.'

Dover and Folkestone provided little of interest, but beyond the latter town they passed the rail complex where traffic for the channel tunnel is assembled. Mike recalled that up on the embankment they used to have the tunnelling machine parked, with a 'For sale' notice attached: 'One careful owner'.

'You didn't buy it, Mike, did you? You're filthy rich and you might have wanted to dig tunnels on your estate.'

They stayed overnight at The Imperial in Hythe. In the

morning they started westwards on the coast road, passing a long, long fence. Mike, who had friends in the army, told her that the whole area between that fence and the sea was devoted to weapon training. 'They have practice ranges for all sorts of rifles and machine guns and rocket launchers and so on. The MOD has several similar places, and whenever a chunk of the army is sent overseas, they are sent to one place or the other to check that they can still shoot straight.

'I've been inside once', he said. 'At slack times they allow civilian rifle clubs onto the ranges. I used to be a fringe member of a club and spent a miserable day there, trying to find shelter from the rain and the wind. I failed.'

They passed what seemed to be the main gate and peered through. There was not much to see. Just rough grass and scrubby bushes. There was also a concrete road and a guard house and a building labelled, 'Short Term Weapon Store'. Half a mile further on, they turned inland through West Hythe and climbed up to the high ground around Lympe Castle. They walked along the Old Sea Cliffs and enjoyed the marvellous view over Romney Marsh and the sea. The shooting ranges were still visible. Nshila commented that soldiers leaving home today had a different experience from her romantic image based on 'Goodbye Dolly Gray' and 'Lily Marlene'.

'No leisurely, tearful partings, then, today?' She asked. 'Just furious shooting practice all day, dump your weapons in that shed we saw, and pick them up for a pre-dawn start next day?'

'Something like that. But soldiers will always find somewhere to drink on that last evening and they certainly still sing.'

The old sea cliff does not last long. They turned south at St Rumwolds Church and were soon down on the low ground, over the Royal Military Canal and onto Romney Marsh itself. They passed Burmarsh and Newchurch and St Mary in the Marsh and Ivychurch and Brenzett. Their talk was dominated by Nshila trying to discover what it felt like to be really rich.

'I can't tell you much. I've always been rich, but somehow without noticing it. It all seemed just natural. I might describe it better if I had ever been poor.'

In the early afternoon they debated whether or not to cross Walland Marsh by footpaths and come to Rye from Camber. In the end they walked from Brenzett towards Appledore until they struck the old railway line dead straight like a Roman road, and walked along it towards the town. They left the railway line where it passes under the road from Playden and scrambled up the bank. It was a short walk then through the Landgate, along the High Street, into The Mint and up the passage to the back entrance of The Mermaid.

A different world then intruded upon their holiday. The Mermaid had a conference in residence, yet not exactly a conference because it was a private group, not an organisation. 20 people who all shared a common anxiety and had got together to share experiences and seek for a solution. Amongst them were Gerald and Miranda Schein - well known to Mike and acquaintances to Nshila.

It was impossible to ignore them, and the two were soon drawn into the conversation. The subject, it turned out, was protection of their teenage children. They all had boys and girls between 15 and 21. They were all worried about the number, and seriousness, of the temptations now open to youngsters. They felt desperate about their inability to provide understanding, or advice, or discipline, or whatever was necessary. The group had been got together by Louise and Martin Adamson who had lost their daughter, Hazel.

'I don't say "lost" meaning "dead", Mike.' This was Louise speaking. 'I say "lost" meaning that we have no idea at all whether she is alive or not, or where she might be. She got deeper and deeper into the drug scene, spent less and less time at home, and disappeared one morning at 6.00am.'

Jeff Thomason joined in. 'Half of us here were friends or acquaintances of Martin and Louise when it happened. The others are friends of friends and have similar anxieties. Martin and Louise got the group together because they are desperate about the loss and because it seemed that people with the same problem might be able to help each other.'

Mike was startled when Nshila joined the conversation. This was surely outside her normal range of interests. They were all seated on the terrace behind The Mermaid itself, where Mermaid Passage runs through the hotel, broadens out and runs down between garden walls to The Mint. Some birds were very vocal behind one of those walls - disturbed in some way.

Nshila asked, 'Are you sure that the danger is really serious? I can quite see that Martin and Louise are shattered by their loss, but surely children have been revolting against parental values since time began. The ones who disappear are the extreme cases. There can't be too many of them.'

'We think it's serious. We think that things are much worse than before because people are richer, and the temptations are more varied, and "getting away" is so much easier.'

A man named Terry Waters joined in. He was a very large man and obviously not comfortable on the white, decorative metal chairs provided by the hotel. He spoke while leaning backwards against an upright post of the pergola. 'Look, when I was a boy we had enough money for a few rounds of drinks on a Saturday night and alcohol was the only substance we could abuse. Except that a few people tried methylated spirits. The very worst that could happen was getting picked up by the police for "drunk and disorderly".'

Miranda Schein continued on the same theme. 'Teenagers today can get so drugged that they lose all self-control and can be pushed into almost any ridiculous action. It's no exaggeration. I once got a call from my daughter at 11.30am. She had gone out the evening before to a party in Reading. She was calling from Paris. She had been present at a bust-up between boy and girl. They had been booked on a trip to France, the boy was left with a spare ticket, and my daughter had decided to console him by going instead. Kids do those things without thinking. They don't even need a passport.'

'And there are signs that serious criminals are getting interested. It is so easy. Pose as a young, successful businessman, for instance, and ask a few excited, drugged girls whether they would like a short flight in your executive jet. Get them inside it and they won't have a clue where they are going.'

By dinner time, most of the members of the self-help group had arrived. Somehow, Nshila and Mike became attached to the party, sat at one of their tables, and took part in their evening session. It was not the evening they had planned. This group had spent a full day searching for ways in which they could relate better to their children, and extra input was welcomed. Mike became involved because he was known to be rich and perhaps have the financial resources to set up a snatch operation – were he a man of criminal intent. He might be able to guess 'How the enemy worked'.

Some of the questions he could answer easily enough. 'Could the owner of an executive jet fly wherever he wanted to?' 'How closely was his flight monitored?' 'Could he carry passengers without anybody knowing?' 'How expensive was it?'

To other questions he could only give informed guesses. 'How could victims be prevented from contacting the authorities?' What would be the purpose of the operation?' 'What would be the final destination?' 'Were there any standard methods by which criminals seduced teenagers?'

A few questions could only be answered by the fact that some humans will sink to any level of depravity if there is enough money in the transaction and they think they can get away with it.

Nshila took little part in the discussion, but paid very close attention – particularly when one or two people were named as possibly being associated with this sort of crime One of the names was Grant Toppley. Driving back to London next morning Mike asked her why the subject grabbed her so.

'I can't really explain it to you, but it ties up with a problem I am working on and it has given me some useful insights.'

Chapter Ten

The Legacy

Nshila was much influenced by the evening in Rye, and the added credibility it gave to what she had learnt at her meeting in the London Eye. There really were criminals capable of snaring teenage girls and there were markets to which they could be delivered. Previously she had been aware that such things might happen, but had inclined to the view that young people who were stupid enough to get into the drug scene had only themselves to blame. Now she had learnt at first hand about a disappearance and had seen the grief of the parents. These had not been neglectful parents. They had provided a stable, happy environment for their daughter and had lost her to a very nasty form of crime. And Grant Toppley had been named. Mentally she edged closer to accepting the assignment and passed messages to the would-be clients asking for more data. A few days later she received a disc from the clients with full personal and biographical details. One of his addresses stuck in her mind; it was adjacent to a conference centre where she had attended a desperately boring seminar on the formation of ox-eye clouds at sea. 'Principal residence', said the text, 'Feathermede Hall, Framlingham, Suffolk'. There was also a London address: 21 Denham Drive, Walthamstow.

She made a provisional commitment to the assignment, stating that she had enquiries in hand to confirm the nature of Toppley's activities. If these agreed with what the client had reported, then the deal was on.

And then, two days later, a messenger arrived from an out-of-town courier service with a package for Ms N Ileloka. The sender had not known the right address but had been given directions, and a personal description of the addressee. The messenger was also required to ask a personal question to which only Nshila could possibly have known the answer. 'How many

runs did St Alban's have on the board when it started to rain?'
It frightened her. Whoever had framed the question knew more
about her than she wished. It referred to a cricket match between
her school and stronger opponents in which she had engineered
a draw by making it rain. She was soon to find out who this
knowledgeable person was. Inside the package were two large
brown envelopes and a normal sized white one. The white one
had a return address on the back, showing that it came from
Alabaster, Stroy and Clegg in Milford Haven.

> Dear Ms. Ileloka,
>
> For many years our firm has acted on behalf of the late Daffyd
> Shane. Mr Shane owned a small shipping business carrying goods
> to Ireland and the Scilly Isles, but also carried out unconnected
> trading operations of a nature never disclosed to us. These involved
> substantial absences overseas.
>
> Mr Shane always attached great store to completing such
> operations to the satisfaction of his clients. While any operation
> was incomplete he was accustomed to leave details of it, sealed, in
> our offices. On completion, he would remove and destroy these
> details. His instructions were that, should he die while any such
> operation was incomplete, the documents were to be forwarded to
> you with the accompanying covering letter.
>
> Mr Shane did not have your exact address, but he
> provided us with directions based on conversation with a third
> party, alleged to be friendly with you both. We are hopeful that the
> directions will be sufficient to reach you.
>
> We shall, of course, be very happy to assist you in any activity
> that will further Mr. Shane's last wishes.
>
> We remain, Madam
>
> Your Obedient Servants,
>
> Alabaster, Stroy and Clegg

The thinner of the two brown envelopes was of high quality
and fastened in a very traditional manner. It had a scarlet splash

of old-fashioned sealing wax on which a personal seal had been impressed. Nshila could not be sure of the design. There seemed to be a circle with a sharp, protuberance at one end. She read the letter with growing amazement.

Dear Nshila,
Unless your information network is absolutely top class, my name will mean nothing to you. But you will know who I am when I remind you of the Latin American Police Chief who was shot on the steps of his Headquarters, and the absconding banker who was apparently eaten by a shark. Likewise the shipping magnate who perished in a refrigerated container while it was being carried on one of his own boats. They were all my doing.

We are (sorry, we were) professional colleagues.

You don't know me and the only reason I have some awareness of you is that information gathering has been one of my high priorities. I can't say that my knowledge of you is extensive (you are almost as careful as I), but it is enough to give me a great respect for you as an honest, competent and reliable craftsman. (I am too old to learn modern terminology and call you a craftsperson.)

I am in my late fifties, and I have a family history of heart disease. It is therefore possible that I might die with an uncompleted contract on hand. I would hate to leave unfinished business behind me; it has been a point of honour all my life that, having taken money to do a job, I should not fail my client.

I have therefore formed the habit of writing down all details of any on-going contracts and leaving them with my solicitors. If I die while on the job, the solicitors have instructions to forward the envelopes, with this letter, to a named individual. That individual may, perhaps, feel able to complete the work on my behalf and, of course, take the fee. When I complete a job, I remove and destroy the envelope. So, at any time, there might be no envelope resting with my solicitors, or up to three different ones. (I don't believe in having more than three projects active at the same time. Usually it is just one.)

For some years my named individual was Alf Groschen, of whom you have probably heard. If so, you will know that he suffered an unfortunate accident last year when the poisoned components of a salad were placed on the wrong dish. He will not be able to carry out my wishes.

Of those currently active in our profession I consider you to be my best hope. I have no doubt at all about your skill, but I recognize that picking up somebody else's contract may not appeal to you. I am, after all, asking you to accept the research I have done rather than do it your own preferred way. If I were alive (which I won't be if you get this letter) then I would certainly accept your decision. My hope, of course, is that you will find challenge and excitement in any contracts I leave behind, execute them with panache and enjoy the money they bring. Should you accept a contract, there will be no difficulty with the client. I have made recent clients fully aware of this minor risk to my health, and it is accepted that should I pass away, a competent successor will take over.

I shall sign now with my true given name. I have not used it in this professional context for many years.

Your sincere admirer,

Owen Llewellyn Jones
(a.k.a. Daffyd SDhane

She got herself a stiff drink and went outside onto the roof garden – and blinked because of the bright sun. When she had sat down to study the package the day had been overcast and dull. Light rain had been falling The sun had broken through the clouds while she was concentrating on the letters and the world was now bright and fresh. She went inside again, found her sun glasses and sat down to think.

What a turn up! Her first emotion was annoyance that anybody, anywhere, should know enough about her to write and deliver such a letter. If Owen Llewellyn Jones could do it, then did anybody else have the capability? A criminal in a spy story would have traced the leak all the way to its source and killed off every link in the chain. Not possible! 'How did you find me?' The first link in the chain was dead! She could only make her behaviour more discrete than ever and hope that OLJ was a single case. After all, he had prided himself on having the best- ever information network.

The next emotion was pleasure that OLJ, a man with all

that knowledge of the assassin's profession – and twenty years more experience than herself – had chosen her as his confidante and professional executor. It was an accolade.

Suddenly she knew what the design on the seal meant. It was a bit clearer on the brown envelope than the other. OLJ must have been a literary type. He must have read The Lays of Ancient Rome and rejoiced in the way Horatius killed the Lord of Luna:

> *'Through shield and skull and helmet*
> *So fierce a thrust he sped,*
> *The good sword stood a hands breadth out*
> *Behind the Tuscan's head.'*

There it was. She could see the circle now as a human head: the protuberance on the left side was the good sword sticking out. What a marvellous seal for an assassin!

There were two decisions to be made. Should she open the second envelope? It must contain details of some man or woman who OLJ had contracted to kill, and details of the client. One option was to reject the whole concept immediately and put the envelope in the fire. That's what her more cautious self wanted. It warned her, 'Nshila. The whole idea is mad and dangerous. Play safe for once in your life. There is no obligation on you to do anything at all'.

'Surely I can open it and read it? That won't commit me to anything'. So spoke her risk-taking self.

'It opens the door', said the cautious self. 'You may find that the contract has exciting elements that you can't resist. Open that envelope and you are exposing yourself to danger. You know how bad you are at resisting temptation. Burn it. Burn it now.'

At that moment the door from the office opened and Gillian Harker appeared.

'Nshila. I need your opinion.'

Gillian was a top-flight meteorologist and when somebody asked for a prediction about the weather she was the one who studied the data and calculated probabilities. But sometimes those probabilities were evenly balanced and one of the things in which The Rain Consultancy took pride was never giving a woolly answer. If somebody had to call off or confirm a proposed event – fete, garden party or fashion parade – the consultancy said 'go' or 'don't go' - no messing – and lived with the consequences. That required a management decision rather than a technical one, and it was down to the boss.

This one related to an extended family gathering at a mansion beside the Thames. Should Lady Vandalstone include the planned regatta in the programme, or cancel it? Rowing boats were to be used, of the Sunday afternoon type, and the young men in the party were to race against each other, with a lady on the rear seat to steer. Several other activities were also planned, but none were quite so much at the mercy of the weather.

Gillian was told to say No to the river outing. It was an emotional decision based on a previous experience. Heavy rain in such circumstances – for a woman dressed in her finest clothes and a long way from any shelter – is very bad news. It's not just that the dress gets soaked; very soon the bottom of the boat fills with water and fashionable shoes begin to dissolve. It also has a bad effect on the man who is supposed to be rowing. He gets upset and impatient, pulls too violently on the oars and cascades water over his passenger.

The decision made, Nshila resumed examining the brown envelope. She turned to a well-proven personal decision making process. It involved jumping forward, mentally, in time and imagining that a commitment had been made – one way or another. The question, then, was, 'How do I now feel?'

Suppose she had burnt the letter. It was ashes and she would never know what had been in it. She would have failed the writer. She would have run away from a challenge. Some frightful evil-doer might live to do further evil. She would have missed out on a substantial fee. At that notional future moment, she imagined herself feeling shame. She also imagined herself feeling relief. Two contracts at the same time would be very hard to handle.

'Relief, girl?' Her risk-taking self came in aggressively. 'That will very quickly give way to feelings of shame. When did you ever run away from a challenge? Will you really do it for the first time now? Open the brown envelope.'

The decision making process required her to jump forward down the other route. She imagined she had opened the envelope. She knew the identity of some major evil-doer. She had a responsibility to do something about it. She had two contracts running at the same time. She had one target that she had not fully vetted herself and must accept a dead man's judgement about the other.

'You won't like that will you?' Her cautious self started. 'You like to be in control don't you? You like to manipulate the odds so that they favour you. You won't like picking up decisions made by somebody else. You'll feel frightened, won't you?'

'Rubbish. What's wrong with being frightened? It brings out the best in you. When did anybody hit the heights without being frightened? Get on with it, girl. Open the envelope

CLIENT: *Gives her name as: Norah Constance*
COMMENT: *Very unlikely to be her real name. This woman told me that she is an employee of a large organisation that is well able to pay the agreed fee. The reasons for wanting this death suggest that the organisation is either a government agency or a trade competitor. My research suggests the former alternative to be more likely.*
HOW TO CONTACT: *Coded messages displayed at the internet chat room owned by Hobbyenthuse.*
COMMENT: *Messages are recognised by the inclusion of words 'polyvalent' and 'asphyxia'.*
TARGET: *Gerald Tetherman.*
COMMENT: *Description and photograph supplied. Tetherman has a distinctive appearance on account of a short, wide nose and very heavy eyebrows. He also has*

minor weakness in his left leg and limps slightly when tired.

TARGET ADDRESS: *Dutch Elm House, Littleforth Avenue, Bristol.*

COMMENT: *I have confirmed that the target sometimes resides here. However, he travels a great deal and research indicates that he rents caravans on two separate caravan parks. These are at Lowestoft and Poole. It appears that he also owns 'Hazeldean', Byswood Road, Epping.*

REASONS FOR ASSASSINATION: *The client alleges that Thetherman is a critical link in a hard drug import chain. Most of the imports are thought to be up-market designer drugs with unpredictable side effects. Tetherman is believed to accept significant consignments and organise distribution to local operators. He appears to have contacts inside the police force and to learn from these sources which operators have been identified, and which are still safe. He directs supplies to the latter group. On rare occasions he has recruited a new distributor. The authorities have never found Tetherman with drugs in his possession. The information comes from a dealer who was arrested in France and, under interrogation, named Tetherman as one of the people to whom he despatched goods. It is thought that Tetherman operates other forms of business as well, because drug-related activities are intermittent. It is not know what such other businesses might be, nor under what names Tetherman is known. He simply disappears from the drug scene, and then reappears.*

COMMENT: *By persistent observation I have confirmed that Tetherman does receive supplies of hard drugs. These are re-packaged into smaller lots and hidden at his two caravan sites. They are fixed to the chassis, not of his own caravan, but of other vans whose owners are not in residence. I feel fairly sure that my client is a government agency. I don't see how a competitor could know of the confession to French police. On the other hand the information would quite naturally be passed to an appropriate agency in England. I think that Tetherman may use Dutch Elm House as a base at which to discard one identity and assume another. I once observed two 'arrivals', with two weeks between them, when my operatives recorded no 'departure'.*

FEE £250,000

COMMENT: One half of this amount has already been deposited in my account with The Rural Borders Bank plc. They have instructions to expect an identical sum from the same source within one year. If there is no such deposit, then the original sum is to be returned. But if the second deposit is made, then the entire amount is to be made available to the person named in a sealed letter held by my solicitor. If the named person does not claim the money within one further year then it must be paid to the Alumni Fund of my old university.

A fine man! Nshila was impressed. What integrity! After a few necessary checks she would visit that chat-room to accept the assignment. Commercially it was great; most assignments have to bear major costs just to win the business in the first place. All this needed was execution.

Chapter Eleven

More Lives Than One

Public ideas about a private enquiry agent rely on fiction. Novels describe one seedy room with a dirty half-glass door. Inside, the detective secretes a whisky bottle in one drawer of the desk and a gun in another. The name of Nshila's preferred agency, Snakesmith and Company, would have fitted well with that image.

The reality was different. The offices occupied seven tastefully furnished rooms on the first floor of 1, Harrowby Street, not far from Marble Arch. The building occupied the corner site with Edgware Road and had the main entrance upon it, but one of those quirks that beset London addresses had determined that the number on the door should refer to the side street. Vic Snakesmith liked the arrangement, since he saw the Edgware Road as down-market. His name was one he was proud of and had turned to advantage. He frequently referred to his grandfather, who had been a Smith in both senses, operating his own village forge until progress made it hopelessly unviable. Then he turned to making the most beautiful wrought iron animals, of which the very best were snakes. On his death, his oldest son honoured his father by changing his name to Snakesmith. He said, 'There are millions of Smiths in the world. I am going to stand out.'

It was ten days since he had received the commission from Nshila Ileloka, and Vic had abandoned his executive desk to sit at the coffee table with two of his operatives. He was not in a good mood.

'You two have fouled up. Surely you have enough experience to hand over surveillance without a mistake. How did it happen? And tell me the truth. I don't want to find out later on that one of you skived off to lunch before being relieved.'

Paul Mycroft was indignant. 'It wasn't like that at all, Vic.

Derek followed Tetherman's car all the way from Marlow and it never stopped. He saw the car turn into Dutch Elm House and he parked up a lane opposite that gave him a view of the front drive. He saw Tetherman get out and walk up the steps.'

'Do you confirm that, Derek?'

'Yes.' Derek Naseby was emphatic.

'Where did you pick him up yourself?'

'We knew he was stopping overnight at The Compleat Angler at Marlowe, on his way back from Lowestoft to Bristol. I watched him check out, and followed. Somewhere around the Leigh Delamere service area I phoned Paul, who was in his car, returning from Poole. I told him that Dutch Elm House had to be the destination. Paul gave me a time for his likely arrival there and I promised to maintain surveillance till he arrived.'

'Did he arrive before or after Tetherman went into the house?'

'After. At least half-an-hour after, because I listened to a news programme on the car radio, and I followed the commentary on the 1.30pm at Newmarket.'

'Were you concentrating properly all the time? Could Tetherman have left without you knowing?'

Derek was exasperated and aggrieved. He was not used to having his vigilance doubted.

'No way, boss. You don't have to look at a radio, do you? Not like tele is it? Anyway, Dutch Elm House has only one driveway, with automatic gates that have to be opened by a signal. They move slowly. I wouldn't have missed it.'

Vic Snakesmith thought for a moment. He believed his enquiry agency was one of the best, and he hated mistakes. It looked at if Paul and Derek had made an error, but good operatives were hard to find and both of these were experienced. There might be another explanation.

'Paul, how many times had you seen Tetherman before the time when you met Derek outside Dutch Elm House?'

'Just once, and that was at a distance of about twenty yards. But I had the photograph you gave us, and Derek described him for me; told me what he was wearing, and so on. And he also said that Tetherman might be walking with a very slight limp.'

'I said that because there was something strange in the way he moved when he got into the car at Marlow.'

'Paul, I suppose that when the man you thought to be Tetherman came out to the car again, he was wearing different clothes from those Derek described.'

'Yes, he was, but you would expect that if a man was at home for a few hours after a long journey and then had to go out again. He had a hat in his hand, but he did not put it on, and I saw his face quite clearly through my glasses. I never doubted that it was Tetherman.'

'Was he limping when he came out of the house?'

'Now I think of it, perhaps, yes. But it was hardly noticeable.'

There was silence for a minute while Vic considered other possibilities. He fiddled with the ornate glass ashtray that rested on the coffee table, and almost dropped it. Then he addressed Paul Mycroft again.

'After you took over the surveillance, and followed Tetherman, is there any chance that you lost his car for a time, and then picked up a similar car with a similar number plate?'

'None. None at all. When there was little traffic I kept a good distance behind him, but he was never out of sight for more than a few seconds. What's more, there was a splash of white paint on the off-side rear wing. I suppose some vandal had scrawled a message on his car and he had not wiped it all off.'

'Let's move on. When did you first begin to feel any doubt about the identity of the driver?'

"Nothing upset me till we were just south of Stroud. I was a bit surprised before that, of course, since we rather expected him to be going to the caravan site at Poole and he turned north out of his gate instead of south. But it was only a guess and not enough to worry me. But he turned into a place called Beverly Hall on the outskirts of Stroud and while I was waiting I checked with an agency to find out who owned the place. The name I got was Glyn Everett, the athletics star from ten years ago who now sponsors athletic clubs in the west country. He did not seem the normal type for Tetherman to cultivate. I thought, "What are you doing here mate? Not your scene, is it?"'

'Later on, as I understand it, you had another reason to worry.'

'Yes. An hour later he came out of Beverly Hall with another man. They each got into their own car and drove to a local garage. The owner was outside, adjusting one of his pumps, and I heard him speaking to the Tetherman fellow. But the name used was different. It sounded something like Mr Botley or Mr Hopney. I could not make it out exactly. But it was definitely not Tetherman. Then I looked at the photograph again, and the description you gave us, and began to wonder if the hair colouring was slightly different and maybe the beard cut slightly shorter. Then I got in a panic and phoned in. But I did hear Glyn Everett calling "At the stadium, then, in an hour from now". I told Veronica that when I rang.'

The door swung open and a secretary came in. 'Vic, I've got Mrs Cavendish in the waiting room. She's dead keen on employing us again to check up on her husband. It seems he rushed off this morning without a decent explanation and she's talking about his old tricks and leopards not changing their spots and so on. You said to let you know if she turned up.'

'Yes, I did. I don't have time for her right now and I don't care for her business. She has had us follow him four times, and four times there has been no contact with any woman. Tell her the truth and get rid of her. He has fled from her ear-bashing and gone racing. Horses give him less grief.'

'I can't say that.'

'No. But you can wrap it up nicely. He is not, repeat not cheating on her with another woman and it would be a waste of our time to follow him.'

Paul and Derek had been talking at the window. They came back to sit around the coffee table with Vic. Paul re-started the talk.

'Vic, I know it seems that we lost Tetherman, but have you got nothing more at all? What happened after I phoned in?'

'I was out of the office when you rang, but I was back in time to ring our associates in Gloucester and they were very helpful. They had a man on retainer in Stroud, and he said that 'the stadium' might mean the athletics track that has just been opened on the Nailhurst road. He got there about ninety minutes after your call and saw two men sitting in the front of an empty grandstand talking to somebody in a tracksuit. He thought the tracksuit man must be an athletics coach, and he recognised one of the others as Glyn Everett who is well-known locally. The other man matched the description we had given him.'

'So what happened? Don't tell me he gave up and went home?'

'No. He did well. He saw all three men leave the stadium and walk to one of those bar/restaurant places. It was one of the Granary Chain places and quite crowded. Our man got close. It seems that the coach fellow had arranged to meet his wife there, and the other two wanted to talk with him longer. So the coach introduced them to his wife. The names he used were Glyn Everret and Grant Toppley.'

'How do you read it then, boss? If the man Paul followed from Dutch Elm House is not Tetherman, then Tetherman could be anywhere. How did we locate him before? Surely we can we do it again. We should start with the caravan site at Poole.'

Derek Naseby described another possibility.

'It might just be that Tetherman and Toppley are the same person. We have found people leading double lives before. You'll have to give us some direction, here, Vic. What do you think we ought to do?'

'Immediately, nothing. I need both of you for another job. For myself, I am going to talk to the client who asked us to follow Tetherman and report exactly what happened. This is a shrewd client who has given us a lot of work. I have to play it straight. This development may alter the brief.'

The same three people sat round the same coffee table next

morning.

'I spoke to the client last thing yesterday. Things are better than we expected. There was criticism because we mistook the identity, but extreme interest in the possibility that Tetherman and Toppley are one and the same. It seems that the client has some prior knowledge of Toppley and has provided us with a description and some addresses where he might be found. The description – there was a photograph too – fits Tetherman well. The brief is still to find and watch Tetherman, but there is a big bonus for establishing whether or not this is a case of dual identity.'

Paul Mycroft thought it a hard task. 'How are we going to do that? I can't see any reliable method.'

Vic Snakesmith saw no problem at all. 'You, Paul, will find Toppley and stick to him like glue. You, Derek, will do the same for Tetherman. We know enough about their addresses and interests to provide possible pick-up points. If they are not the same person then both of you will identify your target with no more delay than is usual at the start of surveillance. I will get your reports, and it will be obvious that Toppley and Tetherman are different people, being followed in different places. If they are the same person, then one of you will have a long wait before your target appears, but when he does, then you will find your mate tagging along behind him. It will be dead boring – for one of you – but it won't be hard.'

Nshila approved the plan suggested by Vic Snakesmith, but she also mobilised Zach Kawero to check the biographical details of the two men. His research was illuminating. It showed that Toppley was real and Tetherman was not. They both had driving licences, and bank accounts and telephone numbers and e-mail addresses, but when it came to National Insurance Numbers and Birth Certificates, Tetherman was lacking. What did he do, she wondered, when he had to be paid for a deal and the payer wanted to account for VAT? Perhaps he never did honest deals at all! Perhaps he was always paid in cash or favours or deposits in a Swiss bank account. Whatever the answer, Tetherman was a shadow figure.

And just two days after Zach had reported, the news came through from Snakesmith. Derek Naseby had found Tetherman quickly, and followed him to both his caravan sites. Paul Mycroft had chosen the sports club that Toppley visited most often, and endured five days of fruitless watching. On the evening of Day Six he had finally seen Toppley arrive. Greatly relieved, he had entered the Crested Crane, nearby. He was waiting to be served when a hand fell on his shoulder and Derek Naseby said. 'That's it, mate. You can buy me a beer. It's was a long drive from Lowestoft.'

So it was extraordinary, but true, Nshila thought – the most unusual situation of her life, but also the most humorous. Two government agencies paying money to kill the same man, neither of them knowing what the other had done. Would everybody see it as humorous? She certainly did. All those clever people not knowing and she only aware! A line of poetry came to her.

"For he that lives more lives than one,
more deaths than one must die."

Amused and excited, she visited the chat room and signed up.

Next morning reality struck. Excitement had made her pay too little attention to the practical difficulties. Each client would be expecting a body and there would only be one to show. Perhaps she should abandon the idea and play a straight game. The deed being done, she could collect the fee from Client One and explain to Client Two what had happened. There would be no need to provide a body, though she could hardly ask Client Two for her full fee.

That was commercially disappointing, but she saw another, more serious, disadvantage to telling the truth. It would reveal to both clients that the different strategies they had followed to find an assassin had led to the same person. The convergence might endanger her security.

The alternative was to let both clients remain ignorant of

what had happened, and to sustain that illusion she would have to collect two fees. Did that worry her? Not really, she discovered. Both clients had agreed a fee, both would have got what they wanted. If she ended up feeling guilty, she could always give the money to a charity.

But she would still have to provide two bodies.

She confronted the problem on a Sunday morning. It was marvellously quiet and she drifted between the office and her flat wearing her favourite housecoat – bright blue with Chinese dragons all over it. She saved all the meteorological material currently on the display boards and opened a new program offering decision trees and flow charts.

Quite soon she realised that this method was useless. It required her to make detailed entries that were not yet possible. It was a time, rather, for identifying broad-brush concepts. She reverted to pen and paper, struggling through possible and impossible ideas with amendments and deletions all over her work. Several pages got torn from her pad, crumpled up, and thrown into a corner. Rasputin, not normally a playful cat, decided to chase these around the room. Finally, she identified three distinct lines of approach, though each of them could clearly have variations.

Number One. Death with no corpse at all. A person could be killed in such a way that there was no body to identify – as might happen in an accident at a dangerous location, or an explosion. If one client believed the dead man to be Toppley and the other believed it to be Tetherman, both would be satisfied.

Number Two. One body, re-used. If Toppley, say, was killed and the death was verified by normal procedures, then the corpse could be stolen for re-use, as Tetherman. This idea had several variations, based on the use of one body, somehow rendered unidentifiable after the second use.

Number Three. A death and the illusion of a death. Toppley, or Tetherman, could be killed and the second death could be imaginary. A witness might testify that he 'saw' a death in circumstances that could not be verified.

The next step was to examine the difficulties posed by each strategy. What were they? Could they be surmounted?

The first strategy called for an observed (or presumed) death, an irrecoverable body and two separate witnesses, each of whom believed the victim to be a different person. Building up the deception would be complicated and small details might be missed. If, for instance, death was caused by swimming from a dangerous beach, whose name was going to be found on the pile of clothing left behind? It would be disastrous if the shirt said Toppley and the trousers said Tetherman. She passed on to the second strategy.

It might just be possible to steal the first corpse. There are extensive procedures that follow a death, especially a suspicious one, for which the body has to be available. But there's a window of opportunity when the coffin lid has finally been nailed down but has not yet been buried or burnt. This looked better than the first strategy. What about the third?

Could the second death be illusory? She had included this strategy because she remembered her success in luring Kevin Carruthers to his death in a dis-used mine shaft on Bodmin Moor. He had certainly seen her- or believed that he had seen her. But that was not the same as creating an image of somebody other than herself that was visible to more than one observer. Had she ever managed that? Yes. Once, long ago, with appalling, exhaustive effort, aided by strong words learnt from Kwaname and since forgotten. There had to be a better and more reliable way of making a death illusory - maybe a technological means, but she didn't know it.

Stealing and re-using the corpse of Toppley looked the best idea, and she began to list ways and means of doing it. But the task was hard to focus on because her analysis had highlighted annoying gaps in her own skill. She did not know how good she was at creating illusions, or at influencing the minds of other people to control what they saw. Worse still, there were huge areas of magical science that she had never attempted; such as Voodoo and the creation of Zombies. Like other pupils, she felt regretful that she had not sought knowledge harder. She remembered talk about Kwaname. How he had been seen in different locations, miles apart, at much the same time. It was commonly believed that he could arrange 'appearances' that were indistinguishable from reality. How convenient it would be if she were able to kill Toppley and resurrect the body in Zombie form under the Tetherman identity. She could then direct it to perform some suicidal activity and the contract would be fulfilled.

She gave up, and it was time for physical action. She dressed in tracksuit and trainers, took a taxi to Hyde Park, ran for an hour, and then walked briskly back all the way through the West End. Tired by the experience, she flopped down with a Chinese take-away and a bottle of rough red wine. She switched on the television, which proved instantly soporific. But all the time her thoughts were back in the hut under the Baobab tree, and the need for greater wisdom.

Kwaname invaded her dream - as if the spirits controlling them both had responded to her need. The venue was unexpected. She was waiting, in her dream, on the pavement in Cannon Street and a red bus came to a halt in from of her. It was one of the old Route-master buses, with a conductor. He was standing on the platform – and it was Kwaname himself. He looked exactly as she had known him and wore tribal dress rather than London Transport uniform. He put out a hand to help her aboard. He spoke, 'It's time, Nshila. Dig. You need the box'. That was all. And suddenly it was Kwaname no longer. It was a man in a white helmet saying, 'Demolition will be starting after lunch, Ms Ileloka.' Adjusting instantly she told him, 'You've got the wrong building'.

It shook her. Never before had he appeared to her. She had felt his presence during the days she spent in the hut during the cattle thief episode, and once she had heard him speak; just three words, to which she could attach no meaning. But this manifestation was quite new. In her waking state she recalled very clearly what he had said, and knew the words to be important. Where was she to dig, and what box was she to look for? Kwaname knew nothing of London. He must mean his own very distant hut.

Chapter Twelve

Learning

Nshila took stock of the situation. Was there any immediate crisis? No, because arranging an assassination always takes time and neither client would be pressing for action yet. Did her lack of skill matter? That was doubtful. She believed that she could operate her second strategy (kill, steal and re-use) with her present resources, but that was not a good reason to ignore a chance for personal development. Experience had shown that whenever she acquired new skills, new opportunities opened up. An up-graded Nshila might be able to execute the second strategy better than one who had not made the effort. It might also make the third strategy viable. The deciding fact was Kwaname's appearance to her. It was effectively a command – like the many he had issued when she was a girl, and which she had never disobeyed. He knew that she had a need, even if she herself was doubtful. He knew that a big moment had been reached.

Yet she was still not completely convinced about killing Toppley. She felt a need for more evidence of his evil-doing, and she had an idea how to get it. Should she pursue it? Did her acceptance of the Tetherman contract make it a waste of time? She had accepted the case made by OLJ for killing Tetherman, and since they were one-and-the-same man it seemed superfluous to research Toppley further. If Tetherman was to die, then Toppley would die also. But she was uncomfortable. If Toppley had not been thoroughly investigated – and OLJ knew nothing of his existence – then it might be that something existed that was hugely to Toppley's credit. It might be so significant that it justified his survival, and that of Tetherman too. She must, after all, know more.

What could be done immediately to further the project? It was frustrating. An overseas trip took time to arrange, and

98

the ruse envisaged for data-gathering about Toppley involved a scheduled event and a fixed date. She was frustrated. She wanted action. She thought of her friends in the police. One of their mantra is the command 'Do something'. The worst thing that anybody can do in their world is nothing. It does not matter too much if the 'something' is wrong, at least it is positive. Indecision and inaction are crimes. Nshila felt like that. But what action was possible? Her risk-taking self had an answer.

'What do you mean, girl? Nothing positive you can do? Rubbish. You can increase your skills by practical experiment. You know what you need to brush up on. Go to it.'

'No, you don't.' Her cautious self was on the alert. 'We've had too much of that. You'll overreach yourself, take one risk too many, and get carried off by the devil. Be sensible, woman, just once in your life.'

She started preparatory action. 'After all', she told her cautious self, 'There's no harm in reading things up, and getting in the necessary materials, is there? I don't have to use them. I can always give up the idea.' Her risk-taking self said nothing, knowing it was winning already.

She racked her brains to remember the things that were said about Kwaname. She reviewed the actions she had seen him take. She assembled all the texts that deal with projections and illusions, and refreshed her knowledge of hypnotism. She studied the literature about hallucinatory drugs.

A prime requirement for materialisation or projection or illusion was accuracy. The witchdoctor must know the subject of the apparition, and the intended observer, and what that observer would expect to see. No suitable subjects came to mind. Nobody was as real to her as Maurice Tate, the schoolboy with whom she had fancied herself to be in love. But suddenly she saw a sealed letter left ready for posting beside Gillian's desk. The postman! She knew him well. Could she conjure up an image that was at least visible to herself? It would be a start.

So late that night she was in the shed on the roof surrounded by books and smells and potions and striving to put the right degree of authority into her commands. The postman delivering to Eastcheap in the summer normally wore sandals and pink socks. He had ordinary blue trousers, which sagged at the front because of a slight beer-belly. A dark blue pullover half covered a heavy leather belt. He wore no tie and had a short neck. His face was round and slightly flushed and always smiling. On his head was a knitted woollen hat.

She spoke the incantations, moved a wand in time to sombre music from a DVD and peered through the smoke at the spot where the image was due. She got the feet right. Then she built him up gradually through the socks and the trousers, concentrating intensely. Things did not appear clearly, of course, but began with a cloud of murky gas that was gradually forced into shape by the power of her mind. The colour came last. How much easier it would be, she thought, if it was like building with lego bricks. But it did work. She was delighted with the pink socks.

Disaster struck when she got to the belt. She could not remember which way his belt was worn. It was a long belt, with the tongue hanging down. Was the loose tongue falling over his left hip, or his right? For one moment she panicked, and that was enough. There was a flash of light, a noise like breaking crockery, and she was thrown to the floor.

Sixty seconds later she was conscious enough to look at the door. It had been blown off its hinges and fallen outwards onto the roof. And there stood Kwaname in full witchdoctor regalia. 'Stupid girl. Don't meddle. Do as you're told. Dig for the power, girl. Dig in the corner.' And then there was nothing. Just the debris of the attempt and a full moon, and the broken door and silence. She got to her feet, and staggered out, treading on the door and feeling it wobble under her feet. It must have fallen on a stone or a brick that prevented it lying quite flat. She looked at it. When she had seen him, Kwaname had been standing on the floor, not on a wobbling platform. The door had been round his ankles. Where were the breaks in the door that allowed this to happen? Nowhere. His image had been totally spiritual.

Something hot and sweet. She debated strong tea but decided instead on whisky and hot water and sugar. The mixture relaxes one and helps the thought process. What had he been trying to say? Obviously he meant to reinforce his instruction to search in the hut, and this time he had added 'Dig in the corner'. When had she last seen him? Before she left the village to go to St Alban's. But wait. He had spoken to her later. Memories came back of the time, after his death, when she had been called back to the village to nail the cattle thief. She had spent long hours in his hut building up the mystique that a witchdoctor needs. Amongst other occupations, she had probed the floor for a hidden cache of powerful charms that he had never let her see. She had been probing away with an old spear and suddenly her arms and shoulders had been frozen and his voice – firm and clear from beyond the grave – had said 'Not yet, Nshila.' Surely that was the meaning. Hidden in a battered old tin box, buried in a smelly, deserted hut beneath a baobab tree, thousands of miles away, was some talisman that would empower her to complete the present work. Perhaps. But what difficulties there were! The hut might no longer exist. The tree might have fallen and become firewood. The tin box might have rusted away. The place might be impossible to find. The site of the village might have moved so that even the previous location was in doubt. Yet she knew it must be done.

She accepted that she was going. Now she began to plan. She had to devise a solid cover for her visit, and a different personality, and arrange transport from the capital out to the village, and hire at least one helper. Fourteen days, or maybe twenty-one, would be needed. She could start immediately after the event relating to Grant Toppley. That was a charity dinner that was somehow sports related. Gillian, through her badminton connections, could provide a ticket. Nshila would attend, learn what she needed about Toppley, make a decision and fly out a few days later.

She thought back, then, on the failed experiment. Had she learnt anything useful? Yes. She knew she could build an apparition, visible at least to herself, and she knew that extreme accuracy and extreme concentration were needed. Before she started, she had to have complete confidence and a perfect minds-eye image of the expected result. But could she make the apparition visible and credible to observers? That she still didn't know.

She rejected the idea of further experiment, but took solace in harmless desk research about her other great area of ignorance. Sooner or later it might be useful. She typed 'zombie' into a search engine and got'

'the bokor prepares.........

.....a concoction of mystical herbs, in addition to human and animal parts......administers the potion..........the victim is rendered insensible, succumbing to a comatose state resembling death.......taken to a hospital........the morgue.........buried in a grave.

the bokor.....

..........raises the victim after a day or two and administers a hallucinogenic concoction called the "Zombies cucumber", that revives the victim.........past personality is entirely absent.........easy to control and used for farm labour and construction work.'

Wow! Theoretically she could make herself a biddable unskilled labourer to carry out simple tasks. Like what? Re-decorate the flat? But how would Rasputin react? Would a cat know that there was something strange here?

Another website added to her knowledge. This time she used 'voodoo' as the key word.

'Today, there are two virtually unrelated forms of the religion:

- An actual religion, vodun practiced in Benin, Dominican Republic, Ghana, Haiti, Togo and various centres in the US.
- An evil, imaginary religion, which we will call voodoo. It has been created for Hollywood movies, complete with violence, bizarre rituals, etc. It does not exist in reality.'

It left her confused. Which parts of voodoo belonged to which tradition? If something was strictly a piece of fiction created for Hollywood, then presumably it would not work. A practitioner might spend vast quantities of time and effort in a doomed activity. Yet if any of the zombie stuff worked then it was a magnificent tool. She put the subject aside for study at a later time.

Chapter Thirteen

Charity Dinner

Gillian Harker knew that she was seen as excessively conscientious and apt to take on worries that were not her problem. She herself sometimes saw her employer as too relaxed about the details of the work. 'This is science, Nshila', she would say, 'not a lucky dip.' Peter Grace reckoned she was ridiculous. He reacted quite sharply when she interrupted him one morning to start moaning. Nshila was out of the office.

'Hold on a moment, Gillian, I can't do two things at once.' Peter was concentrating on the coffee machine tucked into the space between the door and the chart table. It was a unique machine, produced several types of coffee that were actually pleasant to drink – not just an excuse for taking a break. It never went wrong. Neither Gillian nor Peter had ever before worked in an office that owned anything that good. Spares were thought to be unobtainable and it was treated with great care – almost like a talisman.

'I hope you don't agonise like this over other parts of your life, Gillian. Why should you care if the boss is a bit careless and lazy and distracted from time to time? It's her business. It's doing well; we get a good salary, we enjoy the work. I am a lot happier here than I was sewing mail bags in prison.'

'Happier, I can believe. Mailbags, I won't. Prisoners spend their time, now, taking OU courses or learning skills to help them when they get out.'

'Shows how little you know. But don't change the subject. Why are you so angry with Nshila?'

'Because she won't concentrate on the things that matter. She's become preoccupied about some personal project. I had serious doubts about three forecasts I was making and I needed her opinion. Did she give it? No. Just said, "I'll trust your judgement, Gillian." I don't want her trusting my judgement all the time. She's supposed to carry the can.'

'You could ask my opinion instead.'

'Big joke! You're great at massaging the feelings of a client, but you don't have my knowledge and you don't care about the details. I might trust you to steal a car, but not to interpret data.'

'Why do I think you're in a bad mood?'

'Well, there were two things this morning, before she went out. First, she refuses to go and visit the organisers of the Five Counties Show. They have a series of coordinated events planned over a wide area and want minimal risk of disruption. They wanted 'the principal' to visit all the intended locations and attend two committee meetings. She says, "Stall them" or, "You could go, Gillian" or, "Write and tell them there would be no great benefit".'

'She might come round if you leave her alone. What was the second thing?'

The door bell rang at that moment. Not two tasteful notes. Not a fancy musical tune. Not a persistent buzzing. Instead a series of loud clangs from one of the items Nshila had brought with her from Africa; the bell from the lead cow of a herd. Gillian opened the door to find the caretaker of the building, who would normally be in his box in the entrance hall. He was puffing mildly from climbing the stairs.

'Here's the letter. Your boss sweet-talked me into promising that when it arrived I would bring it up straight away instead of putting it in your pigeon hole. It doesn't look important to me, but that's what she wanted.' Thanking him and closing the door, Gillian looked at the letter and turned to Peter.

'You wanted to know about the second thing. Well, this letter is about an event called the 'Arrivals of the Season Dinner'.'

'What arrivals? What season? What dinner?'

'Nshila has got a mad idea about sponsoring some sport, or sportsman or sportswoman. She's been asking me about sporting opportunities for young people. All because I am very keen on badminton. The 'Arrivals Dinner' is about young sportsmen and women who have begun to make an impact. Nshila wants me to get tickets and take her along as my guest.'

'Can you do it?' Peter was curious. He had never seen Gillian as a 'fixer'.

'Probably. There are people in my club who have the right connections. In fact this envelope probably has the tickets.'

'Give me a few details.'

Gillian obliged. 'It's organised by a group of youth clubs and takes place once a quarter. They get a celebrity speaker and charge £75. Five young people are given awards for sporting achievement. They are the 'Arrivals'.'

Peter postponed comment till he had offered Gillian the biscuit tin. It was a normal part of the morning coffee routine and the two took turns to buy supplies. This time they had a minor row because Peter had eaten all the chocolate ones and left Gillian with a choice of digestive or ginger nuts. She liked neither. Peter spoke again about the dinner.

'It sounds a good idea. A nation needs to spend money finding and developing new talent. Do you think Nshila wants to support some young black hopeful and has to find out how things are done? And who is the celebrity at the event you are going to?'

'It's an MP. A man called Grant Toppley. He has a bad reputation politically – very right wing – but works very hard in the sports development scene.'

The tickets had been arranged by a friend of Gillian's whose younger brother, Oliver Oates, belonged to the club hosting the dinner. So they were a party of four; Oliver and his sister, Gillian and Nshila. Gillian found herself looking forward to the event, though Nshila said no more about why she wanted to attend.

The tables were round, and were set for ten people each. Nshila and Gillian were placed opposite each other, too distant to take part in the same conversation. Next to Nshila on her right was Hilda Benn, who looked like – and was – a shot putter. Then came a string-bean fellow who did pole-vaulting - Will

Longland. After him was an earnest young man name Max Cole who was games master in a school, and then a man with an eye-patch who obviously wanted to look like a pirate. He was on Gillian's left, and Gillian later reported that he was one of the financial backers; a sportsman who had lost the eye in an accident and received massive compensation. On Gillian's right were her friend and her brother and a pair of identical twins. Their sport was tennis, and they were the men's doubles partnership of a sports mad university.

But Gillian noticed that Nshila seemed to talk less than usual. She spent all her time asking questions and drawing other people out. She appeared to be in information gathering mode; assessing what must, for her, be an unfamiliar world.

There were five 'arrivals' to be honoured. One of them had been nominated by Max Cole. Once this was realised, the others became interested in his views and the conversation focussed upon him. He spoke quite forcefully.

'It's all very well to give youngsters recognition at an event like this, but they have mountains yet to climb in order to be world-class. I worry that in many cases there won't be enough money to keep them motivated through the extra years of effort.'

'I agree', said one of the tennis players, who were named, confusingly, Gordon and Gregory. 'There are several isolated initiatives like this, but no coherent national strategy for promoting excellence.'

Nshila put a question. 'Surely it is a good sign that we have an MP interested in this project. I mean, our speaker tonight, Grant Toppley.'

There was silence for a moment. Then the one-eyed pirate spoke up. His name turned out to be Graham Sadawi. 'I don't think that Grant Toppley is a good advertisement for anything. I think it was a mistake to invite him.'

Hilda Benn thought the same way. 'I agree with you, Graham, but I know he has his circle of devotees. Is there anybody round the table who is enthusiastically pro-Toppley? We should hear the other side.'

Nobody spoke immediately. Then Gillian's friend Amanda

offered her view.

'I think he has great charm, when he cares to use it, and gains too much influence over the young hopefuls who are close to him - it's especially true of the girls.'

'Oh! Come on! You're getting close to saying that he seduces them.' Oliver Oates wanted to avoid any conflict. It didn't stop Amanda making her case.

'That's not a thing I can claim to know. All I am saying is that I don't like the closeness of the relationships he gets into.'

'That does not mean that they are immoral, does it? He may be a bit weird, but you can't deny that he does a great deal of good for sporting people.'

Hilda Benn, sensing that nobody would be deeply offended, put her thoughts more openly.

'I think he is harmful, sometimes. I know two girls who have been seriously scared by suggestions he made to them. And one girl from my club went off to his training camp in Spain and has never reappeared.'

There is a time at such events, after the dessert, when people get up and move around and chat before settling down to the coffee, brandy and the speeches. It used to include cigars, of course, but at this dinner the smokers were confined to a single table as far away from the others as possible. The break allowed an opportunity for realignment; people not sitting down again in the places they were at before. Gillian got the tennis players, who had at least some understanding of Badminton. Nshila stuck close to Hilda Benn and managed to get Amanda and Max Cole on her other side. When the event was over, Nshila thanked Gillian enthusiastically for fixing the tickets and disappeared with her new acquaintances.

Next day she told Peter and Gillian that she was feeling tired and stressed out and planned to take a three week holiday, starting almost immediately. Could they manage without her for that long? Gillian avoided saying that she had effectively managed on her own for the past month. They reviewed the work on hand and saw no serious dangers. Two days later she was off.

Chapter Fourteen

African Adventure

Three days after the 'Arrivals Dinner' Dr Wilfred Scoon, headmaster of St Albans, was sitting in his study five thousand miles away. The study of a headmaster looks much the same all over the world. He sat behind a large desk that would have been impressive in a bankers office, if properly cared for, but was actually covered in books and tattered papers and had scratch marks around the bottom where a previous headmaster had tethered his dog. Predictably, Dr Scoon sat below a rather mediocre portrait of the founder. Less predictably, the wall also carried a photograph of the President, in splendid military uniform, and the headmaster's membership certificate of the ruling political party. The national flag stood in a mahogany holder in one corner. Had it been in England, the windows would have been closed against the rain. In Central Africa they stood wide open.

Seated in front of the desk were Fred Mbwele and Abel Mubala. They were uncertain what might happen; they were clearly criminals, the damage of their drunken vandalism proved it, but they had officially left the school. This was their first day of freedom from its discipline. Could the headmaster do anything terrible to them or not? Dr Scoon enjoyed their uncertainty because he knew exactly what was going to happen and it suited him well. He started with some knife twisting.

'You two are going to get a well-deserved punishment, in addition to your present appalling headache. You're not going to like it one little bit.'

'No, Sir.'

'You are fixed up with a temporary job with the mining company, I believe? Two month's work at a decent rate of pay, and valuable experience. That's right, I think?'

'Yes, Sir. And we're both very grateful to you for fixing it.'

Fred considered politeness and courtesy were the best way to avoid or mitigate whatever might be coming. It had no effect on Dr Scoon. He allowed a moment of silence while he looked out of the window and watched his language teacher climb into a taxi. Then he spoke.

'Well, it's cancelled. The company phoned me yesterday. They were very apologetic, but their exploration programme has been altered and they don't need any temporary staff. They will probably have to lay off some of their permanent people. You are unemployed, boys.'

Fred and Abel said nothing. Their headaches were instantly worse.

'Bad news, I fear,' said Dr Scoon.

'Yes, Sir. Very bad indeed.' Abel had nasty visions of two friends from whom he had borrowed money, and one young woman he had invited to a very expensive event. He would have to make some embarrassing excuses. Dr Scoon might have been reading his thoughts.

'And you don't have any money, do you, either of you?'

'No, Sir.' Fred answered for both boys. 'Is there nothing else you know of, Sir?'

'Nothing that either of you deserve.'

Fred looked up sharply. He sensed an opening. If there were no possibility at all of a job, the headmaster would not have qualified his comment. He was not sadistic enough to dangle an unobtainable carrot.

'But that means you do have something, Sir, even if we don't deserve it. Please. Give us a chance. We can't be the first people who have trashed half the school on their last night. I can remember what the leavers did two years ago.'

That, of course was a fact well known to Dr Scoon. His response recognised it.

'Quite true, but you two are today's culprits.' After a pause, 'Have you got the humility to work for a woman?'

'Yes, Sir. If the money's right.' Fred was the one most

eager to seize the opportunity.

'Then maybe you will survive after all. I got two calls yesterday. The second was a request, last night, from one of our alumni. It's a woman, one who left here about ten years ago, went to England for a university education and now owns her own business in the field of meteorological forecasting. She wants to set up some specialised weather-recording points in this country and needs a couple of sensible young men to work for her. It will last about three weeks.'

'It sounds great, Sir.' Fred was sitting forward on his chair, trying to make it psychologically impossible for Dr Scoon to backtrack. 'But why Abel and I, and why doesn't she just fly in and contact the labour exchange, and what would we have to do, and will we be able to do it? And is she black or white, Sir?'

'Ever since you came to us, Fred Mbwele, you have been asking multiple questions. Which do you want answered first?'

'The one about contacting you, Sir, and not the labour exchange.'

'She wants two young men who are well educated and reasonably competent, and reliable in the sense that they won't disappear into the bush if the work becomes difficult. She knew it was the end of our school year and she thought that two boys recommended by the headmaster would be better than whatever turned up at the labour exchange on the day she arrived. She wanted it all fixed in advance. What she actually said was, "I am going to be stuck with these two for a month. I don't want anybody dumb or lazy or gutless. Doesn't St Alban's pride itself on turning out the other sort?"'

'Will she take us?' This time it was Abel who spoke.

'She wants one who has experience of driving a landrover in bad conditions – that's you Abel – and one who speaks Cisindi – that's you Fred. And she wants both of you to be healthy and strong, because there may be some heavy physical work involved. If you are asking whether I have doubts about recommending you both, it's a big 'Yes'. Fred especially so. You have done some fairly stupid things in your time here. But you are also resourceful, and neither of you is ever boring. Again, the records show that this woman was pretty troublesome when she was here so maybe you will get on alright. Don't let me down.'

From the moment Dr Scoon had mentioned working for a woman, Abel had been listening intermittently. His adolescent mind was speculating about what this woman would be like. His preferred reading matter was a rather lurid magazine that featured curvaceous models in minimal clothing and enticing attitudes. Surely he was not going to be that lucky! He asked about it.

'What does she look like, Sir? Is she doll or dragon or dumpling? I don't want to spend four weeks working for some frightful old hag with thighs like an elephant.'

Fred kicked Abel in the shin and scowled at him fiercely. He did not want Abel's obsession with face and figure to foul up this opportunity. Dr Scoon noticed and approved. Nevertheless, he answered Abel's question.

'Abel, you are a nasty little creature. The best I can do is show you the picture of her final year group from ten years ago. Over here, on the wall. Third from the left in the back row.'

'Looks pretty good," said Abel. "But it might be very different if she has had six children since. She may not be what we see in the photo. Will it be What You See Is What You Get?'

Dr Scoon was still patient. 'She is not married, and I have never heard of any children.'

'Why have you covered up the names, Sir?' Fred suspected he was not getting all the truth.

'Because she won't be using her real name, and she does not want anybody here to know it. Her reasons could be perfectly sound. We have had several political upheavals here, and she might have made a few enemies. The main question is, are you going to take this on?'

Fred answered, before Abel could say anything more inquisitive. 'Yes. Yes. At least this is novel and pays money. What do we have to do?'

'You have got tomorrow and the next day to get everything

together for a month of travel, mostly in the bush. You must also get hold of a second-hand but reliable landrover. I can give you the money for these things because she has transferred funds to the school account. The third day from now, you go down to the airport to meet Flight BA 1359, which is due at 10am. You stand outside the arrival door with a big notice saying 'Isabel Ngombi'. And make yourselves respectable; no frayed jeans or whatever.'

Fred and Abel, both quite smart, were at 'Arrivals' at 9.30 in the morning. They knew, from a telephone call that BA 1359 had left Nairobi on schedule and might even land early because of a following wind. They thought that Ms Ngobi might be on the ground early as 9.45am, and struggling with Immigration and Customs.

Both departments were unpredictable in terms of speed and efficiency. There were days when no official appeared at all and passengers walked through unhindered. There were other days when officials were present in numbers, and were quarrelsome and bad tempered. So the time delay could vary from five minutes to two hours. Bad tempered was also the right word for Fred, who believed that Abel had not done his share of the preparatory work. Abel had apparently decided that Isabel Ngombi was not going to be too far over the hill, and he had insisted on buying various things that he believed a smart woman might appreciate. While Fred was choosing the right sort of portable stove, and working out how much fuel would be needed, Abel had been in the chemists shop purchasing perfume and hair spray and bath salts and patterned tights. And he himself was ponced up like a television presenter. Fred heard him rehearsing his greeting. 'Mizz Ngombi? I am Abel Mubala and it's going to be a great pleasure to look after you. Do let me take your suitcase. By the way, this is Fred Mbwele, who will be with us.'

At 9.30am people – a large number - started coming through the double doors that were the exit from customs, but none of them looked like Isabel Ngombi or noticed the placard. The stream of people shrank to a trickle and the two began to worry. Then both doors were forced open and a porter pushed a trolley through. On it was a small wooden crate, plastered with customs clearance labels. The woman walking behind was obviously Ms Ngombi.

Pleasantly normal. This was not the sexual exhibitionist that Abel had hoped for. Nor was it the widespread mother-of-five he had feared. She was about five foot eleven, slender and upright. She had a strong face, full of character. She looked as if she was accustomed to getting her own way, but lines at the corner of her mouth suggested humour. She was dressed in a simple brown trouser suit and low shoes; an outfit that looked smart, but was convenient for travelling. She seemed a bit tired, quite naturally after a night flight. She also looked angry.

Abel lost out. The porter said, 'this is as far as I go,' and shoved the handles of the trolley towards him. Isabel made it worse by saying, 'Give the porter a tip, will you. I don't have any local money.' So Abel was standing between the shafts of the trolley, searching for change, and Fred was the one who said, 'Welcome, Miss Ngombi. I'm Fred Mbwele and my friend is Abel Mubala. We're the ones Old Fretful chose to help you.'

'Don't be disrespectful to your headmaster.' She spoke firmly, but there was a twitch at the corner of her mouth. She realised she had made a friendly move by recognising the headmasters nickname.

'Sorry, Miss Ngombi. It's just habit.'

'Break it, then,' she said. 'Anyway, Good Morning, Fred. Good Morning Abel. The first thing I want you to do is get this crate hidden away in the back of your landrover before it causes me any more trouble.'

Abel stood up with the trolley and started forcing his way through the crowd. Fred asked, 'Was there trouble with the customs, then?'

'Yes. The things in the crate are harmless meteorological measuring devices, but the customs staff had no idea what the names meant and asked question after question. Then some senior police officer stuck her nose in. She was at the airport to

114

deal with some terrorist scare. A white woman with an officious attitude and no manners. Her badge said Special Adviser Maud Franklin. I can believe that we still need whites for specialised jobs, but why can't they screen out an arrogant cow like her? She seemed to think I was bringing in the hardware for an atom bomb.'

They reached the landrover. Fred and Abel hoisted the crate into the back and pulled down the cover. 'What next, Ms. Ngombi?'

'I have booked into the airport hotel. Take me there, and we'll go over the supplies you have brought, and check there is no shortfall. Then I want to sleep through the afternoon. You two must come back at seven o'clock. We will have dinner, and then I will brief you about the work. We start out tomorrow at 6.30.'

The review of stores went well. The men had collected all the things she thought necessary except for five spades and two pickaxes. They were obviously going to do a lot of digging. Abel went off to make the purchases.

Promptly at 7.00 they entered the bar and looked around for the woman they had met that morning. She was nowhere to be seen. They were just sitting down at a table near the door when they heard, 'Over here, boys.'

What a difference! They had been conditioned to expect this high-powered businesswoman from Europe. They had forgotten that she had been born in their country in a rural village. The person at the end of the bar was dressed in the manner of any wealthy African woman; flowing, brightly coloured cloth and a matching headscarf, tied to give her an extra three inches.

'Surprised are you, boys?' It's so long since I dressed like this that I had quite forgotten how comfortable it is. Do you like it? I searched all over London for something and finally struck lucky with a French website. Then I spent a weekend in Paris making choices.'

'It's magic, Mizz Ngombi. You look like our Prime Minister's wife at a state occasion.'

'Thank you, Fred. St Alban's still teaches people good

manners.'

Over dinner she explained the work. Looking back, Fred realised that there were some inconsistencies and inadequacies in her story, but neither he nor Abel knew anything about meteorology, and they felt a bit overawed anyway by her strong personality. She explained the project in a way that her two new helpers would grasp.

'Meteorology is about studying the weather, and it can sometimes tell you what is going to happen. Weather phenomena move around the world according to the atmospheric situation around them, and whatever is going to hit you tomorrow is in existence somewhere else today. If you know where it is, and which way it is moving, you can predict whether it will hit you or not.'

Abel started fidgeting at that point, just as he had done in hundreds of lessons at St Albans. He got the same nasty look from Ms Ngombi that he had received from his teachers. Fred, embarrassed, made faces and gestures intended to stop him. Politeness was more important now than it had been in the classroom. Ms Ngombi went on.

'The farther away a weather system is, the longer warning you will get if it does happen to be coming your way. So people are experimenting with collection of data from very distant parts. So far as the UK is concerned, this country is very distant indeed, but my company thinks it is worth finding the facts, sending them back to London, and seeing what, if anything, we can do with them. It may turn out to be a waste, but it is not terribly expensive.'

'Is that crate full of measuring instruments then?' Practical things, physical things, were more Abel's scene.

'Yes. They are not very fancy or expensive. A remote collection point is not large, and you will see that what we leave behind us does not look much more than a wooden box on a stick.'

'How does the information get from here to London?' Abel again.

'That's the clever part. I have fixed a deal with a satellite company. My data goes up to the satellite and bounces down to London. For them it is a tiny part of their traffic. To me, it is very useful. One of their directors owed me a favour and the fee is low. I shall be the only one getting this data, and one day it may be valuable. You could say that I am flying a kite, commercially.'

The men had a last drink together after she had gone to bed. Abel was less impressed than Fred.

'She's a bit too clever for me, Fred. I'm not sure what I was hoping for, but that serious commitment to the task is a bit heavy. Not to mention the technical knowledge. Impressive woman-wise, of course.'

'You were never the brightest of us, were you? I think you missed most of the sophisticated signals. She is intelligent and knows her business and she has a keen sense of humour.'

The party left as intended at 6.30am the next morning. They had a good map, and the first installation was to be seventy five miles west from the city. Roads in the country were good near the big towns, and between them, but got rapidly worse in the rural areas. They got to the first destination about 9.30am but had then to choose a precise spot for her equipment. Isabel Ngombi explained the requirements.

'These remote stations are not going to be visited, so we must do everything possible to secure them against accidents. We don't want them to be easily seen, and attract human visitors. Nor do we want animals rubbing against them to mark their territory. And we certainly don't want elephants trampling them. So look for places that are hidden away a bit, and where there is no reason for animals to come. We will never put one close to a waterhole.'

So the three split up, and scoured different areas. If Abel or Fred thought he had found a good place, he called her. Often she rejected it, so the whole morning passed before a site had been approved. By then it was really hot, so they spread the canopy of the landrover to provide shade and ate lunch. Then they rested. They restarted their work at three o'clock. Theoretically, digging a single hole for a post ought not to take too long, but these were stout posts that had to go down a long way. 'When the rain comes,' she said, 'places that now look secure can become a sea of loose mud.' The pole also required three props to support it.

When the post was fixed, she had to assemble her equipment, bolt it securely into the housing, and fix the housing on top of the pole. The thing looked rather like a dog kennel on a tripod. Were they finished? No. 'One way of keeping this thing safe,' she said, 'is to camouflage it.' So they had to paint it all in a colour that merged nicely with the surroundings. That usually meant dull brown, or dull green, or a greyish blue colour if the thing was against the skyline.

Abel asked, 'How do we find it ourselves, if we want to?' He learnt that he had to take compass bearings on it from two easily identifiable spots – and found that he lost status when Ms Ngombi realised that he had no idea how to do it. Painstakingly, she showed him, saying, 'It's quite possible that nobody will ever want to come near this thing again. But just in case, we must have the bearings.'

On the first night of their trek there was a modest hotel, and it served a simple but well cooked evening meal. They were all glad of it. For the second time she wore African dress. It was time to become less formal.

'All today, you two were calling for 'Mizz Ngombi' to come over and inspect a site. It's better if you call me Isabel from now on. Informal will suit us better. But just remember that I'm paying you.'

They travelled on the next day, and Isabel explained that they would set up about ten stations before turning back to the city. It would be one station on most days; two if things went well. The night at the small hotel was the last taste of luxury. After that it was unstaffed government rest houses, or sleeping in tents beside the vehicle. In those conditions, three people develop some sort of relationship. One feature, an amusing one to Fred, was the near-adoration that Abel displayed. Back at school he had viewed women entirely as sex objects. Now he was attentive and obedient and very keen to please. When fixing the camp site, for instance, everything had to be made just right for her. On her side, Fred detected amusement mixed with a slice of harmless cruelty. Twice she sent him off on unnecessary errands; but errands that still demanded hard work, and it seemed as if she was playing with a toy. Fred sensed that she had been in that position of power before.

His own reactions were different. He found her an attractive and entertaining woman, but remained suspicious. There was something about her that he was unable to define, and it made him nervous of any emotional commitment. On the other hand he found that they had both studied English literature at St Alban's and that the course had not changed much between their times at school. They were fond of similar texts, and could exchange quotes from sources as varied as Beatrice Potter and T S Eliot. Even one of the teachers from her day was still there in Fred's time. They talked of Mrs Van Jaarsvelt with her thick Afrikaans accent and her habit of bursting into tears when she read something beautiful. Fred quoted an anti-feminist line:

'For graves have learnt that woman-head
to be to more than one a bed.'

Nshila saw it as a strategic skill rather than an insult.

They drove westwards day by day, setting up the stations. Fred and Abel became quite skilled in site selection and digging and painting. They finished the ninth station in the morning, and after the usual rest Isabel suggested that they drive on towards the last place marked on her map. That evening they camped on the edge of an escarpment, overlooking a plain. There was a river in the middle distance.

Next morning Isabel said, 'I am a bit tired today. I think I will trust you two with the whole job. But we have a great view from here, so we can talk over the possible sites before you go.'

It took them half-an-hour to make the decision. The plain was almost flat from the bottom of the escarpment the whole way to the river, and the lush vegetation made it obvious that there would be flooding in the wet season. The station had to be safely above flood level, so there was only, perhaps, half a mile available from the foot of the escarpment outwards. There was also a large village, with gardens around it. That further restricted the available locations. Then Isabel pointed out that the village looked new, and had possibly been moved from an older site.

Fred and Abel tried to identify that older site, thinking that if it had been abandoned then few people would go there. Isabel herself was the first to spot it. She pointed, and said, 'Do you see that huge baobab tree? Look carefully a hundred yards to the right of it. There are patterns on the earth where huts had once stood.'

'I've got it', said Abel. 'And I can see that there has been a hut right there beneath the tree. Its not quite part of the village, is it? Perhaps somebody special lived there. If we worked there, we would have a bit of shade over us.'

'Put it there,' Isabel said, 'but work quietly and avoid being seen if possible. I don't want too much local interest.'

That evening they had a better than usual celebration dinner. Isabel insisted on adding a few special herbs to the pot, things that she had found during the day. She said that she remembered them from her childhood. Fred did not much like the result and ate little. Abel made a pig of himself and told Isabel how marvellous it was.

That night, Fred had a foul dream and woke up after midnight. This was an unusual experience for him and he wondered whether the cause lay within the dream or whether something external had caused it. Certainly, something was different. The light outside was very bright, but lifting the tent flap showed him a full moon, at present free of clouds. Not the light, then. Suddenly he realised that when he looked out he had seen the flap on Isabel's tent open. Was she there? Had she gone out? Was she perhaps in danger?

He got out of bed and went outside. His own tent flap

made a noise as it fell back behind him and he suddenly knew what had disturbed his subconscious mind. It was deathly quiet. That was extraordinary in the bush, where animals of one sort or another can always be heard. And he could feel a breeze on his face, but not a leaf was stirring; neither leaves on the trees nor fallen ones. The moonlight was so strong that it threw dark shadows, and some of them recalled shapes from his dreams. It was scary. He felt unsure whether he was awake or asleep. Then Abel started snoring and Fred knew he was awake.

He looked down onto the plain and tried to locate the spot where he had been working. It looked different; the shadow of the tree partly obscured their newly erected station and he could only see part of the dog kennel bit. Nothing of the support was visible. A thin cloud moved across the moon and the light changed again. Was there something moving down there? An animal? A person? He concentrated hard. Yes. There was a human figure. It moved, the moon came out again and he recognised Isabel. What was she doing down there? What a crazy time, Fred thought, to go and inspect the work he and Abel had done! Surely not! Another movement. Was there somebody else present? That was harder still to work out. There was a shape, a human shape, but things could be seen through it. Fred could see a large square stone that Abel had sat on while they ate their lunch. If the shape was real it should have hidden that stone from view. Fred was scared, but fascinated. What was happening? Now Isabel and the shape seemed to be standing face to face. She seemed to bow her head before it. A cloud over the moon again – this time thicker, so that for a moment he could see nothing. Brightness once more,, but nothing strange to be seen under the tree. Only Isabel – clearly Isabel now – walking back towards the escarpment and carrying a tin box. It was not a box Fred had seen before. Now noises returned; a lion growled in the distance, leaves rustled, a jackal called, a dog barked in the village.

Fred turned back and lay down in his tent. If something supernatural had happened, he wanted no part of it. He certainly didn't want Isabel to know that he had observed her. He slept,

121

but in an extraordinary manner he picked up the sequence of his earlier dream. In the morning he was more confused than ever; had the incident been real or not? He remained in doubt for two days, until they were re-arranging some of the equipment in the landrover and he had to move some of Isabel's personal baggage. Hidden underneath a blanket was a large tin box – dirty and rusty as if it had lain long in the ground.

The trip back to the capital was uneventful. Fred and Abel said goodbye to Isabel at the airport and were well pleased to find that the envelope she gave each of them contained the full agreed payment and a generous bonus.

That was the end of the affair for Abel. But for Fred there was an epilogue two years later when he attended his first alumni gathering at St Albans. He was studying the annual photographs on the wall and saw the name that had been covered up by the headmaster's hand. Nshila Ileloka, he read. Not Isabel Ngombi,

A voice spoke behind him.

'Admiring us, are you? Our year was a very good one. That's me, in the centre of the back row.' Fred followed the pointing finger and saw a younger and fitter version of the portly white man, apparently about 30, who was now beside him. Patrick Quinn was the name given underneath him. Fred pointed to Isabel/Nshila, and asked what he knew of her. Patrick had plenty to say.

'My boy, that is one fellow alumnus that you don't want to mess with. If you ever meet her, run the other way fast.'

Fred said nothing about his adventure with her, but pressed for details. His experience had left him liking and respecting her, but awake to the fact that she might have a darker side.

Patrick told him, 'You'll always get conflicting views about her. She was very clever here at school; top of the class more often than not, and often coming up with questions the teachers found hard to answer. She had plenty of friends, but there was always something a bit weird about her. Most of the black students were keen to embrace European culture in a big way. They saw it as the best way forward. Nshila was different.

She never saw it as superseding her tribal values, more as an extension of what she knew or a comparison point.'

Other alumni moved in to study their youthful images, so Fred and Patrick moved aside. They took one of the window seats that looked out onto the front drive. Fred could see the statue, still missing an arm, that he had vandalised on his last night at school. He had more questions for Patrick.

'How did you get that idea? What did she do to make you think that way?'

'Quite a lot. She certainly knew something of tribal witchcraft and she did some astonishing things. She would have been expelled if anybody could have proved them. But nobody could, because there was no physical evidence.'

'I don't understand. Give me an example.'

'A boy was found smoking by one of the teachers – Mr Doubleton – who confiscated a gold cigarette case that had belonged to the boy's father. The boy told everybody that he would break into the teachers study and get it back. He was friendly with Nshila at that time and she told him he had better have an alibi. Nobody quite knew what she meant. What happened was that the teacher entered his study unexpectedly, just as somebody was disappearing out of the window. He jumped to the conclusion it was Maurice Tate, the smoker. Anyway, the cigarette case was gone.'

'So Maurice was in real trouble?'

'No. That was the weird thing. Another teacher had been sitting at the window of her bedroom marking papers and she swore she had seen Maurice, on the bench beside the cricket pavilion, mending a model aircraft. There was a huge argument about it. Doubleton said that she had been wrong about the time. He said it had been too dark to see clearly. He said that because Maurice was known to make model aircraft, Mrs Capstick had assumed that it was him that she saw.'

Patrick went on. 'None of the arguments shifted Mrs Capstick. She was convinced that she had seen Maurice working at his aircraft for a full twenty minutes, and that covered the time of the alleged break in. Of course, Maurice was dead lucky to hear what Mrs Capstick had seen before Doubleton accused him. If he had denied the story without claiming to have been at the cricket pavilion he would have been lost.'

'What happened?'

'Mrs Capstick won. The most Doubleton could get her to say was that fading light made her last view of Maurice a bit blurred. He became, she said, 'slightly fuzzy at the edges.' But when Doubleton kept on grilling her, she burst into tears and that was the end of it.'

Fred apologised to a passer-by who had nearly tripped over his outstretched legs. He tucked them under the window seat and encouraged Patrick to finish.

'It was confusing. But the person who was most confused was Maurice. He knew he had broken in, he knew he had not been sitting beside the cricket pavilion. He could see no reason why Mrs Capstick should lie to protect him. Yet she seemed to be speaking from conviction. She had really seen him – or believed that she had seen him. Maurice did the sensible thing. He got the cigarette case out of the way by having the groundsman take it to the local pawnshop. He adopted Mrs Capstick's story in full.'

'Why should anybody connect Nshila with all that?'

'I'm not sure that anybody but me did. But I knew a bit about Nshila because she had helped me in that love potion affair. I knew she had some degree of power. I knew she had spoken about an alibi. And I watched her. I could see that she was utterly washed out for two days afterwards. It was as if she had exerted herself in some activity that tested her to the limit. Then there was that curious statement about 'going fuzzy at the edges'. If somebody with psychic power was able to create an illusion, then it must require massive concentration. If the concentration could not be sustained, then logically the illusion ought to fade.'

Fred remembered what he had seen, or perhaps imagined, as he looked down from the escarpment in the middle of the night. He put this story beside it and wondered more about Isabel/

Nshila. Who was this woman he had spent a fortnight working for? One conclusion he reached was that the whole business of the weather stations had been a charade. Her objective had been to gain something from the shadow figure underneath the baobab tree, and to do so secretly. Physically, the gain must have been the tin box. Spiritually, it might have been knowledge and advice and power.

Chapter Fifteen

Too Many Roles

On the flight homewards, Nshila reflected on an enjoyable experience. It had been expensive, but the rust-eaten biscuit tin was in the overhead rack; no way was she going to risk its disappearance into the hold. She had just been able to make out the letters 'H, U, N, T, L,' but otherwise had not examined it. She had also learnt much from that meeting of minds with Kwaname. The boys had been fun, and it was terrific to be really warm for three weeks. Nothing had gone wrong. The data from the measuring stations might really reach her, and might even be useful. Not least was the sensuous pleasure of the Afro-outfit and the way it fell around her in mind-blowing colours.

Her happiness took a blow. The flight had a scheduled stop at Nairobi and was routed subsequently over Italy and France. There was a lightning strike of air traffic controllers in France and the flight landed at Milan's Linate airport to await the re-opening of air space. The announcer warned of delay that might be as much as twenty four hours. The airline staff explained the arrangements made for the passengers. Contrary to her expectations, Nshila slept quite well in her hotel room. Another ameliorating circumstance was arrival at Heathrow at the civilised time of 10.15am instead of the usual pre-dawn horror. She phoned the office to tell Gillian she was back.

'Thank heavens for that. Get here quickly. I really need you.'

Not a welcome reply. But understandable, she knew. If a person leads a double life then the problems will double also. She reminded herself that The Rain Consultancy had become the most important part of her life, however much drama and excitement the other activities provided. She needed the respectability attached to being a successful businesswoman. She needed it to grow and prosper. Supporting her staff was necessary. But she was not, after all, going to make a relaxed entrance to find Gillian and Peter right on top of the job and indifferent to her return. She was not going to enjoy a light lunch of cheese and white wine and pass the afternoon in a long pleasant dream.

The taxi delivered her to Eastcheap, she dumped her gear in the flat, unpacking nothing except the tin box. She made a coffee and asked Gillian what the problem was.

'Two things. I don't know which worries me more. We have had a very aggressive complaint from Lucreford Council about our recommendation for their historical pageant. We got it wrong; the whole affair was washed out in torrential rain and they want their money back. The woman on the phone was really nasty. She talked about legal action. I said that we would investigate, and that you would call her back yesterday. But she called herself, and I explained your flight was delayed. Then I left early to avoid any second call.'

Nshila relaxed a little. She had coped with worse crises before and had strategies for dealing with complaining customers. No business was so good that it had none at all. She spoke calmly to Gillian.

'I am not going to panic about that. We have been wrong once or twice in the past and I have a few strategies up my sleeve. What's the other problem?'

'It's Peter.' Gillian was agitated. Obviously this was the thing that worried her more. 'Last night he said that he was off to meet some old friends, and it seemed to me that he was edgy about it. He has not shown up today and I'm wondering whether the "old friends" were people he met in prison. If people like that urged him to meet for a drink, he would find it hard to refuse. He might be in trouble.'

'Come on, Gillian. Why so pessimistic? He has plenty of friends who are not ex-convicts. And I could give you five reasons for lateness without even trying.'

'But his timekeeping is normally OK, Nshila. You know it is.'

Nshila thought it over. While she thought, she wandered round the office touching familiar objects that she was glad to see again; her MBA certificate that hung on the wall and was slightly crooked, the paperweight that had a snowstorm inside it, the ashtray carved out of Welsh granite, the six inch dice that had a different 'fortune for today' on each face. She spoke to Gillian again.

'There has to be more to it. Something must have happened to give you this idea about bad company.'

Gillian responded. 'Yes. Sometimes he mentions people he met in Parkhurst, and one of the names was Bert Gettily. Peter spoke of him as one of the most inventive men he had ever met; forever devising clever scams to part people from their money. I took a phone call for Peter yesterday. I didn't get the name clearly, and I passed the call over without thinking. This morning, the name Gettily came into my mind, and I realised it was the name given over the phone. I'm sure it was in that phone call that Peter agreed to the meeting.'

Nshila sat down at Peter's work station and gave her mind fully to the problem.

'So you think that Peter met up with some old mates last night, and either they involved him in some criminal activity or they beat him up because he refused to join them. Is that it?'

'Yes.'

'I still think you're building an absurd fantasy. But have you done the obvious things like ringing his home number, and his mobile?'

Gillian was still agitated and started to twist a handkerchief into knots, a habit that came out when she was unusually worried. It always annoyed Nshila.

'Of course I did. The home number diverted to his mobile, and that had the usual recording about the person not being available to take the call. You may think me an idiot, but I also rang one or two hospitals to see if he had been admitted. Negative, of course. I thought of going to his digs, but they are a long way out and I did not want to leave the office.'

Nshila got up and toured the space again.

'You think, don't you, that he is lying unconscious in some hospital bed or locked up in a police station?'

'I do. I know I don't have much reason. I know you are probably right, and there is nothing wrong at all. I've told myself not to be stupid, but I still have this grim conviction that he's in trouble.'

What a mess! There Nshila stood, just home after a tiring flight, with the tin box sitting unopened on the cooker in the flat – niggling at her mind every minute – and Gillian being hysterical over what might be no problem at all.

But it was unlike Gillian to be that bad. Nshila decided it was time to call in a few favours. She told Gillian to try some more hospitals and herself put in a call to a county police force. She was lucky, and got Detective Inspector Bill Waterhouse, who was delighted to hear from her. When she congratulated him on his promotion he said that a big factor in the change had been the removal of Maud Franklin. What could he do for her?

She explained her fears for Peter, and the remote possibility that he might be languishing in a cell somewhere.

'Checking that won't be a problem. I have enough friends in the Met to find out if anybody called Peter Grace was nicked last night. There are only so many stations where people suspected of minor offences are held. But if he used a false name then I'll get nowhere, and if he is charged with anything serious then I am helpless.'

That was all Nshila could ask for. 'Bill, if you could check for the name it would be great. I feel pretty sure you will get a nil return and that will suit me just fine. In the unlikely event of his being charged with something then I'll get my solicitor onto it.'

'I'll call you back.'

Gillian's hospital enquiries all proved negative, so Nshila switched her attention to the other problem and called up the meteorological data upon which GO sent to Lucreford Council had been based. She could see what was wrong; a weather front had changed both speed and direction together. Commercially, of course, The Rain Consultancy was completely safe because all publicity stressed the degree of uncertainty attached to weather prediction. No customer could be unaware that from time to time a prediction would prove wrong. However, every failure was annoying, and Nshila sympathised with disappointed clients. The core feature of her strategy was to let complainants moan as long as they wished, pick up clues about their circumstances and find the best way to calm them down. She rang Lucreford and got through to the lady who had spoken with Gillian.

After five minutes conversation it was clear that the anger, and the threatening attitude, were rooted in personal concern. Lucreford Council was a socialist-dominated body and this lady had gone out on a limb by paying money to a private organisation. That organisation had failed. She wanted something to say in her defence.

'Mrs Sandcote, I really am very sorry that we got this one wrong. But I have called up the data on which we based our forecast and I am quite sure that any other expert, public or private, would have said the same. In our business there are certain experience-based rules that we apply. But they can't be foolproof because the forces we are dealing with are extremely complicated.'

'What do you mean?' Mrs Sandcote wanted more detail.

'Well, the conventions we work to say something like, 'If 'this' condition is true and 'that' condition is untrue then there is an 80 percent probability that "so-and-so" will happen'. In this case any competent meteorologist would have given the advice we gave. There was no justification for doing anything else.'

Mrs Sandcote was still resentful. 'So I might as well have got free advice from a government agency and not wasted money on you. It seems that you don't have much to offer.'

Nshila indulged in a brief coughing fit. It was a good way to buy thinking time, and sometimes inspired sympathy.

'Sorry about that, Mrs Sandcote. I can understand how you feel. But we do have a good reputation, we do give clear advice instead of hedging our bets, and we do give close attention to each and every customer. You would never have this conversation if a government agency had let you down.'

She was disturbed at that moment by Gillian. 'Nshila, what's this dirty old tin box doing on top of the cooker?'

This was a bigger and more immediate crisis. Nshila abandoned the phone call. 'Mrs Sandcote, I'll have to call you back. I've got a crisis!'

Sometimes, not often, the coffee machine failed. When that happened, Gillian and Peter were accustomed to go into the flat and use the kettle. It had happened at a bad time. Nshila rushed through and snatched the box from Gillian's hands just before she opened it.

'It's special, Gillian.' She had no time to think of a better explanation. 'It's a special present to me from Mike Fanshawe. He found it in the attic and for some strange reason I'm not to open it, nor anybody else, until 31st October next year. God knows why. But I promised him. I swore all sorts of terrible oaths that it would stay sealed till that day.'

And then the phone was ringing again. Bill Waterhouse was on the line.

'I've found him, Nshila. Get down to Bow Street Magistrates Court and you may be able to sort it all out.'

'What's he done, Bill?'

'Possibly nothing. It seems he was with a group of three other men, known villains, when a robbery took place. It sounds like an old-fashioned smash-and-grab. There's some doubt about whether your man was really involved. Get down there quickly and exercise some charm. He might not be charged.'

'Thanks very much, Bill, I owe you. I'm on my way.' Nshila put down the phone and dashed into her flat to change.

Gillian was left to phone Mrs Sandcote and explain the delay. It took Nshila fifteen minutes to get out of her heavily creased travelling gear and create an image likely to impress policemen and magistrates. Then a taxi ride, frustrating attempts to find the relevant people, and a meeting with Peter in a secure interview room below the court room.

131

Peter was apologetic. 'I ought not to have gone. I know that. But those three were all good to me in Parkhurst and you can't ditch your friends like old socks.'

'You can, and you should.' Nshila was in no mood to accept excuses. 'But this time you met them. What happened?'

'Most of the time nothing but old mates' talk. They did not really believe I was out of the crime scene, but there was no talk of current projects and no pressure on me to join anything. We drank for a time in The Carpenters Joint and then took Bert's wheels to go to the Goat and Thistle over at Bethnal Green. We were all a bit drunk. The rest was Ginger's fault. He's a mad impulsive creature, quite unable to balance risk against benefit. We passed a ticket agency that advertised discount tickets for pop concerts. Ginger shrieked, "I want those. Huge re-sale value. Stop the car." Before I knew what was happening Bert had pulled over. Ginger and Tom had broken down the door and were grabbing books of tickets. I was in the back seat on the drivers side. I got out fast and left them. I wanted out.'

'Obviously you didn't get away.'

'No.' Peter replied. 'A police patrol car turned into the road, which must have been a one-in-a-million chance. They saw Ginger and Tom getting back into Bert's car and shooting off in a haze of burnt rubber. One policeman got out and the car set off after Bert.'

Nshila was puzzled. She was also uncomfortable. The chairs provided for visitors were of poor quality and hers had a big crack across the seat. 'If you were not with them, how did you get taken up?'

'I was standing around, uncertain what to do. I reckoned that if I ran away it would suggest guilt. Unfortunately, somebody who had seen the incident pointed me out to the policeman, saying he had seen me get out of the car. I didn't deny it, and allowed myself to be arrested. I thought that the less trouble I caused, the better my chance of not being charged.'

'So you were not actually involved at all; neither in the planning nor the execution nor the escape. Is that right?'

'No. There was no planning to be involved in, and as soon as the action began, I bailed out. There's hardly a case against me, but they want to pressure me into naming the other three. I'm not going to.'

'I know one of them, because Bert Gettily gave his name to Gillian on the phone.'

'Don't you dare pass it on!' A flash of anger from Peter.

'Curse your stupid schoolboy loyalty. You're not in a position to lay down rules, are you?'

'If you name any names, I'll deny them.'

Nshila set off to try charm on the policeman handling the case. Another shock. It was a woman. A hard-faced creature who looked about forty five and was built like a sumo wrestler. Charm would be useless. But maybe she was practical enough to face reality. Nshila introduced herself as Peter's employer.

Her approach was direct. The wrestler was likely to be busy and long-winded diplomacy would probably not work. 'I know you want Peter to name names, but I don't think you have much hope. He's a stubborn sod and he thinks there is a good chance your case will fail. Is it really worth your while to press on?'

The wrestler had an answer ready. 'With this magistrate, "Yes". I know his style.'

It was time to be a bit more aggressive, Nshila thought. 'Maybe the odds would change if I got my own lawyer involved. I want Peter out of here badly, and if it costs me time and money, that's just too bad. I'm serious.'

The wrestler thought for a moment and gave in.

'Alright. If it matters that much. There are more important villains than your Peter. We'll drop it. And I might even get a lunch break for once.'

Neither employer or employee were at their best in the taxi back to Eastcheap. They were soon shouting at each other. Nshila was very tired, and said rude things about stupid macho adventures and immaturity and lack of self-discipline. Peter, still rather hungover and faintly smelly from his night in the cells, told her she was insensitive and shallow, and didn't know the meaning of loyalty. Suddenly, they both ran out of steam and started apologising. Belatedly, Peter expressed gratitude for the rescue.

Nshila sat down on a bench in the lobby of the Eastcheap building. A rest was needed before the next crisis. In a short space of time she had been listener (to Gillian) apologist (to Mrs Sandcote), guardian (of a treasure), rescuer (of Peter) and adversary (to the sumo wrestler). The tin box had been far from her thoughts while at Bow Street, but now made a comeback. Where had she put it after she had snatched it from Gillian? Her mind was a blank. She took the lift, rushed up the extra flight of stairs and burst into the office. She never reached the flat, for Gillian put her hand over the phone and waved urgently.

'It's Mrs Sandcote. Asking if you are free yet. She has to go out in a few moments.' Gillian spoke into the phone again.

'She has just come in, Mrs Sandcote. Can you hold for a moment while she gets the papers?' Nshila took a few deep breaths and cleared her mind.

'Hello, Mrs Sandcote. I'm so sorry I had to break off our talk earlier on. It's been a really grim day here. Crisis after crisis. One of the staff managed to get an electric shock from a table lamp.' A harmless lie, she thought to herself.

It got a bit of sympathy. Mrs Sandcote said that she had made enquiries about the weather prediction business in general and was willing to accept that even the best advice could sometimes be wrong. But the council had lost a lot of money. How about a refund, or a reduction of the fee? That, thought Nshila was just not an option.

'I'm sorry, Mrs Sandcote, but we never give refunds. Doing so, even in an exceptional case, would be very dangerous for us. Our policy loses us a few clients, and we don't like that at all, but the alternative is worse. Every business has dangers, and this one goes with the territory. An offer that we can make, and I will make it to you now, is to waive any fee at all if you should use our services again. It's a one-time offer, of course.'

Mrs Sandcote moaned on for some minutes, and even had the gall to ask if The Rain Consultancy would put the offer in writing. Reluctantly Nshila agreed, and Mrs Sandcote rang off, satisfied.

'That was brilliant, Nshila. I could never handle a conversation like that even half as well.' Gillian's praise was welcome.

'And I don't have your skill as a meteorologist. Maybe that makes us even.'

Then Nshila was into the flat and looking for the tin box. Relief. There it was, balanced on top of the refuse bin beside the sink. The light was falling on it in such a way that she could just make out more letters on the side, – 'H, U ,N ,T L', and after a gap, 'M, E, R.' A few days later she did some desk research and identified Huntley and Palmer as biscuit manufacturers – long defunct – of Reading in Berkshire. How had the tin reached the hut under the baobab tree?

Chapter Sixteen

I Can Do It!

The afternoon brought no new crisis. Gillian left work. Nshila toasted some crumpets for tea and fell asleep in front of the television. It was not till late evening that she set the tin box on the coffee table and thought back to that midnight meeting. Had Kwaname really been present, physically or spiritually?

She had been aware of a shape that looked human in outline but had blurred edges and left the background dimly visible through it. Not physical in any normal way, she thought. But the emotional and spiritual impact had been tremendous. Moses must have felt like that, she thought, meeting God on the mountain top, or Elijah meeting him in the cave. And she had heard, or felt, the words, 'Touch and feel. Watch in the smoke.'

Mixed up with her fear had been a pleasurable awareness that Kwaname was pleased with his pupil and proud of what she had become. She recalled that feeling as she opened the tin box and began an inventory;

A long piece of cord with six different types of knot at irregular intervals.

A mud and glue cast of a man's foot.

Ten small round stones, each of different texture and colour.

An old tobacco tin labelled Cape to Cairo Shag and full of powder.

A second tobacco tin containing powder of a different colour.

A large metal saucer that had obviously been used for heating things.

A broken part of several different personal possessions.

A flat stone about four inches long and two wide. It was covered with curious markings.

Where to start? She remembered being called back to the village to deal with the cattle thief problem. She had been in the hut then, recalling what Kwaname had taught her, and had found that handling his materials brought memory and understanding where none had existed before. They had their own curious power. And now his message was, 'Touch and feel. Watch in the smoke'. Perhaps she must heat one of the powders in the saucer, hold one or more of the artefacts, and gaze. It was worth a try. But which artefact?

The African adventure, she remembered – and the appearance of Kwaname in the shed on the roof - had started when she had tried to create an apparition. Might any of these articles be relevant? An apparition, she reflected, is a thing of two parts; the reality and the seeming reality. Amongst the items before her were some that were one half of a whole. Could that be a clue? There was half (the hilt) of a knife that had once belonged to her half-brother Shumba. There was a single earring, which she remembered swinging with its fellow on the schoolteacher. There was a strip of scarlet cloth which was the exact colour of a scarf flaunted by Samuel Chiluba's wife. The other items she did not recognise, but always it was possible to imagine another part that might match it.

One part of an object in one place, another part in a different place. Was that a parallel with part of the owner being in one place and another part of the same owner being in another? She took a lampshade from a bedside light, tore off the fabric and used the frame as a tripod to support the metal saucer. She put a candle underneath and a spoonful of the first powder in the saucer. Cupped in her hands was the single earring.

She waited. And waited. And waited. Nothing. Except that Rasputin emerged from the bedroom, sat down before the blank television screen and gazed at it.

She tried the other powder. Bingo! A heavy, sweet smell and plenty of grey smoke. A greater darkness forming within the smoke; gradually, a human figure. Definition was poor, but she knew the school teacher because of her unusually long neck and narrow waist. The earrings were flashing above her shoulders. She was leaning her bicycle against the tree in front of the school.

It faded. Another shape appeared; Kwaname himself. He was staring at one of the earrings lying in his cupped hands, just the way Nshila held it now, and the metal saucer was making smoke beside him. A scene appeared in the smoke. First came the tree beside the school, then the teacher and the bicycle; a picture within a picture. Then the smoke of Nshila's saucer dispersed, the image was lost and Rasputin left for the roof garden.

Is it easy to interpret dreams and visions? If the explanation is given at the same time then it looks dead simple, Nshila thought. Like Joseph and Pharoah and the seven fat cows and the seven scrawny ones. Good years followed by bad ones. Stockpile your food now, Pharoah! Not so easy in other cases. She struggled with her experience and groped for a theory about creating apparitions.

- The original of the apparition must be a real person.
- The apparition can only appear in a place where the real person has been.
- The creator of the apparition must possess some article that the real person possessed or held when present in the place concerned.
- The creator of the apparition has to concentrate on the stolen article and will the apparition into existence.

Did the creator of the apparition also have to perform some special ritual or speak special words? That was unclear. But perhaps if she met the other conditions then the words or ritual would be revealed. She knew enough to launch an experiment.

There was still a contradiction. The conditions had not existed when she created Maurice Tate, or herself (for Kevin Carruthers) or the partial postman. It was a mystery. But from now on she would follow the instructions.

Gillian was not very tall and enjoyed wearing high heels. However, in the office she often kicked them off and wore bright pink slippers instead. When Peter commented on them, she said that they were her favourite colour and that she had two identical pairs, one for the office and one for home. Here were the materials needed. Gillian had frequently sat on the swivel chair in front of her computer. She had frequently been wearing the pink slippers. She had left them under the chair.

Nshila hesitated. She knew that she had what her police friends would call 'previous' for experimenting thoughtlessly. And there might be dangers. Suppose that creating the apparition somehow detracted from the real person. Suppose that while the apparition lasted, the real person lost some capability. Suppose the person was driving a car in difficult conditions and their concentration failed. It was a nasty thought. 'It will only be a very short appearance,' she told herself, 'just enough to prove that it works.'

She made the smoke, stared intently at the two slippers lying across her hands. She pictured Gillian in her swivel chair and waited for the spirit to give words. It did. The words came soundlessly into her mind – as if her ears had been by-passed. She spoke them slowly, with gravity on a falling cadence. The amazing thing was that after speaking them, she couldn't remember them! Perhaps the spirit was only allowing her a one-time use, like some computer programs do. All she could remember was something of the metre and the stresses. It approximated to the last line of one of her favourite poems;

'Both the yeares, and the dayes, deep midnight is.'

Something happened. What? She was in the flat, and the door to the office closed. She pushed it very slowly open, telling herself, 'In a second from now I shall know! This is my last moment of ignorance!' And she knew. It was there!

She remembered some of those other 'first times'. The first time she rode a bicycle successfully without falling off. The first time she swam the length of a pool without putting a foot down. The first time she wrote a piece of computer code and it worked. The first time she completed the crossword puzzle in The Times or The Guardian or the Telegraph. 'I can do it! I can do it! I can do it! Excitement! I must find somebody to tell!' She was looking at a high quality image. If she had been entering the office in the morning she would have spoken to it.

And then an awful doubt hit her. Perhaps it was only the image creator who could see it. Perhaps another person would just see an empty chair. She had no third party to ask, but she rushed out to the roof garden, grabbed Rasputin and brought him in to look. Wow! It all took place so fast that she saw nothing. But her ears were ringing with the yowling noise that a cat makes when it is terrified and the scratches on her hand took two weeks to heal. He had seen something alright!

The apparition faded, but she knew now what to do. More, she knew how to unlock the secrets from the tin box. She picked up the flat stone and looked at it with a magnifying glass. On one side was a well-defined Egyptian scarab symbol; the dung beetle. So at some time in the past this stone had been in Egypt, or a place under Egyptian influence. How extraordinary that it had found it's way to sub-Saharan Africa. It must be terribly old. On the other side was a crude representation of a man, and on his shoulder was a dark, animal-like shape pointing forwards with it's arm. In front of the man were four scratched drawings. There was a tree, and a deep pit, and a river and a koppje. The thing on the man's shoulder was directing the man where to go. Instantly The Companion came to mind. This stone had to be an illustration of his higher skills. How might it work? She remembered the direction finding devices that featured in old films about World War II, particularly the ones about submarines. A signal was sent out, and if it encountered a ship it bounced back and was audible to the sender. When the signal was loudest it showed the direction in which the target lay. The Companion could inflict discomfort and unease. Perhaps it could vary the intensity so that the subject found relief in going the way the companion directed. If the subject tried to go in any other direction, the discomfort and unease returned with intensity. Yes, it would work. In a subtle way the subject would be like an arthritis sufferer who is constantly twisting and turning to find a position that minimises pain.

This was all so clear to her that she almost abandoned the idea of looking in the smoke. She was about to put the stone away when she remembered how little Kwaname had actually said. Just eight words. They must be important. She would be stupid to ignore them. She burnt powder again and was rewarded. There stood Kwaname. He had the stone in front of him but he was also tying knots in a cord. As he tied each knot, he touched one of the scratched images on the stone. He must be determining what experiences the victim was to undergo. It looked as if The Companion could be accurately programmed and would give the operator precise control of the victim.

Time passed. An hour after midnight she got up from the settee and staggered to her bedroom. Surprisingly, she slept really well and woke refreshed. Rasputin had overcome his fear and was lying quietly across her feet. In her calmer state of mind she realised that she had gained a huge amount of information and a major increase in power. More options were available. But they also made it harder to decide about their use. And she still had lingering doubts about eradicating Toppley. Knowledge gained at the 'Arrivals Dinner' had left her almost convinced, but not quite.

'I must switch off', she told herself. 'The mind is a marvellous piece of machinery. If you stop worrying about a problem and concentrate on a different subject, it will work on subconsciously and come up with a solution. I am going to spend today on something completely different and let my subconscious do its job.'

She got what she wanted. But in an unexpected way. When she went out to the office, rather late, she found Gillian shifting furniture around. This was unusual behaviour, since Gillian normally liked order and stability; everything in it's accustomed place. Immediately Nshila worried that her experiment might have had side-effects and altered Gillian's personality.

'What are you doing?'

'Getting ready for Simon Sullivan, of course. We must have a work station ready for him.'

This was terrible. Gillian had been influenced into hallucinating, and imagining non-existent people. Nshila asked, 'Who is Simon Sullivan and why is he coming?'

The answer relieved her fears. 'Don't say you have forgotten, Nshila. He's the schoolboy coming to us for two weeks work experience. Don't you remember how your brother twisted your arm to make you take him? It was only four weeks ago.'

Nshila struck herself on the forehead. The gesture was uncharacteristic and showed an unusual loss of control. 'Now you remind me, yes. But I can't face it at the moment. I am going to opt out. You and Peter must meet him and organise a programme. I'll go up the West End for some extravagant shopping. See you later.'

Chapter Seventeen
Work Experience

Simon Sullivan lay back in a battered armchair, enjoying the comfortable squalor of the Sixth Form common room at St Finnegan's. He reflected on the work experience issue. Some placements, he imagined, were dead boring and had no value except getting one out of school. Most, perhaps, had some value and a few were terrific. He felt sympathy for the staff who had to arrange them. It must be tough, twisting the arms of employers to take young people who knew nothing of the work and had to be provided with activity for two weeks. If they managed to gain any useful skill in that time, then they were off back to school and would never be seen again.

He felt he had been dead lucky. He had been scheduled to work in the local hospital in the section that fixes appointments, but he had protested that it sounded dull, and his housemaster had come up with a better idea.

'Look, Simon, I have a sister who runs a weather prediction consultancy in London. It's only a tiny firm, but their work is interesting and up-to-date. You could call it state-of-the-art. Naturally, computing is a huge element and you are good in that area. If I leant on my sister enough, she might take you. She owes me a favour or two. The problem, of course, is that you would have to stay in London. Could you manage that?'

Simon could barely conceal his joy and his thoughts raced ahead. Wow! A fortnight in the big city, his driving test passed last week and his Mum unable to use her car because of a leg in plaster! A few phone calls, suggested by his housemaster and his sister, Nshila Ileloka, got him fixed up with cheap accommodation at a youth hostel. It did not sound exciting, but it was a secure address and would do him for the limited time he expected to spend asleep. Apparently most of the users were keen young sportsmen and sportswomen, signed up to a prestigious training programme. Hardly his scene, but some of the girls might deserve a second look.

On Day One of his assignment, he was standing outside the building in Eastcheap. Old and unimpressive, it seemed, and dwarfed by modern structures on either side. The list of tenants in the foyer said 'The Rain Consultancy. Fourth Floor and Stairs.' The lift took him most of the way, and the stairs were right in front of him, tastefully carpeted. He found a brass handle at the end of an ornate bell rope and pulled. It produced a loud brassy clang, repeated twice.

The door was opened by a woman looking rather like his elder sister, Alison. An English rose type; fair hair and a pink complexion, conventional clothing and a pearl necklace. It was not a type he hugely admired, because Alison was forever telling him what to do, generally from a position of profound ignorance. The first exchanges with this one seemed to indicate a similar bossiness. They took place on the threshold, even without the door being shut behind him.

The English rose said, 'you are Simon Sullivan?'

'That's me. Good Morning.'

'Well, you're late Simon. We start here at 9.0am. Didn't Nshila tell you? It's now a quarter past.'

'I'm sorry, it was a bit difficult finding the right tube.'

'Maybe, but if you have come here for work experience, the first thing you have to learn is that employers expect punctuality.' Simon didn't like this very much, but opted for the polite response.

'I'm sorry. I'll remember what you say.'

'You do that. I'm Gillian Harker and this is Peter Grace. We both work here for Nshila Ileloka. She's out at the moment.'

Peter Grace looked a real character to Simon. His face was swarthy and one eye protruded slightly, giving him an unbalanced appearance. He had the blackest eyebrows Simon had ever seen and a great deal of black hair. It was quite thick on the back of his hands and there was more visible again where a shirt button

144

had come undone. He looked to be in his late twenties, which would be right for Gillian also. He took a more friendly line.

'Hi, Simon. Welcome. Don't take too much notice of her. She's fiercely loyal to Nshila, and if Nshila tells her to treat you firmly, that's what she'll do. Gillian's alright underneath.' Gillian's reaction was a feminine toss of the head.

Some of Simon's friends had told him that the first morning of their work experience was spent hanging around like a spare part. Here, he found, a programme had been worked out in advance. Gillian explained some basic facts about meteorology, saying that air pressure was constantly changing and that areas of low pressure had great influence. Apparently they caused winds to circulate around them in an anti-clockwise direction and those winds brought different types of weather with them. After quite limited instruction she set him down in front of a computer and showed him how to call up weather charts. She directed him to one that covered the west coast of Scotland.

'Try this, Simon. Take note of the wind directions shown and imagine how the high pressure areas and low pressure areas are going to move. Guess what the weather will be like in Ullapool tomorrow. Then we will talk about it.'

Simon enjoyed himself. It was fun puzzling out why the prediction for each day had been made, and tracing the influence of different factors. He learnt a lot quite quickly, through being allowed to experiment with the models. By noon he had got four predictions wildly wrong, one half-right, and one nearly perfect. Gillian made no criticism of his efforts, usually saying something like, 'One of the things I didn't tell you was that so-and-so always has an effect.' She fed him additional knowledge at the time he was ready to grasp it, rather than overloading him with instruction too early.

Something he noticed about his colleagues was that while Gillian was very professional and always used the correct terms, Peter was more colloquial. When Simon heard him talking to clients on the phone, it was all laymans language. Gillian would speak about depressions and circulating winds; Peter's version was more earthy. Simon overheard one conversation.

'Look, Mrs Grandle, imagine you are sitting in the bath and you pull the plug out. Imagine that you are facing north. The water goes down the hole in a spiral, right? On the side nearest to you, which way is it going? Left to Right. Of course. Now imagine that the plug hole was magically moved so that it was behind you. Which way would the water now be going on the side of the plug hole nearest you? Right to Left? Yes, you've got it. That's what the winds do around a depression.'

Which of the two, Simon wondered, would an enquirer find easiest to understand? Perhaps different enquirers would have different answers. He was learning something about communication skills.

He also enjoyed the coffee break – good quality coffee, and chocolate biscuits as well.

And then, as he was beginning to wonder about lunch, the door opened and three hat boxes advanced into the room. Behind them was a tall, elegant black woman, out of breath and excited. She started talking before the door had closed behind her.

'Hullo, everybody. I've bought some hats.' Pretty obvious, Simon thought.

'Nshila, why? You don't wear hats.' Gillian had clearly been taken by surprise.

'I'm going to start, Gillian. I need to be more adventurous.'

Simon was mildly impressed. Neither his mother nor his sister had any reason for their buying decisions. This woman apparently had a purpose of some sort.

'Show us. The boxes look expensive enough.' Gillian had overcome her surprise.

Simon, forgotten till that moment, was introduced and welcomed, and drawn into a half-an-hour examination of expensive hats bought by his new boss. Nshila and Gillian modelled them, enthusing wildly and sometimes diving into Nshila's flat to fetch some accessory that might enhance the image. Peter obliged with critical and unflattering comments

146

like, 'Do you really want to be mistaken for a dustman?' His comments were treated as infantile and ignored. Simon did rather better, having been through similar sessions with Alison and his mother. He thought the black pill-box thing with the veil looked fantastic on Nshila, but voted down the wide-brimmed hat in pastel pink. He thought Nshila needed bold colours but that the pastel pink looked tremendous on Gillian. He was undecided about the feminine version of a bowler hat in vivid green; it was dramatic, but somehow 'over the top.'

Simon had already decided that the story of his first day would go down well in the junior common room. More was to come. It was lunch time, and Nshila was still on a high. 'The firm will buy us all lunch. Where shall we go?' Peter wanted to go to Simpsons, but the women overruled him and the four of them went to a riverside restaurant at Blackfriars. Nshila decided it was time to talk to Simon in a half-way serious manner, and put the usual polite questions about school and home and the arrangements at the hostel. Her brother was mentioned, naturally, and he learnt that bossiness in elder siblings is neither a sex thing nor a national thing nor a race thing, but universal. Simon heard a lot about Masuko's much-resented efforts to set Nshila on 'the right path'.

The amount of work done that afternoon was limited, but subsequent days were the reverse. Simon learnt plenty of technical stuff, but what interested him most was the way clients talked to these three. Their principal requirement was, obviously, weather prediction, but they also wanted to talk about whatever event they had scheduled and they responded eagerly to sympathetic interest. He came to feel that if he were a client he would ask The Rain Consultancy for advice rather than anybody else. Not because their advice was sure to be better, but because the experience would be more enjoyable.

He categorised the three of them into common types. There are the workers, he considered; the people who really love the nitty-gritty of the job. That was Gillian. There are the outgoing characters whose job it is to charm the customers. That was Peter.

And there are the decision-makers who don't appear to do all that much practically, but are comfortable giving directions and will accept responsibility. That was Nshila.

Gillian and Peter told Simon that he was lucky to have seen the girlish, frivolous side of Nshila. 'She's not like that very often. When it happens, it's usually a way of escaping from complex problems that are getting on top of her. She sort of sheds her usual personality and adopts a playtime one. Normally, she is a serious, rather driven person, and she can be quite nasty if she thinks you have been idle or careless.' Simon never saw any evidence of that. What he himself experienced was a great deal of understanding and sympathy. She was a really good listener.

That must have been why he told her –ten days later - about some rather worrying developments at the Youth Hostel.

'When I arrived I was given a rather dreary room, despite the fact that several others were empty. I was told they belonged to six girls who were away for a short time at a sports training camp in Spain. A few days later a party returned and those rooms – all except one - were occupied. The majority of people in the hostel were girls, and they mixed little with the ten or twelve men. But my room was directly above Sarah Mycroft. She was a leader amongst the girls and they often gathered in her room, chattering so loudly that I could easily hear. They argued a great deal about Jennifer Price, the girl missing from their group of six. It seemed that she had accepted an invitation from the organiser, a man called Toppley, who was a sponsor of the sports initiative to which they belonged. It had meant travelling further east with him, and the girls were worried because they had not seen Jennifer since.'

Simon explained that he had grasped the conversation clearly, but had not been able to identify any of the voices except for Sarah Mycroft. He repeated parts of what he had heard.

'It's not our worry. Jennifer is over eighteen and quite entitled to go adventuring with dirty old men if that is what she wants. She wasn't kidnapped, was she? She told you, Eileen, that she was taking off.'

'She did so, but since then I have worried that she was not quite herself. She is into drugs in a mild way, and might be persuaded to try something new.'

Simon mentioned that Eileen spoke with a strong Welsh accent. At some future meeting he would probably be able to identify her.

Nshila interrupted Simon to check how accurately he had heard. They were in the flat, and Peter and Gillian were talking in the office. Nshila pointed out that with just one closed door between them, significant bits of the conversation were lost. How well could Simon have heard what was being said on the floor below him?

He was confident. He said that the girls were talking in quite high, excited voices. He certainly didn't hear and remember every word, but he had no doubt that what he was relaying now was substantially true. He took up his summary again. Sarah, he reported, was addressing a girl called Patricia.

'Oh, rubbish, Patricia! In a moment you will be telling us that Toppley drugged her and hypnotised her into going with him. I suppose he was going to sell her into slavery in the Middle East, was he?'

'Rubbish, you say! But you read about such things happening. You tell yourself that your own situation is quite different, but how do you know? Myself, I reckon that Toppley is a very nasty piece of work. He is generous with money, I agree, but you can afford to pour money into sports sponsorship if you get a few healthy, high class white girls to sell down the line.'

None of the girls in the hostel took any action, Simon reported. He thought that Sarah had too strong a hold over them, and she had convinced them there was nothing to worry about.

Nshila took his story seriously. 'You are worried, Simon, I can see that. But why? You were told nothing directly and there is nothing you can do.'

Simon was not re-assured. 'It looks like that, but remember that I live on the Kent coast with major routes to the continent. There is a regular inward flow of illegal immigrants, and you

149

also hear rumours of traffic in the other direction.'

'That's still not a convincing explanation for your worry. Is there anything more?' Nshila felt she had not yet heard everything.

'Yes, but it's all so vague. I go to various local pubs with my friends, and in one of them I heard two people next to me talking. One of them was, I knew, an immigration official. He mentioned people about whom he had suspicions, but no facts. Toppley was one of the names. It meant nothing to me then, of course, but when I heard the girls speaking about him, then I remembered.'

'So you think this really could be serious evil, do you? Could it be as bad as Sarah Mycroft acting as a Toppley stooge, selecting likely victims?'

'I can't see Sarah as an accomplice. But I do think this Toppley fellow is into something very nasty. Exploitation of young women is a possibility.'

His story ended all doubt in Nshila's mind. Suddenly she was annoyed with herself for holding back so long. Yet perhaps she had been right. Until now she had had no personal connection with the affair – she had not had the name of a victim who was in any way close to her. Jennifer Price was not close, of course, but Simon had made her a focal figure. Nshila felt deep concern for her and intense hatred for whoever had exploited her, Toppley or any other.

She thought for a while, filling the silence by re-arranging the flowers in a vase that stood on her bookcase. Clearly, she had to offer Simon some sort of advice. He was in that uncomfortable situation of suspecting evil but afraid of being wrong, concerned not to make an idiot of himself. Possibly she could relieve his guilt.

'I can't give you very much help. But I suggest you ask around at the hostel and find out as much as you can about Jennifer Price. Ordinary stuff, like where she comes from and what she does for a living and what interests she has and who her friends are. Things that you might be asking about if you were keen on her and wanted to meet her. Give me everything you get. I have friends in the police and I will ask them to find out if she is on the missing persons register. I will get my brother to help by asking questions locally. Nobody will see anything strange in a schoolteacher being concerned about the welfare of a young person. That will be a start. If Jennifer is on the register then people will listen to us when we make suggestions. If she is not, then we shall have to think again. But at least we shall have done something.'

Simon felt happier, having something positive to do, and a more experienced person to share his worries. He was unaware, of course, that by naming names he had just made Toppley the approved target of a competent assassin.

Two more events lodged in Simon's memory from his later days at The Rain Consultancy. He was alone in the office when the doorman rang through, asking him to come to the main entrance and sign for a 'Recorded Delivery' parcel. It was a small box, posted in Pakistan, and described on the customs declaration as 'Handling Device – value £25.' The customs people had not bothered to open it. When Nshila came back, she grabbed it instantly and disappeared into her flat.

When he finally cleared up his work station he found some papers that had fallen down behind the desk. One of them was a receipt from Majestic Milliners of Bond Street for three ladies hats. Total cost £1,427, paid for by credit card.

Nshila still felt badly about the rather ineffectual suggestions she had made to Simon. She wished she could have done more. The thought niggled at her from time to time.

Chapter Eighteen

Decisions

The tale Simon told matched what Nshila had learnt at the 'Arrivals Dinner.' Some of that had been forgotten during the African adventure, but now she concentrated and recalled it.

During the break at the dinner she had sought the company of three people who seemed to have first hand experience of Toppley's activities. Between them they knew of three girls who had vanished; one a year ago, and two six months ago. The first step of the process seemed to be close friendship with Toppley, based on advice and encouragement about the sport concerned (frequently helpful) and on financial support. Then came an invitation to 'My training camp in Spain.' This was supposed to be for a fairly short time, two or three weeks, and the big attraction was the expected presence of a major sporting star who happened to be 'our visiting coach for that fortnight.' The place was real, and some girls had returned with glowing reports. These encouraged other people and made the invitation look safe. But a few girls had mysteriously disappeared.

Nshila asked about contact between these girls and their friends in England. Surely anybody who was suspicious would attempt to communicate. Of course they did, she was told, but telephone communication was seldom satisfactory and callers were told that the person asked for was 'in a training session' or otherwise unavailable. Then the caller would get an e-mail, apologising for failure to take the call and assuring the caller that the sender was having a splendid time. Toppley had grasped the fact that e-mail does not demand an immediate response in the way that the telephone does. There is a time lag between message and reply. With speech, one thing said is expected to link directly to the previous thing said. Electronically, this requirement is relaxed and it does not seem quite so strange to the enquirer if the reply deals with other matters of interest and perhaps ignores the original question. Toppley sent e-mails that appeared to come from the lost girl but actually came from him. They radiated happiness and goodwill but never contained useful answers.

The last strategy, if an enquirer looked like a serious threat, was a message, even a letter extracted by force, saying 'I have met this marvellous Spaniard and am going to marry him. I love you deeply, but don't make contact again because I know you won't approve and it will make us all miserable.'

Re-living the conversation made her decision simple. She sent an acceptance of the Toppley contract down the communicative chain. She was committed to the double death situation.

How was she going to do it?

There were still problems to be resolved, but she felt more adequate to the task than before. Her awareness of need, her experiments, the Kwaname vision and the homeland trip had brought a considerable increase in knowledge. In particular, she saw an application for The Companion – the souped-up companion that she now knew to be available. He could be used to drive Toppley into some high-risk area where accidental death was common, and would arouse little suspicion. She needed to try out what she had learnt and practice her control of the spirit. Who should be used for practice? Not Zach again, that was absolutely out. Why not Toppley himself? She could see two advantages. Firstly, one or more preliminary experiences would condition him to obey The Companion. Having learnt how to minimise the discomfort by yielding to pressure, he would do so more readily when it was important. Secondly, if he were observed to behave oddly while in his normal environment, the behaviour leading to his death would arouse less comment.

She spent more time on the contents of the tin box, especially the knotted rope. It seemed that the practitioner must carry out careful preparation if the best effects were to be realised, and some of them involved contact with the victim.

She worked through the whole sequence, reflecting again that magic can be hard work. Was it possible to cut a few corners? Unwise. Minor details may be vital. For one Voodoo spell, she remembered, the practitioner needs the gland secretions of the bouga toad. It never worked with any other toad.

Nshila resolved to stick rigidly to the proper procedures. She read, she thought and she watched in the smoke. She acquired detailed knowledge of how the knotted string affected The Companion, and she devoted one full day to a live experiment.

The first thing she learnt was that it was not essential for the practitioner to mark the target himself. If a physical mark existed, that would do. It could be a birthmark or a permanent scar. Toppley had a scar on his right wrist, she knew.

The Companion could also be directional. The intensity of nastiness could be varied so that if the target moved in the direction the witchdoctor prescribed, then the nastiness would lessen. If the target moved any other way then it would get stronger. The Companion could act like a sheep-dog.

Another capability was controlled by the knotted string. Both the knots and the length of string between them had significance. The knots had to be quite large; they had to be linked to places the victim must visit. This was done through a spell and a physical connection. The latter was achieved by tying the knot whilst present in the location, or by concealing within the knot some minute item taken from it. The distance between the knots dealt with the passage of time – about five minutes to one inch of string. There was an obvious likeness to a spark running down a fuse from one small concentration of gunpowder to another.

There were other complications. The sequence had to be initiated at a place and time where the scheduled activities were possible. If, say, the first experience was to take place in fifteen minutes in Trafalgar Square, it was no good lighting the fuse when the victim was in Slough. And initiation depended on the victim being, unknowingly, in possession of the string. It had to be in his pocket, or the hem of his coat, or in something that he carried.

So working the spell demanded precise planning and organisation. But if that was done correctly then the victim was fully controlled. Only by moving from place to place in accordance with the spell could the victim avoid the discomfort imposed by The Companion.

Nshila took a day out of the office and made her first live trial in the small town near Mike Fanshawe's home. She knew it well, and some of the people. She knew that the minister of a strict religious community walked regularly along a certain route. She slipped the cord into his pocket when he was fiddling with change at the Pay and Display station in the car park at the top end of the High Street. She made him enter, successively, a betting shop, a sex shop and a liquor store. The knots were quite small, so all he did was walk inside, look round him, shake his head and walk out again.

She researched Toppley's likely schedule for the next fortnight and focussed on two trial situations. For each of them she devised a short 'programme' which she would force him to follow. It took her a long time to find good locations and prepare the strings accurately. Having tied and untied knots many times, she visited the beauty parlour for a badly needed manicure.

Returning after the manicure, she noticed the pile of unread junk mail on the small table beside the door of the flat. Most of it went straight in the bin, but at the bottom was the latest issue of AOSTA. The acronym stood for Alumni of St Albans, and the cover advertised an interview with the retiring head. It seemed that Dr Scoon would be sixty-five at the end of the present term and was proposing to live in England. Would she meet him, she wondered?

Chapter Nineteen

Conditioning Toppley

Major Brendan Coggan was Secretary of Boulder Wood Golf Club. He looked the part and acted it well. He was conventionally good-looking, and well dressed. He spoke in an educated way. He was tactful and diplomatic. It does not matter too much in such a post if one is not rich, for some of the members like to feel that the secretary (a paid official, after all) is a bit beneath them. But he must be capable of chatting as equals at the bar one minute and scurrying off to do their bidding the next. It helps when one is a retired army officer; the staff address one as 'Major' and it's the staff who actually do the scurrying off. One receives and respects many confidences, for there are always members who dislike one another. One has to listen to Dr Wolfgang, for instance, saying 'You know what that ghastly little skinhead Waterson did on the fourteenth green?' Later on one must listen to the Waterson version. One of the stranger stories Major Coggan sat through was told by Andy Musgrove.

'Brendan, have you noticed anything odd about Toppley recently?' Andy put the question as he sat down beside Coggan on the bench below the bar window.

'No. I can't say I have. He seems much as ever to me.'

'So he did to me, when we started out. But we were on the fifth tee. Down there beyond the wood.' Andy waved his hand to the right, indicating the small beech wood two hundred yards away from them. 'It was his honour and I was standing quietly to one side while he addressed his ball. Suddenly he dropped his club and exclaimed, "What was that noise?" "What noise?" I asked, "I heard nothing". "A hissing, dragging noise, as if somebody had hauled one large piece of canvas across another". Then he played a really bad shot, hooking into the rough on the left of the fairway. It seemed as if he had turned his head to look over his left shoulder as the club head came down.'

Major Coggan barely reacted. 'I've seen that happen when it was nothing worse than a wasp buzzing around. Or in the evening, down by the fifth green, it might be a mosquito.'

'I might believe that if nothing more had happened. But mine was a good shot, straight down the middle, so we didn't meet till we reached the green. And he looked physically different! Only ten minutes later! He was white, and jumpy, and constantly looked behind him. His putting was dreadful, and when he missed a short put with his seventh he waved his putter behind him as if he was trying to hit something with it.'

Coggan still wanted to play down the story. When he sensed aggravation between members his instinct was to pacify, 'Sounds like migraine to me.'

'Rubbish, Brendan. Migraine has drastic physical effects and you have to lie down. He was normally active, but behaved as if some unseen force was persecuting him. Something which refused to go, whatever he tried.'

Andy continued. 'At the eighth tee, he accused me of fidgeting to put him off. I had been standing quite still, and after his shot he said "Have you got to stand just at the edge of my field of vision and take practice swings when I drive?" I protested, and he said "I saw something moving out of the corner of my eye. If it wasn't you, what was it? There's nobody else around."

'Then we were walking along the tenth fairway and he suddenly said "What's that awful smell? It's horrible. I can't stand it". Well, Brendan, you know that with an east wind we do get a whiff from the sewage works, but today there was quite a strong breeze from the west. The air was clean and fresh.'

Major Coggan offered another neutral comment. 'Perhaps he has some sort of sinus trouble. That can be very wearing, and make you over-sensitive and irritable.' It didn't satisfy Andy.

'But does it come and go so quickly? After the incident at the lake hole he recovered completely.'

Major Coggan abandoned his playing-down strategy. If he took it any further, Andy would start thinking he was not interested. He changed tack.

'What incident? Tell me about it.'

'Quite suddenly he put down his club, squatted by the water and washed his hands. Then he splashed water on his face. He said nothing about it, no word of explanation, but suddenly he was alright again. I was reminded of the ritual washing that some religions go in for to cleanse them of sin. It was totally weird. And suddenly the paleness and jumpiness was gone. He looked healthy. He hit two perfect drives as the seventeenth and eighteenth, so I beat him by only one hole in the end. It annoyed me. I don't like the man much, and I would have liked to thrash him.'

The final comment was unusually harsh, especially when made by one member about another in front of a club official. Brendan Coggan decided to escape before more was said. He invented a secretarial duty that demanded his attention and rose from the bench.

Polly Camden had a pleasant but undemanding secretarial job at The Manwood Sport and Leisure Club. The building was new and designed in accordance with all modern requirements. So being in a wheel chair was not too limiting. Her previous job had been in a dreary 1930's office block where the doorways were only just big enough and the passages had too many bends and the toilet facilities had had to be specially adapted for her. In her new environment she whizzed around like an express train – so much so that some members had jokingly asked for speed limit signs to be erected. But there was nothing funny about the encounter with Grant Toppley, that she described later to her crony Liz Maybach. It had started with pointless and inaccurate criticism.

Toppley was a frequent visitor to the club, being a sponsor of several young sportsmen, a generous financial supporter of the club itself, and a member of one of the sub-committees responsible for it's affairs. The only unusual thing about the event Polly described was the time; Toppley normally came in the late morning. This time he was early. Polly explained what then happened.

'Can't you put some oil on that chair of yours, Polly? That squeaking sound really gets on my nerves.' As Polly told it, those had been his first words to her that day. No 'Good Morning' or other friendly greeting.

There had been no squeaking sound, she told Liz. The wheelchair was well-maintained and quite silent. The only sounds had been those made by Toppley himself as he sifted through some old records and grunted aggressively when he failed to find what he wanted.

Toppley had behaved strangely from the start of the day, Polly reported.

'You know how one acts when one pushes open a door to pass through it and suddenly realises that there is somebody else behind? The door is just falling back behind you, and you make a half-turn to grab it before it hits the other person in the face? When Mr Toppley came in that morning he acted in exactly that manner, but there was nobody behind him. He cursed, and looked a bit frightened, and said 'Not again!''

Polly also thought that he looked different. Normal, for Toppley, was a slightly flushed face, and a hint of redness in his nose suggesting too much alcohol. Instead, he was very pale and even seemed to have lost weight. His paunch was fractionally less noticeable.

Liz had never liked Toppley and was quite ready to listen to bad opinions of him.

'I didn't take too much notice of his comments about noise, because he is one of the few people around who has difficulty treating me normally. Everybody else takes my disability as a misfortune little different from having red hair or a squeaky voice. I never doubt that they value me as a person and for what I contribute. Toppley is never comfortable with me, and alternates between excessive attention, which comes across as patronising, and irritation at having to modify his behaviour when dealing with me. If I was a nineteen-year-old bimbo it might be different. He is all charm with those, and falls over himself to make them

159

like him. But a thirty-five-year-old secretary in a wheelchair is a non-person in his eyes.'

Liz Maybach nodded her agreement and added her own comments.

'How right you are, Polly. At twenty-nine I'm at the upper end of the age range he pursues, but I get the charm when there's no better target. But if somebody like Angela comes into the room and wriggles her bottom at him, well, I get dumped. But go on with your story.'

'Yes. I was describing the oddness of his behaviour that day. I saw him next in the gym, which my office overlooks. There was nobody there but himself and he was standing quite still in the middle of the floor. Suddenly he turned round as fast as he possibly could to look behind him. He did it several times, but not at regular intervals. It was as if he was waiting for a signal, and when it came he had to turn as fast as possible to see where it came from. Children do that when they are playing hide-and-seek, but there are always two of them present. He was alone all the time.'

'That's pretty weird.'

'Later still, Ellen called out to me urgently from the weight training room. I shot across, slammed through the double doors and saw Mr Toppley leaning against a wall with both hands over his ears, and his eyes shut. So far as we could make out the words, he was saying "Go. Go. Go. For heavens sake, leave me. Stop it. Go." The first thought in my mind that he was having a fit and that Ellen had called me because I have a First Aid certificate. Luckily Mr Toppley pulled himself together and managed to say "It's nothing. I just came over dizzy somehow. It's passed now."'

Liz asked, 'Was that the last thing?'

'No. I saw him hiding in a cupboard. He was inside the one where we keep hockey sticks and long narrow things like that. He was pressing himself into a corner as if to escape something that nobody else could see. I was about to phone Mr Swarbreck for help when he recovered again and mumbled about failing to find something.'

'Finally he did the strangest thing of all. He climbed the stairs to the attic and looked in our glory hole. If he ever needed anything from there, he would have sent somebody else. It would be beneath his dignity to bend down on hands and knees and poke his nose inside to grope for the light switch. But he did it. Then he came down empty-handed. He bent to brush the dust from his trousers, and when he straightened up he was himself again. Some burden seemed to have been lifted. It was like what happens to me when I have a headache. I take a pill, and force myself to do something despite the pain. I get interested, and without my being aware of it the headache passes. I stand up and look around, and move my head to make sure it does not hurt, and say "Thank goodness, it has gone." Toppley was like that.'

Chapter Twenty

Planning Death

Nshila was pleased with the results of her three live trials – one on the Minister and two on Toppley. There had been only one error. Toppley had been meant to enter the cellar, not the attic. It was time to plan the fatal sequence.

There were conditions to be met. First of all, the death of Toppley must do no collateral damage, so directing him under a bus would be a disaster. The bus driver would be deeply shocked and probably feel that he was in some way to blame, other drivers might be distracted and cause knock-on accidents. Nor would it be satisfactory for him to grab hold of a gun and shoot himself; the bullet might go right through him and hit somebody else. Throwing himself off a high building was also out, he could land on a passer-by.

Perhaps the death ought to be private, where there was no risk at all to others. Not a perfect solution, Nshila thought, because he had to be found in circumstances that suggested a violent accident. If he was found lying peacefully in his bed, the client might argue that he had died of natural causes and no payment was due. So getting him to swallow the wrong pills was another negative. It might also happen that death in his own house might not be discovered for some days. She was going to need the body for re-use in the Tetherman identity and any decay would create problems.

What about an accident in his garage, she wondered? Suppose the spirit made him drive into his garage at high speed and crash into the back wall? To make sure of a fire she would need some assisted witchcraft, like an incendiary device stuck to the wall and a few cans of petrol in his boot, but that was the sort of assignment the spirit was good at. No. Another failed idea. Re-use as Tetherman would not be possible if Toppley was cinders.

That reflection reminded her of yet another condition. The best death would be one that entailed fewest post-mortem formalities. She had to keep track of where the body was being held and when the next move could happen. Was the body in a hospital? Was it to be moved tomorrow to a forensic laboratory? Was it in a laboratory already? When would it be released to the undertaker? Was it with the undertaker? When would he get a slot at the crematorium? She felt it would be best if the cause of death was obvious beyond doubt. The process would then be rapid. It would be easier to track, minimising the enquiries she would have to make.

Late at night she hit on a credible method. Not far from Toppleys' house was a fenced off area containing an electricity sub-station. The fence was made of flat, upright metal posts set very close together and clearly meant to prohibit entry. On every side, and on the single gate, was a yellow notice showing a fallen body and a zigzag arrow skewering it from above, with the words 'Danger of Death'. This could be a private killing ground where nobody else would be affected but the event would be noticed quickly. She wrote out the plan in story-form as if it had actually happened, saved it to a disc, and hid the disc in the cardboard box with her high-heeled gold sandals. She had found that writing things out in detail helped her to see the flaws in them, if flaws there were. Review the thing next day, she believed, and you will know if it is good or bad.

In the morning she read the story and judged it inadequate. Toppley could be herded into the sub-station but there was no guarantee that he would touch anything dangerous. She had to set some sort of trap, like resting a long metal rod against the part-open gate in such a way that, when the gate was pushed, it would fall against a power line. Death was then more likely.

If and when the plan was carried out, the Tetherman activity would have to follow quickly. That, provisionally, centred on a burnt-out car, but it had not yet reached the maturity of the Toppley plan. However, she knew of a possible location.

163

Getting out of London by car was always, for her, a frustrating experience. But it got better after crossing the M25. She drove fast around Guildford and enjoyed the view coming down from the Hogs Back. She enjoyed thinking of people who had travelled the road before. Nelson must have done it; off to board his flagship to fight the Battle of the Nile, or start that mad chase to Martinique and back to find the enemy fleet before Trafalgar. Hornblower, fictionally, had also used the route. (She had a habit of confusing stories with reality.) Before that, she thought, Henry VIII must have passed through, on the way to review his fleet, only to be seriously deflated when the Mary Rose turned over and sank.

She was fascinated by the Mary Rose story, without knowing why. When they raised the Mary Rose and there was all that publicity about her sinking, she had wondered whether there was any other history to the ship. The internet said there was;

'Mary Rose was named after the king's sister Mary and the Tudor emblem the Rose. Typical of the larger sailing ships of the fleet with high castles at the bow and stern, she was one of the first ships with gun ports cut out along the side of the hull for the firing of heavy guns.

Mary Rose was frequently in battle against the French. On 10 August 1512 she was part of an English force that attacked their fleet at Brest. The Mary Rose engaged with their flagship, de-masting her and causing 300 casualties.'

She stopped dreaming when she reached Hindhead. She was there to reconnoitre the twists and turns that take the road uphill around the edge of the Devil's Punchbowl. She had a memory of vicious bends at which a car driven too fast might crash through the barriers and fall down a steep slope into difficult, wooded terrain. She was right. Half-an-hour was enough for her to identify a suitable place. She imagined the vehicle tumbling down the gorge, bursting into flames, and incinerating the body.

She also found a deserted woodman's hut that looked ideal for supernatural activity.

Back in Eastcheap, she considered the timing of her operation. In what order must things be done, to what extent could she control their duration, and to what degree was she facing risk?

When should Toppley die? It had to be on a day when he would wake up at his own town house and start off for a known destination. That might well be The House of Commons, for which journey he would walk past the sub-station and hit the main road close to a taxi rank. Days like that could be identified from the schedule of parliamentary business and from Toppleys known interests. Nshila could not control those days, but her research showed that she would have a reasonable choice. Was there any risk? Almost none, because the proposed means of death were supernatural and not recognised by the law.

Once Toppley was dead, there would be an unknown time before she could steal the body. Her plan focussed upon a single moment in the post-death process where she saw a window of opportunity. When would that happen? If she missed it then Toppley would be a body no longer – and an urn full of ashes was no use to her. Accurate data was needed. She must study the procedures and try to identify the undertakers likely to be used. She thought also of 'scrying' – as the Elizabethans used to call it. That old term meant 'overlooking'. She had once had the necessary skill, though she had not used it for years. Was there any risk here? None at all until she had actually stolen the body. Once she possessed it, things would be really serious; body-snatching is a crime in any nation.

That danger would last while she held the body; every minute until it was burnt up in Tetherman's car, and the remains accepted as his. So the time between theft and fire had to be minimised. Did she have everything in place that was needed for that second event? No. She would have to get hold of Tetherman's car and hide it somewhere convenient for transfer of the body. Risk again! Stealing cars can't be done by witchcraft. It can be detected and proved and punished. The theft itself would be easy. A forged letter to his housekeeper – perhaps delivered by a garage mechanic – would secure it. Tetherman, of course, could not possibly be at home because he would already be dead in his Toppley identity. But the longer she had the car, the greater the risk. Might it not be a lesser risk to take the body directly to Dutch Elm House immediately she got hold of it? But then, what would she do with the vehicle used to take the body there? She jotted down a brief schedule;

Day 1   Kill Toppley
Day 2   Steal and conceal Tetherman's car
Day 4 or 5 or 6.Steal and Transfer body: Stage Accident.

Obviously, it was optimistic to hope that a single day would be enough for theft, transfer and accident. The moment of stealing the body was uncontrollable and might happen in the evening. In that case she would have to work through the night. But a one-day operation was the ideal to be aimed at.

There was a preference, she saw, for killing Toppley on a Monday, if parliamentary business allowed. If the schedule extended over the weekend there might be unforeseen difficulties.

Chapter Twenty-One
A Set-Back

A critical day arrived. It was the day before the first of only three suitable dates that Nshila had identified. At first she had discounted this opportunity, because she was due to visit a potential customer at Banbury. Second thoughts prevailed. She realised that if the Toppley death happened early in the day and she moved the Banbury appointment back one hour, then both events could happen. It would do no harm to be located – though later in the day - many miles away from the death. It would prove nothing, but it would be suggestive. It was also possible that the death might not be immediately discovered or that the time of death might be estimated wrongly. Yes. The Banbury event was good rather than bad, and it was also important business-wise. She would take Peter Grace with her to provide a witness for the longest possible time.

On D-day minus three she bought a trade van and arranged to have it re-painted. It was ready on D minus one, bearing the name and logo of an imaginary service company that dealt with water supply, drainage and sewage. Nobody is surprised, she believed, to see such a van parked in a suburban street, with or without workmen visible. Inside the van she placed all those materials needed to summon and assign The Companion.

Later that evening she broke into Toppley's house and put the knotted cord in the pockets of the topcoat he habitually wore to The House. She had considered using The Hand of Glory to get into his house with assured safety – it was still in her freezer in the flat - but it seemed like overkill. She managed by ordinary human methods.

Early in the morning she parked the van in a side street from which Toppley's house was visible. She walked to the sub-station, picked the lock, and propped the gate open with a stick in such a way that it would fall down when the gate was pushed. The gate would then fall back after Toppley had passed and allow the catch to hold it in the normal way. The fall of the stick would also cause the metal pole to fall against the power line. Back in the service van, she monitored Toppley's morning routine through the lights in the windows. She could see when he got up, when he went to the bathroom, and when he ate breakfast. When she judged the time to be right, she placed her drawing of his birthmark beside a photograph of the open-gated sub-station. She burned the necessary incense, murmured the words of the spell, and slapped drawing and picture face-to-face with yet another knotted cord between them. She spoke the final words of power and waited.

Toppley came out of his house and walked boldly down the road like a healthy, happy fifty-year-old. She even heard a tuneless rendering of The Skye Boat Song. There was none of the hesitation and head-turning and general unease that would signal the presence of The Companion. What had gone wrong. Heavens! He was not wearing the topcoat! Why not? It hardly mattered. Maybe the fine morning had suggested he did not need it. Maybe he had spilt something on it and decided it should go to the cleaners. Maybe he had bought a new, heavier suit and the topcoat would not go over it. For whatever reason the knotted string was not on his person and The Companion was impotent.

There was nothing Nshila could do to repair the error. She waited till Toppley had passed, unset her trap, locked the sub-station, and drove fast to the underground car park at Hyde Park. There she dumped the van, walked miles through concrete passages to the Marble Arch entrance and caught a taxi to Paddington.

In the afternoon of that day she learnt that this apparent misfortune had saved her from a major, catastrophic mistake. Had she succeeded, she would have been committed to a series of actions – one of which was likely to fail.

Chapter Twenty-Two

The Pearl Of Knowledge

Peter Grace looked up at the big clock above Platform One at Paddington. It was showing just five minutes left before departure time. He was relieved to see Nshila climb out of a taxi. Relief turned to annoyance when she offered the driver a twenty-pound note and got into an argument. 'What do you think I am, Miss? A bloody cash machine? Dig in that sack of yours and find something smaller.'

Luckily, Peter had coins in plenty. He had also bought the tickets, knowing that Nshila had 'previous' as the police call it, for being late and then queue-jumping at the ticket office. There was a risk that she had already bought tickets at an agency, but he thought it unlikely, and he was right. That pleased him, because the next moment they found new automatic ticket barriers that only accept the small kind. Tickets bought from an agency are the size of an envelope and won't go through the machine. The bearer must look for an official to open the barrier, and often can't find one.

They caught the 10.29am train to Banbury with one minute in hand. When they were settled, Peter asked why he was wanted on the trip and why they were not using her car.

'We're not using the car because I don't want your puerile male comments on the way I drive. And you are coming with me because I expect a puerile male environment where you will go down better than I will.' A short lesson, Peter thought, on how not to be charming!

He felt offended. Days out with Nshila were usually enjoyable, and something to look forward to. As an immigrant, she was apt to notice things about her adopted country that the natives took for granted. Often she had caused him to see familiar sights in a novel way. There was also enjoyment in acting as the

169

male escort of a striking woman. Peter got a mild sexual thrill from it. Something must be bugging her, today. He decided to protest.

'Thanks so much. You make me feel like something very useful and very unpleasant – like an enema.'

'And that's a puerile comment if ever I heard one.' Nshila had still not softened up.

Peter made no reply, and devoted himself to the back page of the newspaper held up by the passenger opposite. The headline said something favourable about his favourite football team, but the small print was just too far away for him to read. It was frustrating. Five minutes passed before Nshila offered an apology and began to explain.

'Sorry, Peter. I had a few troublesome moments this morning, and these people we are going to meet are a grim prospect. It all got to me for a moment.'

Peter switched his attention from the paper. 'Why are they so awful? And if they really are awful, do we want their business? The money is rolling in nicely at present.'

She was about to reply, when Nshila noticed a jumbo jet apparently hanging in the air as it prepared to land at Heathrow. 'How on earth does it stay in the air at that speed? It's magic!' Then, without waiting for a reply, she started a short lecture. She was still a bit edgy, not quite her normal self.

'Did you have business studies classes in Parkhurst? If they had, and you had bothered to listen, you would know that the owner of a business must constantly look for new opportunities. We do well at present, but we can't tell when a competitor might destroy us with new or cheaper methods. Or you or I or Gillian might make some catastrophic error that ruined our reputation.'

A ticket collector arrived. Peter found his ticket easily, in the top pocket of his jacket. Nshila had put hers in one of the many zip-pockets of her handbag and had to search every one. She found a ticket and offered it up – only to be told that it was an out-dated ticket to Bradford-on-Avon. What had she been doing there, Peter wondered. She found another, the right one, and the ticket collector departed, shaking his head. Peter took the conversation back to forecasting errors.

'When you talk about a catastrophic error, do you mean some foul-up like the meteorological office made in October 1987? The great storm that blew down thousands of trees all over the country?'

'Yes. Exactly. An error like that could ruin us. I want us to have a broader base. I have looked at several ideas, and made a few experiments, but not found what I am looking for yet. Maybe you wondered why I wanted remote stations in Africa. It was a low-cost trial move that might yet pay off in terms of early information that other people don't have.'

Peter accepted that, but he wanted to know more about the day ahead. 'How do today's people come into it?'

'They call themselves 'Site-Prep' and their business is preparing the environment for a range of strenuous and sometimes dangerous outside activities. Let's say that a cycle manufacturer wants to sponsor a race for mountain bikes. Site-Prep will contract with them to choose the location, mark out the track, provide marshals, ensure safety, and all the rest of it.'

Peter did not follow the logic. 'What do they want from us? Adventure activities are usually independent of the weather.'

'They want more than a weather forecast. They want an estimate of the state of the ground before and during the event, plus qualitative details of any bad weather. I mean, will any rain be heavy or light? Will there be a driving wind so that people can't see through the rain. Is there a danger of soil slippage at any place along the track. They have to make decisions like, for instance, will competitors under eighteen be allowed to take part? They will be dead scared of Health and Safety Inspectors and of lawsuits. They want to be as safe as possible.'

'Can we do that sort of work?'

Reading was now behind them, and Pangbourne, and they looked out at the Thames valley on their right. Nshila fell silent as she enjoyed the lush greenness of the scene. It was a small river, she thought, by world standards, but up with the best of them as a spectacle. The view gave way to the uplands as the train passed a deserted platform labelled Cholsey and Moulsford, and she produced a considered answer for Peter.

'We can do it as well as anybody else. There is always knowledge somewhere, so we would pay a retainer to a soil composition expert if we had to. And Site-Prep probably don't know yet what can realistically be done. They don't know that, and we don't know the details of what they want. It's an exploratory meeting. Business may come from it, or it may be a waste of time. It's worth looking into because they seem to be shooting for high profile events with big money attached.'

Peter liked the idea. 'It sounds great fun. I'm all in favour of adventurous activities. But you've not given any reason yet for disliking these people. Let's hear it. But not yet, please.'

It was Peter's turn to pause the conversation. They were passing Didcot and he wanted to catch a glimpse of the railway centre. Steam trains were one of his enthusiasms, for his childhood had just overlapped with the last of the tiny, romantic country railways that used to criss-cross East Anglia. The centre fell behind them and Nshila spoke again.

'Gillian picked up the vibrations first. The caller wanted to speak to 'the top man' and when Gillian said that it was actually the top woman, there was a heavy pause while the caller digested the idea. Then, in a rather ungracious manner, 'Very well, then, I'll speak to her.' When I picked up the phone I got this man with a flat, heavy Birmingham accent asking questions about what sort of work we did. Cutting out his limited attempts at politeness, what he asked was 'Do you just sit in an office and play with computers or do you get out into the real world?' I made a big thing of my recent trip to Africa and how I had hired a team for a rugged trip into the bush. So this consultation was fixed up. You are substituting for the heavy mob I am supposed to have hired. You had better take your tie off and let people see your hairy chest.'

At Banbury, their expectations were reinforced by the person and vehicle sent to meet them. The mud-spattered landrover, driven by an unshaven security guard looked seriously down-market. Leaving the vehicle to greet them was also a missing courtesy; the driver shouted 'Over here' and waited. Peter opened the passenger door for Nshila, aware that she was fuming mentally because the driver had omitted this basic courtesy. The vehicle started off with a jerk and Peter hit the back of his head on some piece of equipment in the rear. Instead of turning left into the town, the vehicle drove away from it up the hill and eventually reached a fenced-off encampment round a row of temporary cabins, the type used as offices on building sites. The driver shouted to the gatekeeper 'Got them, Barry. Where's the boss?' Being told, 'Down at the hen house', he drove to the farthest hut, on which was a notice 'Site-Prep Operations HQ.'

'In there, folks,' said the driver, and roared off the moment the door had closed. Inside the hut the visitors found the only woman they were to meet; a girl of about seventeen who was trying hard to look like a super-model and earnestly painting her nails. She wrote names on visitors badges (Ms Ilelanka and Mr Grasse) and shouted for 'Norman.' A man duly appeared, presumably Norman, and led the way out of the hut to a rather better looking one just behind it. A man came to the door, greeting them in the 'flat, heavy Birmingham accent' that Nshila had spoken of. He, and the two others they met, had a strong smell of 'Services' on them; they displayed the attitudes and behaviour acquired in an army or police or security organisation that is almost entirely male and has a 'canteen culture'. They showed no dislike of Nshila, but were uncertain how to behave towards her. They introduced themselves as Bert Enderby, Charlie Hosegood and Kevin Clarke. Bert seemed to be the boss, and did most of the talking.

Possibly because Nshila's clothes said 'money' quite loudly, the manager apologised for the scruffiness of the environment. He said that an out-of-town base was essential for getting started and a respectable office could come later. 'We have got substantial financial backing, you know, but we don't want to waste it on non-essentials. It is a high-risk business we are starting, and there has to be a big pot for "contingencies".'

Nshila minimised any conversational difficulty by upgrading Peter. She said, 'Peter and I are primarily here to find out just what you need. I probably have greater technical knowledge, but Peter has an excellent memory and loves getting his mind around new activities, particularly when they are practical outdoor things. I will listen to it all very carefully, but I won't intervene much.'

Their relief was obvious. The strategy also worked well because Peter eased back into the old macho attitudes in which he had grown up. In the rural world of his boyhood a girl might eventually get herself an education, but only after she had bred two boys of fourteen and sixteen and both were working in the fields. He could assume the old behaviours and remember the right jargon. He enjoyed himself. He enjoyed talking about practical problems that could be solved by common sense and strength and knowledge of human nature; stuff learnt in 'the university of the world'. He felt once more the old camaraderie of a group that does not have to worry about emotions and feelings and esoteric knowledge and government interference. He could feel Nshila getting madder and madder inside herself, but felt he was doing the right thing in the prevailing situation. He got a good understanding of the activities they were into, and ways in which The Rain Consultancy might be able to help them. They did a great many different things. It might be surveying a wooded area for a school orienteering competition. It might be manufacturing obstacles for an assault course. It might be a hill-climb for quad bikes. It might be one or more sections for a motor rally. It might be something for horses.

Coffee was offered after an hour, and Nshila's face registered distaste when she saw spoonfuls of wet sugar being dumped into a dirty mug and covered with muddy liquid that tasted of anything but coffee. There was scum on the surface. However, this was a business conference, and she drank it bravely. During that break Peter talked with one of the hosts in the gents, and discovered a mutual acquaintance. Exploring the link, he revealed that he had done time in prison. Immediately his stock shot up. He knew well that people in law enforcement can like, and even respect, what they call 'an honest villain'. They do, after all, provide employment for those supposed to catch them. They have much to talk about together. It's like two rugby teams that aim to slaughter each other on the pitch but re-live every blow with pleasure as soon as they have a few beers inside them. After the coffee break Peter was definitely 'one of us'.

The discovery also did Nshila some good, because the same host asked Peter what it was like working for a woman, and a black. He explained that this was not any woman, nor any black; that he had met her at a steam engine rally and that they had been friends before he joined her firm. He gave here a good press, 'extremely bright', he said, 'courageous and risk-taking in business. If you get her on your side, you'll be pleased with the deal.'

So the barriers began to come down, and during the afternoon Nshila got more constructive answers to her questions than would otherwise have been offered. To give an example of their work, they suggested going to a site that they were preparing for a motor race; old, disposable vehicles to be driven round a demanding five mile course.

Lunch was poor. It featured the thickest ever sandwiches filled with tasteless beef. The hosts took each sandwich apart and poured tomato sauce over the meat. One of them licked the top of the bottle. Nshila ate nothing except two chocolate biscuits.

And then, along the race track, she suddenly came to life. They were at a point where the track emerged from some trees and swung sharply to the left to run along the rim of a steep gorge. She asked, 'What happens if a car goes over the edge, here? It looks like a nasty death to me.'

Her hosts exchanged glances. The unspoken message was that this woman had only seen such things on the screen. Bert Enderby's reply was polite.

'When the race actually happens, we'll have crash barriers here, set back a bit from the edge. Quite sturdy things. The Department of Transport is busy installing them at dangerous places right now.'

'Will that stop a fast-moving car?' Nshila asked. 'Surely I have seen pictures of broken barriers where a vehicle has gone straight through.'

This time it was Charlie who replied. 'Yes. It can happen. At high speeds, or if the barrier is old, or if a previous car has hit it and damaged it. But it would cost the earth to have completely impenetrable barriers, so we plan the safety measures in line with our risk assessment.'

Nshila wanted to pursue the subject. 'If a car does go through the barrier, I suppose it falls right the way to the bottom and bursts into flames. Right?'

'Sometimes. But it's not certain. In fact it happens a lot less than television suggests. For one thing, cars only carry enough fuel for the race. It's not as if they had twenty gallons of petrol or so.'

Nshila looked disappointed. 'But they still burn, surely?'

'Not every time. I have known cars strike a boggy area half-way down and stop without serious damage. I have known the petrol tank get wrenched off by an obstacle, so that when the car stopped there was no petrol there to burn. There's a lot of chance in it.'

'So when the stories say that the body was incinerated and had to be identified by dental records, that is just dramatic colour, is it? How disappointing.'

The answer this time was a bit longer. Bert had noticed her disappointment. 'Like I said, there is a lot of chance in it. A factor working against incineration is that the rescue services are very good. If you go to the worst known danger points on our roads you will often find that the emergency services have cut a track to the bottom. They can get there quicker than one would think. They put out the fire and the body will be pretty much intact. The person is still dead, of course, but somehow it makes the relatives feel better.'

Nshila asked plenty of other questions, too, but Peter got the feeling that the idea of cars leaping through fences and bursting into flames had sparked her imagination. On the points she raised later, she tended to accept the answers quite readily.

On the train journey back to London, Peter had to endure a fair amount of critical comment about how well he had got on with the hosts. He was quietly amused by it, believing her to be annoyed that he, rather than she, had been the focus of attention.

He perceived it as an endearing feminine weakness.

Chapter Twenty-Three
Necessary Revisions

A lucky break, she thought, back in the flat with Rasputin sitting on her lap. If Toppley had died that morning it would have started a sequence for which she was, she now realised, ill-prepared. The burning out of Tetherman's corpse-bearing vehicle was far from certain. She also felt grateful to Peter. It was his relationship with the Site-Prep people that had made the visit so extensive and interesting. On her own, she might have been become annoyed with them and never learnt those critical facts about crashes.

To what extent had the events of the day altered her plans? The immediate and obvious consequence was that she had time for revision. Toppley had not died. His corpse was not passing through the post-mortem process and was not imposing a tight schedule upon her. It was still going to happen, but not yet. When it did, however, more actions had to be completed within the time scale. Simply pushing a car over the edge of a precipitous slope was not going to be enough. It would not necessarily burst into flames. Even if it did, the emergency services might arrive in time to find recognisable parts of the body.

She made another journey down the A3 to the Devils Punchbowl and was glad to have done so. Scrambling down the route planned for Tetherman's car she found an access track at the bottom exactly as had been described at Site-Prep. Cars had crashed this way before and the rescue services could get to the scene with little delay. It was frustrating; if the Toppley/Tetherman body was found in reasonable condition, a pathologist would know that it had been dead some days. Even a quick look would be enough, and undertakers do more than that when they tart up the body for relatives to view. Her plan depended on the body being burnt away to the extent that only dental records would identify it. Anything else, and questions would be asked like, 'If he was dead before the accident, then where did it happen?' Enquiries might well come to a dead end, because nobody had a reason to connect Toppley and Tetherman. But there was still a risk. Some random enquiry might link the two recent deaths and find that Tetherman's dental records also matched those of Toppley.

She worked all night to find a crash path that was difficult to access. Getting through the undergrowth was a hard task, resulting in numerous falls, numerous scratches and a narrow escape from a broken ankle. Early on she regretted not spending more time choosing her outfit. Twice she was disappointed, but finally found a place where there was a sharp bend, the crash barrier was old and battered, and the likely resting place of a vehicle was hard to access. She also found another useful location; a place from which she could probably see the wreck. She had previously found a derelict woodman's hut that was ideal for the supernatural part of the job.

That left the matter of ensuring a burn-out. She reflected on the many times she had engineered a death by supporting the witchdoctor element with practical action. She could certainly make an image of Toppley/Tetherman and burn it in the right conditions with the right spells. But she had to make the car burn, too. Machinery is less susceptible to psychological pressure than the human mind. The spirits knew how to handle human targets, but could they make metal and plastic burn? Alternatively, could she do anything practical to make the vehicle burn? Not easy. She had to be at the start point to make the car crash through the barrier. It was impossible to be at the bottom also to set a match to the wreck.

And then came inspiration. She had scraped the worst of the mud and leaves and twigs from her clothing and was driving back northwards with the radio on. There was a new flash. A terrorist group in some Middle East country had destroyed a British vehicle with a rocket launcher. The crew had escaped, but the vehicle had been totally burnt out. Here was one way to deal

179

with the Tetherman car. If it did not burn because of the crash she could fire a rocket into it. Could she get a rocket launcher? Her cautious self spoke up. 'You are totally out of your mind! You don't know the first thing about rocket launchers. You don't know what they look like, or how they work, or how to handle them or how many people are needed to fire them. Come down to earth, woman.'

The risk-taking self was having none of it. 'The sequence hasn't started yet. Toppley is still alive. There's time enough for a resourceful person to get a rocket launcher. Make an effort, girl.'

She left the A3 and drove cross-country to Gatwick, where large featureless hotels cater to airline traffic and are accustomed to arrivals from anywhere in the world at any time of day or night. A strange black woman, looking somewhat bedraggled and wanting breakfast at 5.30am was nothing new. Amazingly, the breakfast was good and the coffee was hot. She booked two hours in their 'business centre' and got to work on the internet. She typed Rocket Launcher into a search engine and immediately found pictures of six different types. Three of them needed one operator only - the Bazooka and the Law 66mm and the RPG 7.

Any trawl of the internet provides masses of irrelevant information before the wanted item is found. Nshila was unable to restrain her curiosity and was frequently side-tracked. She wasted time on obscure facts, learning that the Chinese had used rockets against the Mongols and the British had used them at the Battle of Leipzig.

She learnt that there were things called multiple rockets, but dismissed them as too complicated. She wanted single shot weapons, and knowledge of how to get them and how to use them. Not easy. It was no help to find that one could pick up an RPG 7 for a few dollars almost anywhere in the Middle East.

There were enough clues amongst the listings to start her on a brainstorming session. Sitting in the business centre at that featureless hotel, she listed all possible sources, without regard for their practicality;

An army training centre. (She had see one at Hythe.)
A military museum.
A manufacturer.
A para-military outfit in Northern Ireland.
Private collectors of militaria.
A terrorist group.
.
Some of those organisations had websites, but few were directly helpful. Nevertheless, she soon knew the exact location of at least one RGP 7 – in the museum of the Police Service of Northern Ireland. It wasn't enough.

Once again she got distracted, perhaps being a bit light-headed after her night in the woods. Thinking of substitutes for a rocket, she came up with the idea of incendiary bullets. The internet yielded a story so ridiculously incongruous that she had to finish it. Apparently a German Zeppelin in WW1 had fallen to the ground when hit by incendiary bullets. On the ground it had been attacked by a French cavalry squadron with swords. Here was an extraordinary meeting of modern and ancient technology that had some likeness to her own methods, the witchcraft of past ages and the technology of today.

Something else she soon learnt, which she must have known already if she was thinking clearly, was that anything really dangerous like a rocket launcher is only going to be available if de-activated. One stolen from a military museum – even if that were possible – would not work.

Failure made her angry. Surely there was some source of help, somewhere. She remembered getting lost, once, in the City and finding herself in Smithfield Market, outside a shop that sold nothing at all except butchers hooks – dozens of different types aimed at a very specialised trade. It had struck her at the time that every obscure activity has it's own resources. Now, memory took her back to the OU course. She had sometimes wanted to get information without knowing quite where to start. She had spoken instead to firms that were not themselves in the business she was researching, but might have leads to it. It always worked in the end if one persevered. She typed in Weapons Collectors and was rewarded instantly with TANKSAREUS.CO.UK. The blurb showed that they really did sell tanks; warfare tanks, not water tanks or whatever. They were real. They really sold tanks, though de-activated. They mentioned the sort of people they sold to - museums and film-makers and theme parks and adventure camps.

What was the RPG 7 made for? Destroying tanks. These people must have knowledge. She had a starting point. The clock now said **8.45am** She would wait half-an-hour, and phone them. Most people would be at work by then.

She asked to speak to their Public Relations department. They didn't have one, but eventually she was speaking to one of the partners, a cheerful soul named Glen Brockby. She told him she was President of a Historic Arms Society that had been asked to put on a display for a big local festival. Weapons from all periods would be shown, from the middle ages onwards and that something really modern was needed to end the show dramatically.

'What I really want is a rocket launcher – something topical and dramatic like an RPG 7. I am having terrible trouble getting one. I realise that your business is about tanks, but you must know about the things people shoot at them. Do you know anybody at all who is in that line of work and might help me?'

The response was sympathetic laughter.

"Give it up, Mrs Crawford (her assumed name for he call). You will never, never get your hands on a working RPG. They are very tightly controlled. You are wasting your time.'

Nshila had no intention of giving up. At least this man knew something about rocket launchers, and that was progress of a sort. 'No, please. Don't get me wrong. I know a working item is out of the question, but surely there are some de-activated ones around. I mean, if you have a market for tanks, there must be somebody, somewhere who deals in the things used to attack them.'

Her persistence, and her need, and perhaps the fact that

she was a woman drew a positive response from Glen Brockby.

'I might be able to dig up a few names for you. But a de-activated RPG does not really look very exciting. It's just a tube, and a bomb on a stick.'

'I understand. It's a bit feeble unless it does something. If only we had an active one we could make an exhibit that really shook people. We could set up a few targets in a safe place and blow them all to bits. But the world is so regulated now that you can hardly light a match without the Health and Safety Executive jumping on you. We had terrible trouble getting permission for our 'storm a castle' display last year. They objected to our boiling oil, even though it was coloured lukewarm water.'

Glen expanded further. 'Mrs Crawford, something has just come to mind. There's a small chance it might help you. If you could bring your audience here to our site we could blow up a tank for you with a bazooka. Or else we could send you a video.'

'How's that? I thought you said the things were totally illegal.'

'Strictly speaking, yes. But the police get rather bored with inspecting us and things get overlooked. Years ago we bought a tank from the USA and somebody had left a working bazooka and missiles in the storage area. We used it once. A man asked for a tank with a large hole in it. Very impressive it was. The bazooka got overlooked in all the paperwork that smothers our business. It's still there in the storeroom behind a pair of portable latrines.'

Nshila made herself sound excited. She had no intention of visiting, but she wanted the conversation to go on. 'Where are you? Physically, I mean.'

'On the edge of Salisbury plain. Is that too far for you?'

'Yes. I'm afraid so. It would have made a marvellous spectacle. But can you tell me a few names that I might ask about rocket launchers?'

He did so. Nshila expressed deep gratitude, rang off, and waved both hands in the air in triumph. She had located a

183

working rocket launcher.

Next problem – how to steal it. Even though the things they sold were de-activated, TANKSAREUS must have good security. How was one unarmed woman to break through their fence, find the miscellaneous storeroom and lift the weapon from behind the portable latrines?

With the Hand of Glory, of course. Her mind was working overtime. The thing was still there in the deep freezer in the flat behind the Eastcheap office, still in the package from Pakistan. True, her first attempt had proved little about the effectiveness of the spell. Maud Franklin had been unconscious before the candles were lit. Against that, it had been very much a substitute Hand and therefore the test proved nothing. She would try again. The great thing about witchcraft was that it is not legally recognised. Suppose it failed to work, and she was found outside a security fence with a long-dead severed hand and a few bits of wax. Would she have committed any crime? No. And if it worked then everybody close by was going to be immobilised and she could walk in. Breaking and entering? No. The hand would have unlocked everything and she would have walked through an open gate. Where was the crime in that? No serious offence would have been committed until she walked out with the bazooka and a few rockets.

The God of Depression lurks around mankind between 6.30am and 9.30am, especially if a person has been at work all night. He struck hard at Nshila. What on earth was she doing? How could anybody conceive such bizarre and impossible ideas? Was she totally out of her mind? None of this would ever work. It was pure fantasy! And all in an attempt to shore up a plan that was ridiculous in the first place. Momentarily overwhelmed, she put her head down on the desk. She slept.

Dreams. Why? When? Whence? Nobody knows. But in her dream some entity encouraged her. Bizarre? Yes. Impossible? No. There's nothing in the plan that you can't make happen if you work hard and keep your head. And it will be wildly exciting. For a few days you will be 100 per cent alive. In the blurred and unstable dream environment she heard, and sometimes saw the risk-takers and adventurers of the past.

'One crowded hour of glorious life' - *'Infirm of purpose, give me the dagger'* - *'Who dares, wins'* - *'My candle burns at both the ends...will not last the night.........gives a splendid light'* - *'Slave, I have set my life upon a cast and I will stand the hazard of the die.'* - *'The days of our youth are the days of our glory.'*

'Your coffee and sandwiches, Madam.'
Had she really ordered it? But she was pleased to have the tray beside her, and especially for the double whisky beside the coffee cup. She could only have been asleep for a few minutes, but the screen before her showed the revolving diamonds of the screen saver.

She thanked the waitress, consumed the goodies, turned off the machine and left. She had no doubt, now, what she was going to do. Backing out was not an option.

Chapter Twenty-Four

Finishing Touches

Theft of the Tetherman car, she had decided, ought to take place as late in the schedule as possible. So must the theft of the bazooka. Different activities needed different vehicles and there was going to be a transport problem. One vehicle for overseeing the Toppley death, which she already had, another for stealing the body; the Tetherman vehicle for the crash. And at some point she would have to use public transport.

Curled in the armchair in her flat, she studied timetables and maps which she had picked up from the local travel agent, downloaded from the internet or borrowed from Peter Grace. The Berkshire downs seemed open and deserted and were nicely situated between London and Bristol. She worked out a draft schedule.

D-Day Minus Five

Purchase the van needed to steal the body. Take it to an obliging garage to give it the proper identity. Arrange to collect it very early on D-Day.

D-Day Minus One

In the evening, walk to the Toppley house and put cords in the pockets of all likely coats.

D-Day

Pick up the theft van. Drive it to the place where the Water Company van was concealed and swap over. Reach the Toppley house in time to set the trap. Mobilise The Companion as soon as Toppley emerged. Remove all insignia from the Water Company van and swap it for the theft van.

D-Day + X

Using the second van, steal the Toppley corpse. Drive it immediately to the Berkshire downs somewhere near Baydon. Conceal it. Walk to Aldbourne, through which a country bus route wound it's way to Swindon. From Swindon, travel by train and taxi to Dutch Elm House.

Steal the car, and drive to Upton Lovell on the edge of Salisbury Plain and steal the bazooka. Drive towards Reading and sleep in the car till dawn. The 'X' in the schedule had to exist because the time lapse between Toppley's death and the body-stealing window was unknown.

D-Day + X + One and into D-Day + X + Two

Drive to Reading, leave the car in the car park and travel to London for a normal day in the office. Late afternoon, take taxi to Paddington and train to Reading. Recover Tetherman car. Drive to Baydon and transfer corpse. Drive to Devil's Punchbowl and stage final accident. Bury the bazooka and walk cross-country to Haslemere. Catch the train to London for another normal office day.

Satisfied with her plan, she checked the parliamentary calendar once more and confirmed that the next opportunity was just seven days ahead. Should she feel nervous? No. Eagerness and anticipation were her dominant emotions.

Chapter Twenty-Five

The Clients Problem

It was D-Day minus One in Nshila's calendar, a fact unknown to Sir Alfred Munnings, the new Director of the Service, as he sat in his office. He had enough worries without it. Only three days had passed since he had arrived and already he was thinking about poisoned chalices.

The previous director had been retired after an unusually serious scandal. The responsibilities of the service had been reduced, and the budget cut dramatically. Alfred had started life as an accountant and meant to use this area to start feeling his way into the job. He was hearing some of the details from Calder MacFee his Head of Finance.

'Are things really that bad, Calder?'

'They are, Director. The Treasury people have seized on our disgrace as a way to distract attention from their own inefficiency. The budget cuts have been appalling. We are barely able to meet our existing commitments.'

Alfred was scanning the summarised figures, and several items caught his attention.

'What does this heading, 'Facilitations', cover? There's more than a millon set against it.'

'Ah! That's something you must speak to Lachlan Knowles about, our Head of Operations. We have certain areas of knowledge that are restricted to the staff immediately responsible. This 'Facilitations' is a budget controlled by Lachlan personally and I don't know exactly how he spends it.'

'I'm not having that. Get him in here.'

While he waited, Alfred swivelled round in his executive chair, all the way through 360 degrees. It was a habit he enjoyed, now that his status gave him that sort of comfort and prestige. But he was worried, and his privileges made less impact on him than usual. The view of the river, the half-raised Tower Bridge, the fluffy white clouds that promised a fine weekend, the aircraft hanging almost motionless in the sky as they drifted towards Heathrow. They all pleased him a little bit less than usual. That was also true of what he learnt from Lachlan Knowles.

'Director, are you quite sure you want to know?'

'Of course I want to know. What sort of outfit is it where things are concealed from the chief?'

'Previously, Director, this one. You predecessor made it quite clear that certain clandestine activities – however necessary they were – must never be spoken of in his hearing. He wanted to be able to deny all personal knowledge.'

'I'm not like that. If I'm officially in charge I must know everything and accept responsibility. Tell me. Tell me now!'

'Well, Director, there are times when the nation is threatened by individuals or a group that are effectively beyond the reach of the law. It seldom happens, but when it does we have to find a way of removing them.'

'You mean deportation?'

'No, Director, not quite that. Sometimes we have to do more than deport them from our country.'

'Are you talking about assassination?'

'Yes.'

'Appalling! Quite appalling! Stop it! Stop it now! I'm not saying I could never agree, but until I am fully familiar with this service I want all such action halted. Is there anything going on right now?'

'There is, Director. One project is active. Only one.'

'Stop it. Stop it immediately.'

'Yes, Director. But I have to warn you that 'immediately' is tough when we are dealing with this sort of thing. The lines of communication are quite long and at our level we don't know exactly what is happening on the ground.'

'What do you mean?'

'I mean that the assassin needs discretion about when and where the hit is to be made. He also has a need for secrecy. To

189

give you an extreme example, the assassin might be pulling the trigger at this very moment.' Lachlan mimicked the aiming of a rifle and said 'bang' as if he was a child playing in the woods. 'If that happens now, or is due in the next ten minutes, we can't stop it, can we?'

The Director was momentarily lost for words. Perhaps his predecessor had been wise to remain in ignorance. But he had insisted on being told and he had taken a stand.

'Lachlan, get out of here now and do everything in your power to stop it. I don't care if you have to work all weekend or wake up cabinet ministers or crawl through sewers to wrench the rifle from your assassin. Just stop it. Warn the target. Get him protection. Do whatever is necessary. But do it!'

Chapter Twenty-Six

The Day Of The Deed

It was early afternoon on D-Day. Nshila stopped the lift at the second floor of the Eastcheap building and used the Ladies toilet allocated to the shipping agent and the spice importer who shared that floor. She needed a few moments to calm down, compose herself, and freshen up her business identity. The project had gone without a hitch. She re-lived it in her mind.

She had opened the sub-station gate and set her trap. Sitting on a camp stool in the back of the water company van, she had watched the windows of the Toppley house and traced his progress from bedroom to bathroom and breakfast room. She had cast the spells carefully and accurately. She had stabbed her image of the open gate and set The Companion on the job. Toppley had emerged from his house, wearing one of the coats into which she had put a cord. He had seemed to be swatting at something behind his ear. He had looked frightened. He had turned to peer behind him. He had leant against a lamp post, put his head in his hands and groaned. He had even attempted a return to his house, but discovered that it made things worse. He had walked on again. Level with the sub-station, he had stopped abruptly and looked around him.

At that point Nshila had left. She had felt complete confidence in The Companion and only been uncertain about the direction in which the pole would fall. Despite that, she had decided it would not be wise to stay longer. If there was any disturbance and she was found to have been in the area, there would have been questions about why she had not gone to help.

She pushed the brush through her hair one last time, left the toilet and climbed the stairs to The Rain Consultancy.

Mid-afternoon and the evening papers. There it was on the front page. SHOCK DEATH WILL FORCE BY-ELECTION.

Toppley's accident had caused a power failure in the area served by the sub-station, so the electricity people, skilled in tracing faults, had found the body in just half-an-hour. Removing him had taken longer. People with the right skills and equipment had to be found and bureaucrats of different levels had to be consulted. A medical team had been called in case life might not be extinct, but were never needed. Nshila threw down the paper and watched the local television news instead. She was astonished by the scene. The sub-station was marked off with tape. Four vehicles stood there with flashing lights. Officials spoke constantly into mobile phones. A reporter spoke earnestly to a camera, waving his hand towards the scene behind him. The programme finally showed a stretcher being lifted into an ambulance and driven off.

Not many comments about Toppley had been gathered in the limited time available. The Prime Minister had said that Toppley had never been a reliable supporter and the party had a good candidate available to contest his seat. The Chief Whip of the party was an enthusiast for the poetry of John Donne and said 'Any man's death diminishes me', adding 'in this case not by much.' Two teenage girls had phoned the studio to deplore the death of 'a lovely, lovely man'. That was the sum of comment so far.

Naturally, there was speculation about what Toppley had been doing in the electricity sub-station. It was unlikely that he had opened the padlock himself, so it must have been open before and the gate open too. Perhaps he had seen a child or a dog enter the enclosure, and gone in to rescue it. Perhaps he had suspected criminal activity and bravely entered the enclosure to put a stop to it. Police were treating the death as an accident, with no suspicious circumstances.

On the Director's desk was the same evening paper that Nshila was studying. On the other side of the desk sat a tired and frustrated Lachlan Knowles.

'I did everything possible, Director, but it took ages to find anybody who could authorise protection and when I did find somebody he said that staffing problems made it impossible to fix the thing before the day after tomorrow. I tried to find Toppley to warn him, but never made contact. I think I was given the wrong information about where he was going last evening, and the phone at his house seemed to have a fault. I tried again this morning but only got his answering service.'

'But surely you could have called off our operative?'

'I'm sorry, Director. Did you not realise, when we spoke last, that we were using a contractor? These people are very protective of their identity and can't be reached quickly.'

'Good heavens! Are you now telling me that we used a hired assassin? If we are into this sort of thing at all, surely we have somebody of our own?'

The Director was so agitated that he left his chair and paced all around the room. Subconsciously he counted the steps each way and worked out that the carpet really was the right size for somebody of his importance. Lachlan had to turn his head in all directions to maintain the dialogue.

'We don't have many. It's a money problem. They are classified as Executive Officers of a particular grade and they can't be paid above a fixed ceiling. They feel they should be paid a great deal more money than, say, an Executive Officer in Accounts. So recruiting and retaining them is hard. We ought to have three. At the time the Toppley decision was taken, one was in Shanghai and one was sick with meningitis.'

'What about Number Three?'

'Honestly, Director, he was not quite up to it. The report from the training school said that he was hesitant and squeamish. We didn't dare use him. Right now he's having sessions with our psychiatrist.'

The Director allowed himself to collapse into a chair beside the coffee table. He managed to make a dramatic performance out of it, to show his disgust.

Lachlan had worse news to report.

'Sir, there is another problem as well. I think we ought to have Calder McFee to help us.'

Ten minutes later the Director knew the worst. Not only had his service hired a professional assassin, but had done so at vast expense just prior to a massive scandal that had resulted in huge budget cuts. The job had been done, the money was due, and the service was so cash-strapped that it was unable to pay.

Alfred Munnings had a terrible vision. Professional disaster. Early retirement. Less generous pension. No knighthood. A wife who would get more and more shrewish as she waited for the garden party invitations that never came. It had all looked so promising a few weeks ago when Nigel McDowell dropped out and he had become the front runner for the job. Had that crafty old sod heard something that he had not?

He dismissed Lachlan and Calder, telling them to set up a meeting in the conference room at 5.00pm. They must consult all the staff who might have useful ideas.

The Director opened the next meeting. 'Let's be quite sure I have got the facts clear. Somebody in this outfit hired an assassin to rid the world of a man called Toppley? Right?'

'Correct, Director.'

'This was done with the approval of senior management but without the knowledge of my predecessor?'

'Yes. He wanted to be able to deny such things if necessary.'

'A huge sum of money was agreed, and about 10 per cent was paid as a deposit. The money has gone. We can't get it back. Right?'

'Correct again.'

'The job was completed this morning, it seems.' The Director waved the evening paper. 'Toppley is dead, and the remaining money is due to this assassin. Who wants his money. Right

'I'm afraid so.'

'It's only to be expected.'

'And we don't have the money, so we can't pay. Right?'

'Very clearly stated, Director.'

'Knowing what the security services can get up to, I believe most of the story. One bit really bugs me. You say we have no money. Surely every department of every government on earth has got money stashed away under the bed which the treasury knows nothing about. Where's ours?'

'Gone, Director. It is a consequence of the scandal. We paid a huge amount of money on the cover-up operation and then discovered we had bribed the wrong men. So the scandal came out anyway. One of the consequences was intense scrutiny of our accounts by the treasury, and the very tightest of budgets. We can barely pay our staff, and the rows about expenses are endless. We are like small boys lining up for pocket money.'

'The first thing you must do, then, is play for time. Tell this assassin that government payment procedures have changed, or that the computer system has failed, and there will be an unfortunate delay in payment.'

'We will try that, Director. I made the first moves towards contact yesterday, and it's quite possible that by now the assassin knows we have an urgent need to talk. He won't know what about. But we will get some sort of response soon, I believe. Then we can explain the urgency of the problem.'

Chapter Twenty-Seven

D-Day Plus One

The gap year, Nshila reflected. That's what school-leavers have before they go to university. I've got gap days instead; the days between Toppley's death and the moment when I can steal the body.

She had expected the days to be boring. There was nothing she could do to influence the work of pathologists or undertakers or administrators, though she had devised ways to keep herself informed of progress. How could she fill the time? Perhaps by planning the expansion of The Rain Consultancy, using ideas she had picked up on the African trip, and from Site-Prep and other sources. At least it would be constructive activity, and something that could easily be put down if a crisis arose.

Reality was different. First of all, early on D plus One there was a call from Jessop. It signalled the cancellation of slack days and the start of frenzied pressurised days which stretched Nshila to her limit.

'A rather strange message reached me yesterday morning from the client. It was not at all clear, but I sensed a desire to back out of the contract and possibly some concern about the money. I tried to reach you, but failed.'

'Did you take any action?'

'Yes. I passed back a cryptic reply suggesting that this sort of contract is inflexible and both parties must meet their obligations. I think it will force them to be more explicit without us giving anything away. I just said 'Remember the Pied Piper'. Are you with me?'

'I am. He was the fellow who charmed the rats away from Hamelin Town and then charmed the children away when they haggled over his fee.'

'Right. I hope they will interpret it as a threat to use the skills you employed again - but reversed. The Pied Piper said,

'First, if you please, my thousand guilders.'

'Right. They will read that as 'I want my money now'.'
Nshila pondered for a moment. Then she approved Jessop's action and told him to make contact again when he heard more. This time he was to do nothing himself. He must restrict himself to the messenger role.

In the afternoon there were two more telephone calls. The first came from Inspector Bill Waterhouse.

'You remember you asked me to check the missing persons register? Well, I looked regularly for the fortnight after you asked me, and found nothing. But I have been away sick for a time and I now see that the girl you asked me about, Jennifer Price, was reported missing ten days ago. It was reported by her parents, but they delayed three weeks before doing so. They said she was a very independent girl and would be furious if her parents made a fuss over nothing.'

That conversation reminded Nshila of the help she had half-promised to Simon Sullivan. His story had been influential in the decision to take the Toppley contract, but the fortunes of Jennifer had been shunted to the back of her mind. She felt guilty.

And more so when she got the next call. It was from Simon Sullivan himself. He had not forgotten Jennifer at all. He rang to say that his worries had caused him to revisit the hostel where he had stayed, using the pretext of a lost Rolex watch that he feared he might have left in a locker. His news was that Jennifer Price had never re-appeared. The manager of the hostel was worried, but not greatly so because girls did sometimes lose interest in their sport and quietly desert. He admitted that they did not often leave personal possessions behind, but his main concern was re-letting her room.

Could she do anything positive? Nshila felt an obligation, but had little idea how to discharge it. And she still hoped for some relaxation in these gap days.

Without conscious effort, different thoughts drifted together in her mind. She could do nothing about a girl kidnapped and transported to the Middle East. It was not her business. Whose business was it? Government? The Foreign Office? Or a Security Service? There it was – a flash of intellectual brilliance! There was one security service currently eager to make contact with her and apparently wanting something from her! It was a starting point. She phoned Jessop and told him that if and when the client made contact next, he was to set up a meeting.

Chapter Twenty-Eight

What Can We Offer?

It was mid-morning when Lachlan Knowles entered the Directors office – on the second day since Toppley had died.

'Director, I have had two messages. One was late last night and the other just thirty minutes ago. It's mixed news.'

'Give me the bad first and get it over.'

'The first message. It was very brief and seemed to be a threat. Just four words: 'Remember the Pied Piper'.'

'How is that a threat?'

'It's an allusion to a poem in which a magician accepts a fee to save a town from a plague of rats. He does the job, but when he asks for his money the Town Council refuses to pay. So he charms away all the children of the town. Do you see what it means?'

'I do. We ask the man to kill somebody and he does it. If we fail to pay then he kills one of us. I suppose it endangers one of the people we have used as intermediaries.'

'That's possible, Sir. But you would yourself be the most high-profile target.'

'Good heavens!' The Director recoiled in his chair, fear easily seen in his face and manner. He poured whisky from the flask under his desk and gulped it down.

'I asked for the bad news first, and I've got it. What about the better news?'

'That was in the message I got just now. It seems that, despite the earlier response, our assassin is prepared for a meeting of representatives. Such meetings are always risky and he would never agree to it unless he saw a potential gain. There must be something he wants, and that gives us a bargaining opportunity. However, the message said that any such meeting has to take place tomorrow, which gives us little time to work out a strategy.'

Another conference was set up. It took place shortly after lunch, and was attended by all the people who might have useful ideas to offer.

The conference room was set up for a Power Point demonstration when the Director walked in. Waiting for him were Lachlan, Peter Greig, (Finance Officer), Hal Doyle, (Agency Psychologist), Percy Mallingham (Public Relations), Wilf Watson (Chief of Staff), and Samantha Scott (Procurement Manager. The Director had a preliminary word.

'Before we start, let's consider the idea of doing nothing at all. People have defaulted on debts since the dawn of time, and a default puts the ball in the creditor's court. His objective is to get the money, and actions based on revenge are pointless. They won't get him the money. I don't think we should be frightened by a fairy story. After all, this business of the Pied Piper never happened, did it? It's fiction. And if it had, it would be a story of failure because the piper never saw the cash and was lumbered with a whole tribe of children. I can think of three options open to our assassin if we don't pay.'

'What are they, Director?' Lachlan, as the senior person present, put the question.

'One of them is to ignore the debt in anticipation of getting more lucrative business in the future. Tradesmen are always allowing rich customers to run up debts because they believe they will get paid in full one day. Another option is to sue for debt in the civil courts, which an assassin clearly can't do. The third option is to scare the debtor by the threat of physical or commercial harm.'

Hal Doyle was quick to pick up the last point.

'The third course is a big risk for an assassin. Every contract he accepts has dangers, and the more deaths he attempts the worse that risk gets. If he did make an attempt on one of us, it would expose him to danger one more time for no extra money. Clearly, he hopes the threat will bring us into line, but if we call his bluff I doubt very much if he will act.'

Wilf Watson spoke up.

'I think the implied threat is distracting us. It's got us thinking too much about non-payment. Just suppose that we had millions tucked away in our slush fund. Would we refuse to pay for a service we had commissioned? I think not. The problem is our lack of money, and I think we should consider other benefits that we might offer instead. Here's a list. Will you study it?'

Instantly, the screen showed these options;

1. Offer to pay by instalments, allowing an element of interest.
2. Use departmental resources to trace the assassin and kill him.
3. Hire another assassin to kill the first one.
4. Offer some form of payment in kind.
5. Dispute the execution of the contract.
6. Offer employment in the form of a well-paid sinecure.
7. Confess all to the Treasury and beg for the money.
8. Borrow the money from a commercial source, or steal it.
9. Do nothing.

Some suggestions were quickly discarded. Number nine had already been discussed. Number three was regarded as ridiculous. Number two was thought impossible. The Director refused to consider number seven at all. Number five was discussed, because there was no proof that the death of Toppley had really been the work of the creditor. However, majority opinion was against the option because the brief to the assassin welcomed the appearance of accident. The options left were;

Offer to pay by instalments, allowing interest.
Offer some form of payment in kind.
Offer employment in the form of a well-paid sinecure.
Steal or borrow the money.

Peter Greig was very much against paying by instalments

or borrowing the money. He felt that a succession of payments would be easy for the auditors to trace. Also, he argued, the assassin might conclude that the service was buying time in which to uncover his identity. He would surely never agree. As to borrowing, Peter declared that with the present treasury supervision it was impossible.

Hal Doyle spoke. 'I wish we knew something about this man. Then we could do some psychological profiling and anticipate his decision.'

'No chance of that at present.' It was Wilf Watson who answered. 'At one stage in the negotiations Mabel Griffin did have a physical meeting with somebody on the other side – they went for a ride on the London Eye – but Mabel said the contact was a middle-aged professional-looking black woman. There was no way it could have been the assassin himself. He's beyond our knowledge.'

The Director was bothered by the fact that their peculiar problem might not be believed by the assassin. The story might arouse suspicion and antagonism. 'Most people would find it hard to believe that a government agency had trouble finding half a million.'

Percy Mallingham was not wholly convinced. 'It would not be too great a problem if the assassin knew of our situation from his own sources. He might do. He's likely to be well informed about the security services, and we failed to keep our scandal secret. Perhaps he won't see our excuse as incredible at all. We could also leak the information to selected circles and increase the chance of being believed.'

Peter Greig raised his voice. 'I think that might work, because the truth is on our side. If we were hiding something, whoever represents us would be relying on half-truths and evasions. But as things are, he or she can speak with conviction. The truth has a character of it's own and can be recognised.'

The Director cut in. 'We seem to be moving towards some 'reward', to give it a name, that is associated with position or recognition. Maybe like a sinecure post in the service that is well paid but has no duties – or a retainer for services that will never have to be rendered. But won't we have the same old problem over money?'

'That idea is workable.' Peter Greig replied. 'It's workable because new posts are always being created in response to fashionable political initiatives and getting approval for them can be almost automatic. For every new subject that government decides to regulate, there has to be an advisory or enforcement service. If you look at the papers, you will find advertisements for non-jobs with extraordinary titles. Nobody knows what the appointee is supposed to do, but employers want to say "We've got one of those". And holding a sinecure appointment – even an honorary one –can be valuable to the holder marketing-wise. It suggests a degree of status.

'I once had a title as "Honorary Visiting Fellow" at my university. People thought it was a badge of academic credibility and I got things published that would otherwise have been binned.'

Hal Doyle spoke again. 'We don't know what sort of things this assassin values, but if our representative is intelligent and socially skilled, then he or she may be able to pick up hints. And we do know the sort of things we could offer. There are sinecures, and contacts and travel opportunities and service facilities. There are even national honours. I mean, we get six or seven MBE's allocated to our service every year. We can even bring in things from overseas that ordinary people can't get. If we really wanted we could get the odd diamond through one of our people in Russia or South Africa.'

'Now you are in fantasyland, Peter. But I see what you mean.' This was Samantha Scott. ' Our representative should structure the negotiations to cover the widest possible area. It may then happen that she and the other party come up with a solution that neither side had thought of before.'

'Who shall we send?'

'Surely it ought to be Mabel. She's intelligent and good-looking and socially skilled. She seemed to get on well with the black woman she met last time. If the assassin sends the same person, she will have a good chance.'

With minor modifications, that was the plan agreed. No minutes of the meeting were kept.

Chapter Twenty-Nine

On The River

She must have money of her own. That was the first thought in Nshila's mind as she greeted the Dresden doll on Charing Cross pier. She was sure she had seen that black leather jacket in a Bond Street shop window only days ago. It spoke of money way beyond the means of a junior civil servant! Once more she felt sartorially up-staged, being dressed herself as the earlier character from the London Eye.

The meeting had been fixed early in the day because of Nshila's tight calendar. It was now D-day plus Three. All the indications were that her body-stealing opportunity would come on D plus Four, but she was not prepared to take risks. She had thought it all through. Supposing she failed to recover the body, how much would it matter? Since Toppley was also Tetherman, the latter was now dead, which was what she had contracted to achieve. But if she failed to provide a body, it would be a disappearance rather than a death. In that case she foresaw endless disputes – disputes that she could only end by revealing that Toppley and Tetherman were one. That would itself mean more disputes. No, she must stick to her plan, and recovering Toppley was critical. The present meeting had been fixed for a river trip, which offered a reasonable degree of privacy and would allow her to disembark at one of the stopping points if she received vital news.

The Dresden doll was keen to be as informal as possible, and invited the use of her name, Mabel. She was very keen to explain the financial state in which her employers found themselves, and made a good job of it. She suggested that it was not a case of having no money at all, but rather that it could not be paid without the whole affair being dragged into public view. If that happened, she said, various investigative journalists would be searching for the mysterious assassin. Would your principal like that?

Nshila enjoyed the performance, knowing the truth perfectly well herself from her various contacts. She maintained an impassive attitude and allowed Mabel to get gradually more desperate as she met no meaningful response. Then she played her own card.

'There is one thing your employers might manage that would influence my principal strongly.'

'What's that? We really want to get this issue settled.'

'If you can get Jennifer Price safely back to this country, it will make a huge difference.'

'Who? Who is Jennifer Price?'

'You know. You have to know. Your people wanted Toppley dead because he was selling white teenage girls into slavery. You've got to know the names of his victims.'

'I don't. Everything in our outfit is done on a need-to-know basis and I was never in that loop. I was told about Toppley because I had to meet with you, but I never knew any names at all. Truly, I didn't.'

'Well, Jennifer Price was one of the kidnapped girls, and my principal has a special reason for wanting her rescue.'

The launch was approaching Tower Pier and Nshila broke off to look at HMS Belfast. She liked living in a country with so much recorded history. On one side of the river was a fortress using the technology of the eleventh century and on the other was a relic of the 1940's. And both now seemed equally obsolete. She realised that Mabel had been speaking and she had missed something.

'Tell me that again.'

'I don't know nearly enough to respond sensibly. Our service, and our sister services, sometimes get involved in clandestine activities and I can't say it's impossible. I've never been told about such things officially, of course, but one hears rumours. All I can do, if you are really serious, is report back and hope for a favourable decision.'

'Do that. If I learn that your people are making a real effort, then I think I can get my principal to hold his hand for a time.'

Mabel felt immensely relieved, and couldn't completely avoid showing it. Her mission would surely be seen as partly successful, for she had postponed any drastic action by the assassin. Yet she had not spoken at all of the various non-financial rewards that might be available. She talked about them as the launch passed down Limehouse Reach.

Nshila maintained an attentive appearance but felt little interest. Most of the offerings implied some medium-term relationship with the client organisation. She saw such a relationship as dangerous. In her line of business the contact should be minimal. Yet when Mabel started talking about national honours her thoughts became more positive.

'Tell me a bit more about these decorations and so on. My principal has a respectable public identity and contributes to the national well-being in a variety of ways. He might rather like an MBE. And I'm sure he would find it amusing!'

Mabel was keen to explain it all. Her service, like many other government organisations, was allowed to make a certain number of nominations for national honours. Most of them were accepted. There might be a way to substitute the assassin for one of the service candidates.

Nshila pulled back from the idea. It had only been a flash thought – immediate and gratifying, but not possible.

'No. You obviously have to give names, and if you had a true name then your people would be able to identify my principal. If it were a false name, my principal would be unable to use the honour. It would never work.'

Mabel rejoiced internally again. She had found something else that the assassin might value. Providing it looked impossible on the surface, but her service was expert in deception and perhaps a solution could be found. Even if that could not be done, she had established that the assassin did have ordinary human desires. Others might be revealed if the contact went on long enough. She was wise enough to avoid pressing for a future meeting, and duly got her reward. The assassin's representative raised the issue.

'My principal will want a quick response on the Jennifer Price question. I realise that it may not be a complete answer to the problem, but he will certainly need to know your attitude. You will be contacted quite soon and you will have to be ready for an instant meeting. There's a possibility that it might be the day after tomorrow.'

'That's a terribly short time scale.'

'Too bad. You'll have to meet it. My principal is not known for his patience.'

Chapter Thirty
Mistress Body-Snatcher

Alf Hardy had been a miner in the Durham coalfields – all his life until he was made redundant. For a long time he had been bitter. He had taken part in all the protests against closure, and failed. He missed the companionship of men working together in a tough, difficult job. He resented feeling worthless and unwanted. He accepted the redundancy money because it would be stupid not to. A year after the redundancy his wife died, and he left the area to live with his son in the decadent south. He expected no benefit from the move, but there was nothing to keep him in Durham and his son wanted him.

His son and daughter-in-law made huge efforts to provoke him into constructive action, presenting him with brochures for further education and searching out job opportunities. Alf always found some reason to reject them until his son pushed the local paper under his nose and said, 'Here's a job just made for you, you miserable old bugger. Working in a crematorium.'

Alf liked the idea. Coal was black, death was black. In times past everybody had been buried underground. There was some emotional connection with his previous work. Down the mine, there had always been some danger of death. Here it had actually happened. He applied, and he got the job. He liked his fellow-workers, some of whom shared his lugubrious sense of humour. He enjoyed using his strength to move coffins around. Now and again a coffin would bear the name of some well-known footballer. Alf would talk to them,

'That was a great day when you scored twice against Arsenal in the first five minutes. I watched you from the old south stand.'

Alf was on duty at the loading bay where mortuary vans come in from the undertakers to deliver a coffin. Pete Gimman,

Frobisher's usual driver had just driven off after handing over a coffin on which the brass plate said Grant Toppley. He did not immediately put it on the conveyor, but sat down to enjoy a quiet smoke – forbidden inside the building. Then the phone rang. It was the gatehouse, saying that the Frobisher's van was back and checking that he was still on duty. Should they let it in? Alf said, 'Yes.' Maybe Pete had forgotten something.

When the van reached the loading bay, it was not Pete Gimman who got out. It was a girl, and not just any girl. This was a real looker. Tall, slender, black. She had the Frobisher emblem on her jacket.

'Are you Alf Hardy?'

'Yes. Can I help you?'

'There's been a terrible error back at Frobisher's. That consignment Pete has just delivered is not Grant Toppley. We've got to switch immediately or there's going to be a major row.'

Alf had no difficulty appearing shocked. This was unheard of. 'I'll say it's an error! What on earth happened? And how do you come into it? You're not one of the usual drivers.'

The woman explained. 'No. I'm in the office, but my boyfriend is Mick Taylor who works on the coffins. He mixed up two brass plates. He put the Grant Toppley one on the coffin that had Geraint Tinsley in it, and the other way round. You've got Grant Toppley booked in for cremation, but it's Geraint Tinsley in the box. Don't tell me it's in the furnace already!'

'No. He's not due there till 10.15am tomorrow morning. But what an error. Your Mick has to be a grade one idiot. Anyway, I thought the brass plates were put on when the coffins were made, not after occupation.'

'They are. But the engraver let us down and for the past two days we have had to screw them on last thing. Do help me.'

Alf had read books in which women were described as 'wringing their hands'. He had never seen it, but this woman was getting close. She was very agitated indeed. His instinct was to help her, but the manager had strong views about 'irregularities', as he called them. If a mistake had been made, he would want all the procedures worked through again. He would never just swap the two coffins. Not knowing what to do, Alf bought thinking time with a mindless, unhelpful comment.

'Thick Mick. That's your boyfriend. It rhymes, doesn't it? Somebody that dim should never be employed in a business like ours.'

The woman was angry now, as well as worried. 'Rubbish. He's a great guy. But the writing is copper plate and he does not see perfectly without his glasses. And he's not too well. He was exhausted, and he made a mistake. Nobody has found out yet. Please help me. Please!'

Alf was still unable to respond sensibly, and tried a feeble joke. 'Maybe. If I was your boyfriend I would be exhausted too. Can we try, sometime?'

'Oh! Shut up! It's not a time for playing stupid. Help me get Grant Toppley out of my van and Geraint Tinsley into it. Then you can change the plates over and I can get back to Frobisher's before the thing is discovered. You won't meet Tinsley again, his people are using a crematorium up north.'

Alf gave in. 'Alright. But do we really have to rush at it? I know Henry Frobisher well. He'll be at the White Lion now for his liquid lunch. We've got at least an hour.'

Alf had already seen the hand-wringing. Now he learnt that a really angry woman does sometimes 'stamp her foot'. She told him.

'You can't be sure of that. Just get off your backside and help me.'

Alf had a premonition that the next tactic would be bursting into tears. That he could never cope with. 'Very well. Let's do it.'

In a normal delivery situation Pete Gimman would have helped Alf drag the coffin out of the van and onto the platform. Alf welcomed the chance to show his strength and did the whole thing unaided. He thought he saw admiration in her eyes and concealed the pain in his dodgy left hip. He did get effusive thanks, but he got no chance to set up another meeting.

For months afterwards he looked forward to deliveries from Frobisher's and hoped to see her again. It did not happen. She had asked him to promise secrecy about the event, so he didn't talk to Pete or the other drivers. Once, when he was passing Frobisher's, he went into their front office to ask for a brochure. She wasn't there.

She must have got away with it, Alf thought – her and that dimwit Mick Taylor – otherwise there would have been a major row and the grapevine would have buzzed. For him, of course, it seemed a no-risk operation. Grant Toppley he had signed for. Grant Toppley he had got. Grant Toppley, so far as he knew, had become an urnful of ashes by lunchtime the next day.

Chapter Thirty-One

On the Downs

It was early afternoon on D-day plus Four, and Nshila was glad to be driving westwards with Toppley quiet in his coffin behind her. In a side street off the Cromwell Road she had taken off the transfers from the side of the van, and it now had no connection with Frobishers Funerals. Her plan was intact, though the recent extra dealings with the client had not been planned, nor the river trip with Mabel. She thought that she had been lucky to squeeze those events into the days between the death of Toppley and the her present mission. She was committed to meeting Mabel once more, and she might do that on her return from Reading.

In an oversize handbag on the seat beside her was the Hand of Glory, unpacked from her deep-freeze in her flat. With it was a packet of candles, and the cigar cases for holding candles onto fingers and thumb. Nor had matches been forgotten.

Ninety minutes driving saw her high up on the downs above Aldbourne. She rejoiced in the freedom, openness and freshness. Miles and miles of windblown grass and air that cleansed all the grime of the city from the lungs. She felt that the world was hers alone and for nobody else. It seemed less perfect when the black van was considered. Where could it be hidden from view? There were no hedges to be found up there. She found several hollows, but they were mostly too shallow for concealment or overlooked from some higher vantage point. Was there one that had a decent clump of trees to break up the van's outline? She saw one clump with twelve, but a bit far apart. Memory came to her aid. School at St. Albans, and Macbeth in the sixth form. Birnam Wood had appeared to be marching on Dunsinane when the soldiers carried branches to conceal their number. Her chosen hollow had twelve trees, and with the stems of small branches sticking upwards out of the windows the van was hard to spot. She started on the walk to civilisation. She saw nobody and reached Aldbourne in good time for the bus. Country buses don't have the highest reliability rating, so she was re-assured when a woman of about 40 joined her in the shelter. She asked the woman,

'Are you waiting for the four fourty-five?'

'Yes, it will be along soon. George Bangham is pretty reliable.' Obviously, the woman was a local.

Two minutes later, a fine new bus swept round the corner and pulled in. Nshila paid for a ticket to Swindon and sat down in the seat just behind the driver. She heard her fellow-boarder exchanging banter with the driver.

'Off to the city to play the big spender, Ethel?'

'Cheeky old fool you are, George. Any pleasures I get these days are simple, ones like having the children buy me a lottery ticket.'

'You could get off at the next stop and walk up Pickaxe Lane with me. Like you did 20 years ago. The company don't mind 15 minutes delay if I have a good excuse. That would be pleasure, wouldn't it?'

Edith aimed a slap at the driver's face and walked up the aisle to take a seat. The driver called after her.

'Are you sure you won't, love. I wouldn't mind it. Skinny you were then. You've a bit more meat on you now.'

Nshila found herself comparing English rural life with life in her African village. She remembered spying on the lustful adventures of her half-brothers and decided that the basics of life never changed.

The local gossip was less welcome when a shrewish-looking woman got on at the next stop. She saw the driver's friend, marched down the aisle and said 'I've got a bone to pick with you, Ethel Lanigan.'

'Not again, Sally! What's it about this time?'

'It's that Jimmy of yours. He's started chasing after Georgia. I won't have it. She's not for the likes of your Jimmy.'

'What a foul thing to say. Jimmy is a fine lad with a good job. Your Georgia should be grateful for the attention. Anyway, if young people fancy each other, what can we do about it?'

The bus was rounding a sharp uphill bend, and stopped suddenly as a tractor and trailer came in the opposite direction. The tractor and the bus could have passed, but the trailer was an oversize affair with a massive load of logs. Both drivers demanded that the other reverse. Finally each backed a few feet and re-positioned themselves at the very edge of the road. Inch by inch, with numerous warnings to each other, they crept past unscratched. Sally, whose other name Nshila hadn't heard, renewed her complaint to Ethel Lanigan.

'You know quite well what you ought to do. Your Jimmy is a randy kid with his hand up every girl's skirt. He has been boasting in The Crown about how many he has laid. Up on the downs he takes them, at that place they call twelve-tree hollow and thinks that nobody sees them. I don't care about the others, but if he gets my Georgia into trouble I'll see he regrets it.'

'She doesn't have to go with him, does she? She can tell him to get lost. Girls are supposed to look after themselves these days.'

Ethel Lanigan ignored the comment. 'That's as may be. But a decent mother keeps some control over her sons. You should try it.'

'You don't have boys, do you, Sally. Just the two girls. I try to control him, Sally, believe me. But every time I have a row with him he has the same old answer. What was I doing when I was 17, he asks. Why was I thrown out of school? If he is a bit randy, then where did he get it from? Often he finishes by leering at me and saying "Anyway, Mum, you enjoyed it."' Ethel was unable to keep a smile off her face and Nshila thought she heard a stifled laugh from the driver.

'Like mother, like son, eh? Well, you just stop him. If he does my Georgia any harm I will come looking for him. And I won't be carrying a bunch of roses. Georgia came home yesterday with mud all down her dress, and I reckon it was that red mud that you get in twelve-tree hollow when there's heavy rain. The place gets water-logged very quickly.'

'You think your Georgia was saved by the rain, do you?

That it damped them down? That they would have been better off in the back seat of his Escort?'

'Don't you make a joke of it, Ethel. I'm serious. Your Jimmy is a menace.'

There was a good deal more of the same stuff, but Nshila had heard enough to be worried. She had left the van in the hot spot for local lovers and it might be found at any time. She imagined a young man, eager to impress his partner, opening the coffin to show his bravery. Worse, the place was liable to flooding and the van might sink to the axles in soft mud. She had frightful visions of returning the next day to find it vandalised and immovable, and used condoms scattered on the coffin. For a moment her world collapsed. Her cautious self began crowing.

'What a mess you have got yourself into now, woman. The project was far too complicated and you were bound to foul up sooner or later. Get off this bus. Go back to the van, push the body into a hole somewhere and content with the fee for Toppley. It's more than you deserve.'

Nshila had risen for her seat and was asking the driver about the next stop before her risk-taking self asserted itself.

'Sit down, girl. Sit down at once. You can't abandon a big venture like this because a nasty event might – just might – happen. That van is going to be there for 24 hours. No more. Maybe no lovers will go near it. Maybe they will, but the sight of the van will suggest the place is already occupied. What will you feel like later if you chicken out of this one? Sit down at once!'

Sally got off the bus at Liddington and Nshila took the seat beside Ethel Lannigan. A bit of sympathy might be welcome.

'Teenage boys can be really hard work, can't they?'

'Harder than I can cope with, sometimes. Do you have some?'

'No. I'm thinking of my two half-brothers. They caused endless trouble for our family. Their mother tried to control them, but she never had much chance.'

Ethel welcomed that chance to unburden herself. And Nshila found it relaxing. For a while her own mad project was forgotten. The women chattered away till Swindon was reached.

Chapter Thirty-Two

The Watchmans Tale

Bert Bromwich had lived in and around Upton Lovell all his life, and was a fixture in The Golden Grouse. Everybody knew his history, since Bert was a talkative man and difficult to get away from. Everybody knew that he had started as a gardener on the Highwold House estate in the days when the Graddige family had money and status, before the scandal and the mad financial speculation and the sale. When Colin Graddige returned to the area as a confident, self-made entrepreneur, Bert found an audience for tales about Colin, the boy.

'Proper young terror, that Colin was. Riding his bicycle all over my flower beds, climbing trees and breaking branches, stealing my tools to dig for treasure or build himself a fort. What's he up to now? I doubt not it'll cause trouble for somebody.'

Colin Graddige was indeed up to something unusual. He had leased part of the old airfield and was starting a business based on out-dated military hardware to be sold to collectors. It was called TANKSAREUS. It bought de-activated tanks from every nation that made them, or had made them, and sold them to film-makers and museums, theme parks and adventure playgrounds. It did other things as well to get the money in, but tanks were the big feature. In no time at all Colin had 12 different tanks in his compound on the edge of the plain, and naturally the security issue arose. The police started moaning about the security of 'potentially dangerous articles' and the insurers wanted various precautions taken before they would give him cover. Colin objected to it all, arguing that it was quite unnecessary. He told everybody in The Golden Grouse exactly how he had replied.

'Don't make me laugh! How is your thief going to make off with a de-activated tank? How's he going to move it? How's he going to conceal it? What damage is he going to do with it? I have enough difficulty handling these things as a legal enterprise. It would be far harder to do something criminal with them. I don't need your security. I'll put up a strong wire fence, and that will have to do. My partner, Glen, agrees with me.'

The landlord of the Grouse said, 'You'll need a security guard, surely.'

Colin thought about that. Then a crafty smile appeared on his face. He looked round the bar, and saw Bert Bromwich. He walked slowly across the room and sat down beside Bert, with an arm across his shoulder.

'Bert, old fellow, you looked after my toys when I was a schoolboy. How about doing it again?'

It took Bert a few moments to grasp that he was being offered a job. But as he got his slow old mind around the proposition it became very attractive. The money was not great. But he was going to be a Security Guard, with the status and responsibility the title implied. Later, he found out that he was more like an old-fashioned night-watchman, dozing over a brazier. But that never bothered him, because nobody else knew and he could still boast about his importance.

However, the biggest benefit was a domestic one. It removed the threat of being put in a home by his daughter-in-law.

Everybody in The Golden Grouse knew that story. Marylin Bromwich (born Marylin Aspen) had been the cleverest, most devious and most attractive of the girls in Dick Bromwich's class at school. Believing that Dick had 'social potential' she pursued him with determination and married him. At her bidding he jumped through a multitude of social, academic and professional hoops. For five years before the return of Colin Graddige, he had been the dullest of all four partners in the dullest firm of Solicitors in Trowbridge. He never appeared in The Golden Grouse. Marylin had infiltrated the wealthy social set and become part of the coffee morning – fund raising – horse riding set. She was now trying to oust Bert from the family house, saying that he really ought to be in an old people's home. The Golden Grouse had heard Bert moaning about that many times.

'Why does she want me gone? I'll tell you. She wants to re-structure the entire house and make it a place fit for a lady to entertain in.'

At that point somebody would always interrupt Bert and offer to re-fill his glass. They might make some comment like 'Surely it's your house, Bert?' He would resume.

'After my wife died I made the house over to them, just keeping a small part for myself. That's the bit she wants. She has even had architects draw up a plan – though she doesn't know I have seen it. On that plan, my small area has become 'Guest Bedroom One (En suite)' and 'The Blue Room' and 'The Sun Lounge' and the 'Italian Patio'. My workshop has become 'The Gazebo'. The khazi stood there when I was a boy. The place where I read The Beano or The Knockout while my mum shouted for me to come and clean the windows or tidy my bedroom. Marylin is a scheming, sadistic bitch.'

So the offer of employment as Security Guard solved Bert's problems. If he was capable enough to hold down an important job, and earn money, and contribute to the national economy, then nobody could claim he belonged in an old people's home. Also, he could reasonably sleep for part of the day and avoid Marylin and her tongue. Bert accepted the job.

Talking in The Golden Grouse was generally safe, but Bert kept his mouth tight shut about an extraordinary event that happened to him a year later. Nobody would believe him – he was not even sure himself what had happened – and if it had ever got back to Marylin she would have tried again to get him certified.

Bert had been sitting comfortably in his chair inside the security hut, watching a rugby match in Australia. From time to time he had scanned the control board on which a sensor lit up if anything strange came close to the perimeter fence. Most times when that happened, he would take a heavy duty flashlight and go to investigate: almost every time it would be deer, straying down from the plain on their way to eat from the village gardens.

Neither the perimeter nor the main gate were floodlit, because Colin Graddige believed that lights would only attract people. If Bert's patrolling should reveal a genuine threat, he had a line to the police station, and a unique alarm system fitted up by Colin himself. It was an air-raid warning siren from WW2. and it's noise was terrifying. Bert was also provided with a dog; a large German Shepherd called Hilary which looked fierce and barked loudly, but had never been know to bite anybody.

There was a break in the rugby match. The referee was unable to see whether the ball had been grounded, and called for television analysis. Bert looked up at the control board and saw a red light glowing. Something had been detected to the left of the main gate. He picked up his flashlight and went to the door.

It was his habit at such times not to turn on the flashlight immediately. The beam would tell any intruder that he was suspected and cause him to take cover. Without the beam, Bert could sometimes see enough from the light thrown through his open doorway, from moonlight if there was any, and from the movement that an intruder makes.

This time he knew immediately that something weird was up. Beyond the main gate he could see the outline of a tree, and half-way up the trunk were five spots of fire. They might have been candle flames, but they were a bit too tall and burned more fiercely than a candle does. They did not flicker as much as candle flame. It was a still night without much wind, but even so, Bert thought one would expect some of them to blow about. These burnt steadily and brightly. Bert found it weird, spooky and frightening. He could not be sure, but underneath the five lights he thought he saw the outline of a hand. Then he realised that the position of the five flames in relation to each other was just what it would be if the candles were stuck on the fingers and thumb of a hand. Whose hand was it? Where was the body the hand belonged to? He was scared.

Then Hilary arrived. She must have been up at the far end of the compound. She arrived in a hurry, leapt up at the fence and growled. She did not bark. That was another strange thing; she growled, low and deep as if she was uncertain and afraid, but still determined.

Then Bert heard a voice. Audible above the growling of the dog. Either a high male voice or a low female one. Hard to tell. It seemed to come from somewhere to the left of the gate;

' *Open— lock — to the dead man's knock,*
Fly bolt— and bar— and band.
Nor move— nor swerve— joint — muscle— or nerve
At the spell— of the dead man's hand.'

Bert's arm was frozen. The beam of the torch stayed fixed: on a tree stump close to the fence, where he sometimes sat in fine weather. His hand just stopped moving. He felt no pain, but the arm would not move an inch further, nor would any other part of his body. He was paralysed. He could not move feet or arms, or head, nor twist his body one way or another. If his left hand had not been holding onto the doorpost of the hut, he would have fallen and lain on the ground like a statue wrenched from its pedestal. Nothing physical worked at all. He was even unable to move his eyeballs, though the things they were focussed on were crystal-clear.

Bert noticed that everything had gone still and quiet. But was that because his hearing had failed or was it because there were no sounds to hear? How was it possible to still all the myriad small sounds that are part of a country night? He felt menaced by some extraordinary unknown force. What on earth had happened? Was he dreaming or loosing his marbles? Perhaps the green men from Mars had really arrived and were immobilising their enemies before transporting them.

Hilary was frozen, too. She was on her hind legs with her front paws about six feet from the ground, one resting on the fence and one inches away from it. Her muzzle was open as if she was still growling. But she made no sound. Bert and Hilary were both helpless. But some things stayed normal. Bert could hear quiet rustling from the company flag above his head. The thought flashed through his mind that Lucifer would now appear in person.

Somebody did appear. Not Lucifer, but not recognisable either. When Bert froze, he had been looking at a spot well to the left of the gate, so the gate itself was now at the right-hand edge of his limited field of vision. It seemed that a figure of medium height, quite slim, dressed in a long black coat and wearing what might have been a military cap, walked to the main gate and pushed it open. How could that happen? Bert had closed it himself, that evening. He had shot three bolts and put padlocks through all of them.

The intruder went past Bert's right side, showing him that the offices were not the first objective. They were clearly visible from the gate and to reach them a person would have had to go the other way. And suddenly there was sound again – yet different. The natural noises that had been stilled did not return, but noises made by the intruder were clear. Bert heard the prolonged screech that the door of the garage made whenever the left-hand door was dragged along the ground. He heard somebody moving the loose shutter over the main window of the fencing store. That building had no notice to identify it, and people frequently raised the loose shutter to see what was inside. Bert also heard the clang of metal on metal, several times. It sounded as if the intruder had knocked against the portable toilets that were kept in the Miscellaneous Store. What on earth was happening?

It lasted about ten minutes. Then the figure came into view again, dragging what looked like a very large bag of golf clubs. It went to the main gate, and suddenly turned aside to ruffle the hair on Hilary's neck. A Martian dog-lover! What next? Bert then had his clearest view, and felt sure it was a woman. He heard her say 'Tough luck, doggie, but it will all be over in a moment, now.' Then she was at the gate and pulled it close behind her. It wouldn't lock, of course, but she wedged it shut with a brick. Then she faded into the background. The five spots of light moved up into the air a foot or so, just as if somebody had lifted a lantern off a hook. They went out and suddenly Bert could move again. So could Hilary, who dashed to the gate and made a great performance of barking and growling.

Bert thought about sounding the sirens, but then heard a car drive off and thought 'Nobody will catch her, anyway'. Next, he thought 'If I did sound the alarm, what would I tell people?' He had no believable story. What comments would he hear in The Golden Grouse? And he could hear Marilyn's shrill voice; 'The old fool is hallucinating, now. Put him away quickly.'

Still a bit undecided, Bert went around the buildings where he had heard noises. He could see nothing wrong, and nothing was missing. Something had been taken – he had seen it - but much of the stuff in those sheds had been lying around for years. It was unlikely anybody knew what was there and there was certainly no inventory. Bert locked everything up again, and decided to say nothing at all to anybody.

Chapter Thirty-Three

A Quiet Day At The Offce?

Nshila was a bit late leaving TANKSAREUS because she stopped the car and went back on foot to make sure that the watchman and the dog recovered when the Hand was extinguished. They did, though the old man looked a bit bemused and unsteady. She missed the first exit from the M4 into Reading, but was glad that she had done so when she came to the service area at Theale. All that effort had made her hungry.

Sometimes the Gods favour you, she thought. At a service area at 5.00am you don't expect good food. You expect you will be met with fried eggs cooked many hours ago kept lukewarm under heat lamps. You expect cold, burnt toast and coffee that tastes of acorns. Some freak event had changed all that on the morning of her visit. Breakfast was really good. On to Reading station where there was no trouble parking. The train was on time. She found a seat and arrived at Paddington in a good mood. She phoned Jessop and told him to demand a meeting with the client at 2.00pm, and he was to arrange the security.

There were two things more that had to be done. She had to buy a blowtorch, and she had to buy a model car from a toyshop: a model of the Tetherman car. Just in case ignition by bazooka failed, magic would provide a back-up. It would be traditional imitative magic in which the destruction of the likeness ensures the destruction of the real thing.

She attempted the shopping in Praed Street, where the working day had begun. It didn't go too well. She found model cars of many types, but not the Volvo that Tetherman drove. The blowtorch she found easily, but also found a friendly and helpful sales assistant. He didn't see a blowtorch as a feminine tool and didn't believe that she could work it. He offered a great deal of instruction, and insisted on selling her industrial gloves as well, and goggles. He had more to remember her by than she cared for. In a slightly less optimistic mood she walked up to Edgware Road and took the tube, planning to get off at Monument and appear normally in the office as planned.

Gillian Harker was surprised that she had to open the office with her key. Nshila lived in the flat, and when Gillian arrived at 9.00am she was used to finding the door unlocked and her boss at work. Often she also found the sweet, thick black coffee that relaxed her after the misery of the tube. Nshila had taken the previous day off, but had said nothing about being away overnight. However, there were plenty of harmless explanations so she got on with her work unworried.

Peter arrived about half-an-hour later, with some news.

'There has been an incident at Monument Station and the place is surrounded with police. I had to make a huge detour to avoid it.'

'That must be why Nshila is late. She has got caught up in it all. She uses Monument a lot.'

She was right. Nshila arrived about 10.30am - upset and angry and ready to tell the world about it.

'What a stupid performance. Don't tell me racial and sexual prejudice are dead. Why on earth should white men in smart suits be passed through without a question and others be held behind for pointless security checks?'

Peter laughed. 'It's all in appearance, Nshila. If you had been in your usual office gear instead of that casual rig they would have bowed down and said "Carry on, Madam". And as for colour, surely some white people were questioned too?'

He had a point. Nshila was in certainly in casual clothing and looked tired. But Peter's comment did nothing to smooth her down.

'Rubbish. I'll bet they wouldn't have detained you, Peter, and you not only look like a criminal, you are one. I've been victimised by the racial and sexual prejudices of your allegedly impartial police.'

It was unusual for Nshila to see the British as 'them'.

Normally she was fully integrated and would not speak of 'your' police as if she was an outsider. Gillian tried to smooth the atmosphere.

'Calm down, Nshila. Tell us what really happened.'

'It was a bomb scare. A suspicious package had been left hanging from one of the hoods that enclose a public telephone. Somebody had given an order that nobody be allowed to leave. I can't see why. The most likely result if it had been a bomb would have been to get us all blown up together.'

'Yes. It's ridiculous. Somebody must have misinterpreted the order.' Peter agreed with her. To Peter, the police were probably wrong, whatever they did. Gillian tried once again to get at the facts.

'You can't have had much difficulty proving who you are and where you were going. Why should a few questions take a long time?'

Nshila explained. 'I dropped my handbag and it made a strange metallic noise. They wanted to look inside. Then they wanted to know what a professional woman in the city wanted with a blowtorch. The constable had to send for an Inspector to know whether it could be used for a weapon.'

'Well, I'm not surprised they were suspicious. What do you want with a blowtorch anyway?'

'I'll tell you the same as I told them. I want to re-route a few of the water pipes in the kitchen and I resent the fees that plumbers are asking today. I watched a DIY television programme a few days ago and using a blowtorch seemed dead simple. I'm going to try it. And if I make a mess of it, then you can take over, Peter.'

Nshila had left her handbag open on the table, and by this time Peter had taken the blowtorch out to examine it. 'Good product this', he said. 'Your trouble, Nshila, is that you just won't stop experimenting. You're likely to burn your fingers off with this thing.'

'What's wrong with taking risks? Setting up this business was a major risk, and both of you have benefited from it.'

That did not stop Peter from being aggressive. This was a time for laying down the law to ignorant women.

'Did your television programme give you lessons on using it? Experienced people wear heavy-duty gloves and goggles to protect their eyes. Have you got yours ready?'

'Of course I have. Anyway, I am only going to heat up a couple of pipes, pull a joint apart, and join it up a different way.'

Peter was not to be silenced. 'Nshila, I've been here before. Women are forever trying to do things that look simple to them because they have watched it being done well. They get in the most awful mess and end up injuring themselves. My sister tried something like that in the farmhouse kitchen one day. We heard here crying out, and found her sitting in a flooded kitchen with a broken arm. "I was only trying to stop that drip down the wall above the sink." That's what she said. The words, "I was only" are woman-speak for, "I've made a mess of it. Come and help me".'

For a moment it looked as if she might hit him. Instead, she controlled herself and said, 'Very well. If you think you can offer good advice, come through into the kitchen and look at what I am planning.'

Gillian stayed out of it, but the doors were open and she heard most of what went on. Peters voice was the loudest.

'I can't see that what you want will be any better than what you have got now, but if you are determined, then you will have to move those brackets on the wall and re-position them. You will need a good strong screwdriver to get the old screws out. And I mean a big one, because you may not have the strength to get them out otherwise. You need leverage. You will need a drill to make holes in the wall and you need wall-plugs and fresh screws.'

In the end, Peter volunteered to get the things he thought necessary from the hardware shop in Fenchurch Street and went out on his errand. As he left, Nshila added one item to his shopping list. 'Go to a toyshop, as well, and get me a scale model of a Volvo saloon. And don't be too long, I have an out-of-office meeting soon after lunch.'

'What's a model car got to do with your kitchen?'

'Never mind. Just get it.'

While Peter was away Gillian got Nshila sufficiently settled to deal with normal work. She needed her opinion on a request that had come in the day before.

'I am unsure what advice to give the Royal Military College of Science at Shrivenham. They are planning an Open Day in two weeks time and the displays they put on will be different in different conditions. They want us to be as precise as possible about likely ground conditions – not just from the viewpoint of military equipment but also in regard to facilities for visitors. For instance, if visitors can't approach a display on foot because of thick mud, ought they to build a stand? Myself, I don't understand the names of all the bits and pieces.'

'Have you got all the data about recent rainfall, and the best available forecasts and details of the soil composition?'

'Yes. It does not look promising. The soil is poorly drained and there has been more rain than usual in the past fortnight. The bright sunshine yesterday will have dried off the surface, but it will still be very wet underneath and heavy rain now would make things slippery and muddy. But I don't know what these displays they plan are like, in terms of weight and mobility. The difference could be huge - mounted photographs or a field gun.'

A day that had started well was now less marvellous. Nshila had been forced to endure the eager salesman in Praed Street. She had been delayed and infuriated by the incident at Monument. She had been stupid enough to mention the blowtorch and been forced to fabricate a story. She had been compelled to endure a lecture from Peter about DIY skills, made worse because he was right. And now Gillian wanted her help. The client meeting, though necessary, would be another demand on her resources.

The map told her that Shrivenham was quite close to Baydon and might well have similar weather. Instantly her mind was up on the downs, wondering whether the ground under the black van was solid or not. It was a heavy vehicle. Would there be torrential rain? When she got there in the evening, would it be sunk in that soft mud that the woman on the bus had mentioned? And the Open Day at Shrivenham was going to feature military hardware. It would include tanks. That brought the previous night's adventure to mind. Had the watchman fully recovered? Would he talk? What might he say?

Finally, Peter came back. He had a variety of DIY equipment, but he also had the scale model. Her handbag now held the blowtorch and the tiny Volvo that was due to be melted down. She left him in the kitchen and started off for Lincolns Inn Fields.

Chapter Thirty-Four

Good News

The designated meeting place was the north east corner where there is a passage through to High Holborn. Nshila had decided to keep her previous persona, despite having already met Mabel twice. There was little danger of being traced through her appearance, it was assumed shortly before each meeting and discarded immediately afterwards. Also, she chose meeting places that were geographically close to the home of her make-up artist friend. She was visible only for a short walk and attracted no attention.

Mabel was already seated on the bench. She was pleased with the news she brought, and eager to pass it on.

'Things are better than I expected. We have a serious interest in the Toppley victims, but till now there were problems about reliable data. What you have told us about Jennifer Price fills in some critical gaps and makes it possible to devise a strategy. I'm authorised to tell you that significant resources will now be mobilised and that recovering Jennifer is seen as an odds-on bet.'

Nshila was sceptical.

'Given the earlier sob-story about your service being in disgrace, can you expect my principal to take that at face value?'

'Yes. It's true that our service has had its wings clipped, but there are other people with more power. Amongst the secret and semi-secret organisations there is considerable horse-trading and exchanging of favours. We can get it done. We shall be in debt to whoever helps us for a long time, but we think it's worth it. If we get Jennifer back, she may give us valuable information about the people and the methods involved in the trade. It might even get us out of the dog house. We are keen. Definitely.'

Nshila picked up a stick from the ground and made a few futile swipes at the pigeons. She had never liked the arrogant, disdainful manner in which they intruded on human space.

'We still have a problem. The recovery is bound to take time and you can't possibly guarantee success. If you fail, or if it takes several months, the situation between us will not have altered; my principal will have done the work contracted for and you will have failed to pay. How am I going to persuade him to accept that?'

Mabel was not upset by the response.

'Do you remember the other form of 'payment in kind' that I suggested – and you rejected?'

'Yes. The idea of a national honour. What about it?'

'We have figured out a way it can be done. Our service is allowed to nominate five people, and they are always accepted. We would nominate four real people and one imaginary one. If your principal could find a really good hacker, he could get into the computer and write in a new name instead of our imaginary one.'

'But then your people could just look at the name that occupied your slot. It would be a dead give-away.'

'No. At a certain point in the process the names are put into alphabetical order. It will be obvious to our administrative staff that one of our names is missing, but they will have no idea which of the other names displaced it.'

'But the hacker will know.'

'That's true. But surely your principal can find a hacker who is ignorant about him being an assassin. He will know that he has worked a deception, and know that your principal is ambitious. He won't know that the honour is a reward for successful assassination.'

'Is it that easy?'

'Not quite. Every nomination has to be backed by references. There will have to be at least four of them and they must describe a range of public-spirited things the nominee has done. But it's not difficult. Checks are seldom made, but you need to make sure that the papers are given by real people who could speak in support if asked.'

Nshila wanted a few moments thinking time. She said, 'I have had no lunch. I want a sandwich from the snack bar there at the corner'. While she walked there, waited and walked back she kept an eye on Mabel.

'I bought you a coffee while I was there. I like what I hear but how does it help with my uncertainty about payment?

'We accept that point, but we think that it offers assurance of our intent: proof that we are working hard over Jennifer Price and her recovery. You will see that something is happening. We will keep you up-to-date, so far as security allows.'

'Mabel, you know how things are on my side of the fence. I can make sure that the principal knows what you have said. It is way beyond my brief to make promises on his behalf, but the odds are that he will go along with the idea for a time. But long delays would make him lose patience. The best policy is for you people to push forward as hard as you can. We will do whatever is necessary in terms of references and hacking into computers. We will make contact if we feel this plan isn't working.'

They parted amicably.

Chapter Thirty-Five

The last ride

The train that she caught was crowded, mostly with commuters going home and she had to stand. In modern times, she thought, there is no chance of one of these arrogant young men standing up to give one a seat. The blowtorch weighed heavy in her bag. After that, everything went well. The Volvo was present. It had not been broken into or vandalised - or the bazooka discovered. She reached Twelve-tree Hollow on schedule and found the van undisturbed with no evidence of lovers. Time to move Toppley. She positioned the passenger door of the Volvo behind the back doors of the van, opened them and pushed the coffin out, sitting behind it with her back against the cab and shoving the end hard with her feet. Then she started work on the screws, pleased that Peter had insisted on the sturdy variety of screwdriver.

As the screws came out, her fixation with the progress of the task gave way to speculation on the corpse she would encounter. She realised that this would be a 'first' for her. Long ago, back in the village, she had gazed on the back of the cattle thief as he lay face-down in the mud of the creek.She had stayed long enough to be sure he was dead, but it had not been face-to-face in any sense. As for Frikkie Verloppen, there had not been much left of him to examine. And Pullinger, well, he had fallen out of a high window in the ruined tower that formed part of his estate. She had known from the position of the body that he was dead. Now she was due to look a victim full in the face.

She lifted the lid and looked. Not bad at all. He had a full head of hair and a serious face on which one could imagine a smile - a bit like a friendly bank manager . But that was to be expected, for appearance had been a major asset in his villainy. It was the snare in which he caught his prey.

Getting Toppley's body into the Volvo needed all the strength she had. Finally, she used some boards from the coffin as a tray. She got his feet above the door frame and partly under the dash-board. Then she turned the van around so that she could lift the other end of the board up, and rest it on the lip of the goods area. The body was then high enough to be pushed sideways onto the passenger seat. It was over. She reflected that it was worse than stuffing a duvet into a duvet cover.

She threw some of the coffin boards into the undergrowth and took others with her in the Volvo. It seemed to her that if assorted planks were found, and they were not enough to suggest an obvious shape, then nobody would realise they had once been a coffin. It had all made her dirty and dishevelled, which she hated. Knowing about the normal use of the site, she had prepared a notice saying 'Police aware' to stick on the van.

The journey was smooth, uneventful and relaxing. Up the M4 and round the M25 anti-clockwise to the A3. She filled the petrol tank right to the very top at a service station on the Guildford by-pass and drove on to the Devils Punch Bowl. She hid the Volvo off the road and walked to the woodman's hut. Of the many places she had used to practice her art, this one was most reminiscent of the hut under the Baobab tree. Like the hut, it was entirely made of natural materials. Like the hut, it was smelly. Like the hut, it had holes in the roof through which you could see the stars. And it was rural. The only sign of the industrial world was the road, a hundred yards away. She hung up such magical artefacts as she had brought, burnt some incense, and commenced the sympathetic magic that would ensure the Volvo burnt.

The conditions were favourable. The similarity between the model and the object to be attacked was very, very strong. The toy car Peter had found was the right version, the right date, and even the right colour. She cast the spell and lit the blowtorch. That was quite a shock. The sales assistant and Peter Grace had both been right – it was not a natural weapon for a woman. The flame shot out with a roar and for a moment she feared that the whole hut would catch fire and she herself be incinerated.

She nearly dropped the thing on the floor, but found the control knob just in time. She turned the torch on the model car and was delighted with the result. The paint caught fire and the model turned quickly to an unrecognisable lump of metal. No spirit, she thought, could fail to grasp what was expected of it.

She took the bazooka from the Volvo, setting the thing at her 'observation site' – from which she could easily see the probable last resting place of the car and get an accurate aim on the centre of it.

She had almost driven the Volvo out of cover, and into the accident position when she stopped. Crisis! What a thing to forget! Toppley, now Tetherman, was still in the passenger seat! What a give-away if he were found there! How could she have been so stupid? She spent the next ten minutes on a manhandling job. It had been difficult enough to get him into the passenger seat back at Twelve-tree Hollow. Now she had to manoeuvre his limbs round the drive shift and handbrake. But she finally succeeded, wondering whether undertakers became skilled at flipping dead bodies around – like nurses learn to shift live ones.

Finally, everything was in place. Luckily for her the car was an automatic. Had it not been, she would have found that making a car plunge over a cliff while not plunging yourself is a hard task. It's a common scenario in books and films, but how is it done in reality? One idea is that the villain drives the car himself, gets up a good speed, and throws himself out of the door at the last moment. That can go wrong; he might land badly and injure himself so seriously that a get-away was impossible. Perhaps a shoe might get caught in one of the pedals and the villain would be dragged over the cliff with the car. Another idea is that the villain stays outside the car but jams the clutch pedal down with a stick or a brick or the branch of a tree. Then he can get the engine running fast and pull the obstruction away with a rope. The problem with that is the strength needed to push the clutch pedal right down by hand. It's easy to do with the leg when one is braced in the driving seat. It's not easy for a woman when she is leaning in through the door, reaching down with one arm, and holding a stick or brick in the other.

It's much easier with an automatic. She smashed the rear window and hooked a stick round the gear shift. With the car aimed straight at the barrier and the accelerator pressed down with a stone, she jerked hard with her stick. Over it went. It went at a good speed with a lot of noise. She ran to the observation post and was in position behind the bazooka before it came to rest.

An unknown factor, of course, was her skill with the bazooka. Would she be able to fire it accurately? The question proved to be academic, since the spirit did a superb job on the wreck, creating a marvellous pyrotechnic display.

She fired the bazooka anyway! It seemed such a shame to have taken all that trouble for nothing. She scored a direct hit and watched the flames leap higher. Inside her head, her cautious self was resentful of success. 'Stupid woman! There was no need for that!'

She climbed up 200 yards and watched developments. The first car passed without stopping, which surprised her because the smoke and flames from the wreck were very obvious. But it was a winding road and somebody concentrating hard might possibly have failed to notice. The second car stopped. The driver got out, and then reached back into the glove compartment for his mobile. It was obvious from the delay and from his frustrated antics that there was no signal at that remote spot. She saw him drive on another half-mile and try again, parked in a lay-by. The body language was quite different and she assumed a successful call to the emergency services. Anyway, just 15 minutes passed before there was an ambulance at the point where the barrier was broken, and some sort of fire-fighting vehicle bucketing along a track down in the valley.

Something always get forgotten! The bazooka had to be buried, and she had failed to bring a spade! Once again she sensed support from the spirit world, for sticking out below a bench in the woodman's hut was a round wooden handle. What was on the other end? A hoe? A fork? A rake? With her heart in her mouth she drew it out. Not a spade, but the next best thing – a shovel. The job took longer than it would have done with a spade, but she managed it. The bazooka was soon two feet underground.

All that was left for her was to walk across country to Haslemere and catch the earliest train to London. She enjoyed the walk. The English countryside is non-threatening, even at night. None of Africa's dangerous animals. One hears, and sometimes sees all sorts of harmless creatures going about their business. One feels befriended, and at one with nature.

Two days later she retrieved the black van. She went by train to Swindon and took the previous bus journey in reverse. Neither Ethel nor Sally were on the bus, but it was close to being full and she sat behind two aged and dirty old men who were lamenting the incompetence of young people today. She had heard the same conversation often enough back in the village. Soon she was walking up the hill towards Twelve-tree Hollow on a fine, sunny afternoon. The van was undamaged, but there was evidence that lovers had used the site. Was it the boy Jimmy, she wondered? More trouble for Ethel Lanigan? Since she had bought the van quite legally and had all the right documents, she drove it back to London and sold it to a dealer. She lost money, of course.

It seemed to her that she had done well. Toppley/Tetherman had lived more lives than one, and duly died more deaths than one. In both cases there was an inquest, and in both cases the verdict was accidental death. The car accident had worked out perfectly. It had been possible to identify the car as Tetherman's because the engine number was still legible, while the number plates were not. There was enough left of the skull to examine the dentistry, and the teeth were shown to be Tetherman's also. There was no reason to link Tetherman and Toppley, so nobody compared those teeth with the Toppley records.

Two days later it was time to cope with the administration. She sent the Tetherman client an invoice. She expected payment with the usual bureaucratic delays characteristic of government departments. The recovery of Jennifer Price was out of her hands and she could only wait, but the business of a national honour could be moved on. Zach Kawero was the obvious person to do the hacking.

'If you have got a doctorate for a thesis on the myth of computer security, then getting into that database has got to be a doddle, Zach.'

He needed some persuading and he needed payment, but he agreed. Here was one person, Nshila realised, who knew the name that would be substituted in the list. But he did not know about the Toppley assassination. He could speculate about why she wanted an honour and why this elaborate deception had been arranged, but he could never make the critical link. In any case, the Toppley death had been officially classified as an accident. Of course, he would also know the name that he must remove from the list. Could he learn anything dangerous from that? No. It was an imaginary name dreamt up by the client. Nshila felt safe.

The paperwork for her nomination presented no great difficulty. She had more than one acquaintance who was well respected but yet had something to hide. She chose one of them to nominate her and applied pressure. There was, she pointed out, nothing criminal in it. For some years past the government had invited ordinary citizens to nominate worthy people whose achievements they admired. Putting forward her name was totally legitimate. As it turned out, she was never compelled to say 'If you don't, then --.' The words were understood but never spoken. Supporting documents were obtained by variations of this strategy and an impressive proposal built up.

And then, inactivity on two fronts. Waiting for the rescue of Jennifer, and waiting for the moment in the honours procedure where the approved list had been compiled.

Chapter Thirty-Six

Jackpot

On a cold winter morning Flight BA 992 touched down at Heathrow, flying in from Istanbul and various middle eastern airports. Before taxiing to the terminal it was diverted to a secure area and two passengers only were disembarked. 30 minutes later, Nshila and Mabel, unknown to each other and watching from separate places, saw Jennifer Price hurried to a VIP lounge. She looked pale and confused. There was a tearful re-union with her parents and then, with her minder at her elbow, Jennifer gave a carefully scripted press conference.

One month later the press reported a major success by British Intelligence, achieved in cooperation with the police of several middle-eastern countries. The operators of a white slave trafficking gang had been apprehended. Several of their victims had been found and returned to their families. Great credit was due, said one columnist, to Alfred Munnings, who had reversed the downward trend of his agency and played a major part in the triumph.

Two weeks after that, a paragraph appeared half-way down a long list on an inside page of the quality papers. The particular section referred to the MBE.

Nshila Marghrita Ileloka. For services to inter-racial and inter-cultural understanding in social and scientific affairs.

Gillian Harker spotted it when she looked through the paper during her coffee break.

'How will you get it, Nshila? Will you go to a garden party? Will you meet the Queen? What will you wear? How about one of those hats you bought when Simon was with us? Which one?'

This, Nshila thought, will be a hard decision.

Late that evening she talked to Rasputin. 'It's hilarious,

Ras, that I get official recognition for very ordinary services when a much greater service can never be acknowledged.'

Rasputin sneezed.